2ND EARTH

Adversary

EDWARD & EUNICE VOUGHT

Dedication

This book is dedicated to those

who see a need and say “why not”.

Then proceed to make it a reality.

1

The noise in the helicopter is almost deafening. This helicopter is even noisier than the ones that Tim and I used to fly in back when we were Navy SEALs. That is probably because this chopper is a UH-1, and the ones we used to fly in were UH-60 Blackhawk's. They replaced the UH-1 around 1989. We are on our way down to the area that was once known as Miami, Florida to help some of our friends that have a pretty nice settlement down there. Perhaps I should introduce myself, and bring you up to date on what has been happening since last we met. Actually, I should probably explain a little about how we came to be here, in case we have never met.

This may sound just the tiniest bit strange to you, but about fourteen years ago Timmy Nolan and me, I'm Jon Gorman, were going on leave from the military when we started this little adventure. We made it to New York City, and were riding the subway to get to Tim's parents home, when we fell asleep only to wake up in another world. Okay, I know what you are thinking, but I can assure you that I have not been drinking. The world that Tim and I found ourselves in, had all but been destroyed by a neutron war back in 1969. The approximate time that we came here was about twenty years later. The year in the world that we came from was 2010.

The people that survived the war were scavenging for food and shelter just to survive. Tim and I were able to band a pretty good sized bunch together, and move them down to Virginia, where we found a perfect place where we could start a new life. It wasn't easy, but by working together, we have been able to grow our family from sixty members to over five hundred, and are pretty much totally self-sufficient. Of course Tim and I didn't do all this by ourselves. We have been blessed to be joined by some very special people from the world we came from. They have brought with them many of the skills that were needed desperately to allow us to live, and function the way we do. I will introduce them to you, along with our other family members, as we go along.

Many other groups have formed in different areas of the United States, and we have been in contact with some settlements in Europe, England, Canada, Puerto Rico, and Cuba. The settlement in Miami had been exchanging goods with the settlements in the islands like Haiti, Puerto Rico, and Cuba for the past few years, and we thought that everything was going well, until just recently. I will get into more detail as soon as I bring you up to date. As I mentioned, our family has been growing and changing so fast it is difficult to keep up with all the changes. When last we visited, we were still practicing plural marriage. We did that only because we had such a large discrepancy in the number of women compared to men in our settlement.

In the past couple of years we have experienced a large number of men joining our group, and some of the other groups. Some of us think that this may be a result of the strength that the groups now have in defending themselves. When we first settled here, we had to defend ourselves fairly regularly, against groups of men that would come to try to take over the settlement or to steal women. We have always been successful in defending ourselves, in part due to the training that Tim and I had, and the training we have been able to give the other members of our families. We feel that many of the roving bands of men have perhaps seen our way of life, and have decided that it may be better to join us than to fight us. We prefer this as well, we welcome anyone that wishes to join our settlements with open arms. We do watch them closely until they can be trusted, and have not had any reason to send anyone away in many years.

When last we visited I had four lovely wives, and several beautiful children, both biological and adopted. Three of my wives, Robin, Melissa, and Becky have since found new husbands, so Dayna and I are living the way we always wanted to. Please don't misunderstand my meaning when I say that. We were a very happy, large family, and we all got along great. It's just that Dayna and I did not intend to get involved with plural marriage in the first place, but it served a valuable purpose when it was needed the most. We do miss all of the children that used to live with us, but they live very close, so we can visit as often as we would like to.

It was rather funny when Robin, Melissa, and Becky decided to ask me how I would feel, if they asked me to let them marry other men. I have to admit that I had no idea that they were even thinking about this, but Dayna warned me that something like that could come up. I wanted to have a little fun, so when they asked me that question, I told them that I would banish anyone that I even caught them talking to. I thought that I had probably gone a little over the top with that remark, but they seemed to take me serious. Sara, Jenna, and Morgan, who are all like sisters to me, and came from the world that Tim and I did, just happened to come over when I said that.

Sara just laughed and asked who I am trying to kid. She told me that I am getting way too old to take care of four wives, so I should be happy for them, and let them go quietly before they decide to kick my butt. Naturally we all had to laugh, and I admitted to Robin, Melissa, and Becky that I had heard something about it, but that we should discuss it privately. Sara, Jenna, and Morgan all said they think that's a great idea, so we should discuss it. Privacy is one commodity that is in very short supply around here, but we are all family, so it doesn't really matter. I got to meet the men that they wanted to marry, and we called a family meeting to discuss it with all the children that are old enough to know what is going on.

The children did not like the idea of moving out of the house, but since they will be within a house or two, they agreed that they could live with it as long as I am still their daddy. We discussed this very situation when we agreed to try the plural marriage, and felt at that time if we all act like adults, and think of how much it will mean to the other person that we could work it out. That's what we did, it's been a couple of months now, and the children still spend as much time with Dayna and me as with their moms and new daddies. The twins, Tina, and Tammy decided to stay with Dayna and me.

It's funny, but sometimes one or more of the little children or babies just won't settle down, until their moms bring them over so that Dayna and I can hold them and play with them for a while. We all expected that something like that could happen, and as far as I know no one has gotten upset or jealous about it. We are all family, including the new husbands, and since this is new ground for all of us, we just have to do whatever is necessary at the time. The older children spend about an equal amount of time at each of the homes.

That's not the only news around here at this time though. You remember how we love to visit military bases, and to hunt for treasures pretty much everywhere we go. Well we had a new group of people come to our settlement, and asked if they could join us. They had been living in the Kentucky area and had been doing well, but felt that they would like the security of living in a larger community. When they got to see all that we have, they were sorry that they waited so long to come over. They are good people and hard workers, but the most interesting items of information they brought with them, is the fact that there are a couple of former military bases not far from where they were living.

Naturally when our family heard about that, a journey had to be planned to go over and check them out. It was decided that Sara and Gary, James and Jenna, Mike and Morgan, and I would go to see if there was anything that we could use. We were all sure there would be something of value, but we were looking for some specific items that could make our existence easier. Ian, one of the young men from the new group, volunteered to show us where the bases are. We have been through that part of the country several times, but never saw the bases that Ian took us to. We met Colonel Bob, along with his lovely wife, Marie, on the way up there. They both still love to travel around and see the different settlements, and sometimes they even find people looking for somewhere to live.

Anyway we found the bases, and it was like waking up Christmas morning with presents crammed under the tree. We found enough uniforms and other small items to outfit everyone in the settlement, along with several very large fuel tanks that were still almost full. The items that caused the most excitement were the helicopters and the all terrain vehicles that must have been here for trial back then. Tim and I had used vehicles similar to these when we were Seals. They will run on anything that will burn, so that you can take advantage of what is nearby. Sara and Gary got to work almost the minute they saw the Hueys, which is what we used to call the UH-60 Blackhawks.

It didn't take her and Gary long to get one to turn over. It helps that they were in a hangar, instead of being out in the weather. While they were doing that, the rest of us were looking for trucks, to haul a bunch of this great stuff home with us. Once we found several really nice 2 ½ ton stake body trucks, we got to work to see if we could get any of those running. Actually, Mike and I snuck away, and worked on getting a couple of the all terrain vehicles running, just for fun. There were at least two different kinds of these vehicles in the hangar we found them in. There were motorcycles, and four wheelers that are kind of like dune buggies, with automatic weapons mounted on them. Even the motorcycles had guns and rocket launchers on them.

It didn't take us long to get one running and to try it out. The tires on these are the type that can't go flat, unless the tire gets ripped totally apart, and falls off the rim. That buggy is definitely fun to drive. We wound up taking all fifteen of them that we found, along with the twenty-four motorcycles. It is a good thing we could load them into trucks, because we didn't have them all running by the time we had to leave. Between Gary and Sara, and Mike and Morgan, they were able to get three of the helicopters running, and actually able to fly again. I told them that they were more than welcome to fly them back to our settlement, but I was happy to drive one of the trucks.

I am still not sure what caused the biggest stir when we got back. The helicopters, or the all terrain vehicles we found. Actually James and Jenna found some information that could prove to be more valuable than any of the treasures we brought back. Apparently the bases we visited were also sites where the Army Corp of Engineers were stationed. We found filing cabinets full of documentation on alternate sources of energy. There is some information about a company, not far from here, that manufactured all sorts of equipment for solar energy. We visited that facility and found enough solar panels, and other equipment to work a lot more with that source of energy.

We also found information on using the tides in the ocean, or even in a big lake or running river to generate energy. We were able to identify some of the equipment necessary to get started with some of these alternate energy sources. We were mainly waiting for an excuse to go down to the coast to see our friends there, and to try out some of the newer technology we found. Other than that, we made several trips back to those bases and brought back just about everything that wasn't nailed down. When Mike and James came back from their last trip there, they came right to our house and asked what I think about having our own hangar on the farm.

I had to ask them if I was hearing them correctly. They both laughed and repeated their question. I told them that I have actually thought about that quite a bit, mainly because we have so much farm equipment and other vehicles that would obviously last longer if they could be kept indoors in really nasty weather. We have all been astonished at how the metal has changed since the war. We have been here for almost fifteen years, and the equipment made of steel shows very little wear. To get back to our conversation, Mike tells us that they checked it out, and they think we could move at least one of the giant hangars at one of the bases.

Morgan comes in right about that time and asks when we are going back to finish taking that hangar apart and load it on the trucks. Mike told her that she came in just about two minutes too early. We all get a good laugh about it, then they tell me that they found a couple of cranes on the base, and naturally Gary and Sara had to see if they could get them running. Just as naturally, they were able to get them started, which opened up a lot of projects that we couldn't do before. One of which, is taking a hangar apart, and being able to handle the very large pieces of sheet metal and girders that are used in the construction.

It took us nearly five months to move that entire hangar to our farm, and set it back up again, but now we have a place to keep our helicopters and the two small planes we have. We also moved several Quonset huts that we found on the military bases we have visited. If you are not familiar with that terminology, they used to be used as barracks for the military, and for other purposes as well. We never have to worry about having a purpose for a building before we bring them home. We always have plenty of suggestions about how it can be used. Plus the demand totally outweighs our ability to fill the needs, or at least what some people consider a need.

While we were in the process of moving and reassembling the hangar, we had some people from one of the other settlements come and ask if they could join our group. When we asked them why they chose to leave their other group to join ours, one of the men said that he heard we are preparing for a war. He then asked if we are planning to take over the other groups, and make them work for us. I have to admit that I was a bit surprised to hear that kind of talk. Naturally we told him, and those with him, that we will never attack anybody, and we are not preparing for a war.

After that question was asked, many of us felt that the topic was important enough to make sure everyone in our groups and families know exactly what our position is. As our family got bigger we had to add onto the church building we use as a gathering place, but at least we can all fit in there and have a meeting when necessary. We called a meeting of everyone, and explained that although we train to defend ourselves and our neighbors, we do not intend to use our fighting prowess against anyone, that doesn't attack us. And that we are not now, nor have we ever even thought about taking over any other settlement or group.

The question came up, about what we would do if someone did try to take over ours, or one of the other groups that we are in contact with. I started to answer the question, but Sara finished it for me. She told them that if someone tries to take the running of the settlements away from the members of that group, they would be shown that the world we are building has no place for people like that. Those of us, who have survived in this world, do not want to go back to being an anarchistic society, where the strong feel that they can take and do whatever they choose. One of the new people asked how we can keep that from happening.

If you remember Sara, she doesn't have my patience and understanding of human nature. She simply smiled at the gentleman, and told him that anyone who tried that will have to die. I have no idea where these people came up with these questions, but the next question asked is why wouldn't we put someone like that in jail, and work with them to rehabilitate them. By this time I was starting to lose my patience, so I asked them if they have ever seen a jail or prison in their travels. They responded as I thought they would. I continue telling them that we have patterned our society after the bible, and other good books that we have found and read.

If someone does something that hurts another person, they are expected to repent and make restitution. If they do not wish to do this, they will be asked to leave the group. Serious sins, such as killing someone or sexually assaulting someone, will be dealt with as severely as the act itself. We have to be able to trust each other, that goes for every settlement or group like ours, no matter where they are. We don't feel that anyone should have to live in fear of someone around them. We train to defend ourselves in any situation, but we do not have any soldiers, or anyone else whose job in our family is to protect and defend us. Yet anyone in our family can, and will defend against anyone who would destroy our way of life.

We have no idea what those people who came to us expected, because they left the next day. We contacted the group they came from, and warned them about the types of questions they were asking. They tell us that those people asked the same questions in their group. We all hope they learn that if they are looking to beat the system, it simply will not happen, so they may as well enjoy the lives they have. I never could figure out why some people think they have to control others to be happy.

I really can't see why anyone would want to live any other way than we do. We have pretty much anything anyone could want in our world. Yes, we work hard, but we also have a lot of time for recreation, and just about everyone enjoys each other's company. That doesn't mean we don't have some very competitive people in our group. Most of the time, the most competitive ones are primarily concerned with beating me, at anything and everything, not everyone, mostly just the women that came from the same world as Tim and me. I have gotten pretty good at letting them beat me without them knowing it, and once in a while I beat them just to make them try harder.

Mostly I am talking about running the obstacle course we built several years ago, but they want to win no matter what game or sport we are playing. Doc McEvoy and his wife love to watch us compete, and argue good naturedly afterward. One game everybody in the family can beat me at is golf. I can hold my own on the miniature courses we have, but on a full sized course I don't stand a chance. Actually it was a day when Dayna, Sara, Morgan, Jenna, and Lindsay all beat me on the obstacle course, and were harassing me about it, that we received word that our friends in Florida were having some trouble.

At first it didn't sound so serious, but then as we discussed what they told us among ourselves, we realized that it could be pretty bad for our friends and maybe even for us. They told us that they were contacted, by way of the short wave radio, by some people claiming to be the ones they usually do business with from Cuba. They were saying that they would be coming soon to replenish the items that they usually trade, but that there are going to be some changes to their agreement going forward. Our friends contacted us, and asked what we thought it might mean. They were worried because of the tone of voice that was being used, and it wasn't their normal contacts calling.

All of the settlements have worked out a code that we fit into the conversation to show that it is really who the other people are who they claim to be. Just another security precaution we have taken to avoid trouble and the group from Cuba didn't use that code. As I said at first, we didn't think much of it, but the more we talked about it, the more we realized that some of us may have to take a trip down to the tip of Florida, to make sure our friends are not in any danger. That's when we decided to plan a trip down there to check it out first hand. The people down there are very hard workers, but they do not have the numbers we do, and they are not really strong enough to fight off a sustained threat.

2

We have made this trip a few times, to visit and to help our friends down there over the last couple of years, so we know what to expect along the way. This is a big plus, because we know where we can still get fuel, and the best places to spend the night. This is also big, because although attacks are by far fewer than they used to be, they are still a threat, so we have to be prepared for them wherever we go. Naturally Sara wanted to fly at least one of the helicopters down. We outfitted one of the Hueys with full armament. It has twin 30 caliber door guns, and is equipped with rocket launchers on both sides and the front.

When we got it all ready to try out, we flew it into town to a place where there are several hundred cars parked in a large parking lot, and opened fire on those cars in a strafing run. I have to admit, it took me back to when Tim and I were with the Seals, which was not exactly a pleasant feeling either. We decided to haul the helicopter down on a flatbed truck, along with two of the dune buggies and a couple of motorcycles. We decided to take Tim, Gary, Rod, Teddy, Steve, Jerry, and me. Naturally as soon as we decided who is going, Dayna, Sara, and Nickie tell us if we are going they are as well. Then James and Jenna decided that they want to check out that particular group, to see if it would be a good place to try the wave technology to generate electricity.

The first day out we make good time, and get to stop at what was to be our stop on the second day, if we ran into more problems on the road than anticipated. As I said before, we have gone this way a few times now, and have cleared the roads between here and there fairly well. Of course we never know when a big storm along the coast will mess up the pavement, or drop several big trees into our path, so it is always an adventure. On the second day, we were getting close to our friends settlement, when we received a call on the CB radio, that our friends were under attack by the people from Cuba, or at least they assume that is who it is.

We stopped, and decided to go in with a show of force, with the helicopter gun ship and the dune buggies, to perhaps scare the attackers enough to quit and go back home. It only took a few minutes to get ready. Sara is flying the chopper with Tim and me manning the guns. Gary is her co-pilot, and is just as crazy as she is. Teddy and Rod are driving the dune buggies, and the rest of the team is bringing up the rear, and the rest of the supplies we have with us. That brings us to where we first came in.

We are flying low over the road we would have been driving in on, when we see the settlement in front of us. We can also see an open jeep, with a machine gun mounted on the back, shooting into the buildings on both sides of the road. We can also see some armed men, dressed as soldiers following the jeep. I hear Sara call the people attacking our friends some names that are not the kind I want to repeat, then goes into an attack mode with the gun ship. When we get within a hundred yards, she opens fire with the nose guns on this thing, and we can see the trail the bullets are leaving in the road all the way up to the jeep, where the soldiers have abandoned it. It's a good thing, because a bullet must hit the gas tank just right, and blows the jeep up. It lands on its tires in a mass of flames now.

There is a second jeep coming around the corner firing at us, so Tim opens fire from his door gun. They are on that side. I see the guy firing the machine gun fall out the back of the jeep, then the others jump out, as Tim's bullets tear big holes in that jeep. Some of the soldiers walking look like they are getting ready to start firing at us, when Teddy and Rod come around a corner with their guns pointed straight at the guys on the ground. The battle is over just that quickly. The people from the settlement start coming out of their homes just about the time Sara lands the chopper.

Teddy and Rod are gathering up the weapons of the soldiers and stacking them on one of the porches. The gentleman that is the current leader of this group, Roger, comes up to us and thanks us for helping them, then goes over to the one who appears to be in charge of this attack, and asks him why they would do such a thing. The soldier tells him that it is just a matter of time when his people will rule this entire country, then the whole world. Then he turns to us and tells us that we will die for our insolence toward El Presidente. Sara, who is not the most patient person I have ever met, cocks her Sig and asks him if he is El Presidente.

He tells her that he doesn't have to answer to a woman, and I think she is going to shoot him right now. Gary tells her that this guy is obviously not the man in charge. El Presidente would not get his shoes dirty actually fighting a war. He would order lackey's like this guy to do it for him, while he stays home where it's safe. I figure we will not get any straight answers from this guy, so I start asking the foot soldiers what they are trying to accomplish here today. Most of them say that they are only doing what they have been ordered to do. We get lucky when one of the soldiers tells me that he would talk, but if he does his family will be in great danger.

I tell him I will do everything in my power to get his family to safety, if he tells us what is going on here. He tells us that he has come here several times to trade with the good people in this settlement, but a few months ago a man came to their settlement with some men, including the leader here today, and took over. The leader and another nasty looking man tell him to shut his mouth, or he and his pathetic family will be killed as soon as they get back to Cuba. Sara asks them what makes them think they are going back to Cuba. He spits on the ground and tells us we are weak. They have scouted us all and we are afraid to fight, so they will take our pathetic settlements for their leader.

Tim tells him, for people that are afraid to fight we sure kicked his army's behind today. He didn't say behind, but you know what he means. We turn our attention to the one that is willing to talk, and as soon as we turn our backs, a young woman runs up and shoots the leader and the second in command so quickly that we can't do anything to stop her. Sara turns her gun on the young woman and tells her to drop the gun. The young lady hands the gun to one of the other settlement people, then spits on the bodies of the two men on the ground. Roger asks her why she shot those men. She tells him in Spanish that those men attacked her mother and her sister, when she was in Cuba. They were taking her to the home of El Presidente for his pleasure, when she escaped and came here.

Roger tells us that she has only been here for a little over a month, and they had no idea why she came here. The gentleman that is talking to us tells her that her family still lives, but her father was beaten badly for her escaping. Now several others want to talk that the leaders are no longer a threat. We decide that we need some time to discuss a plan of action amongst ourselves, so we put the soldiers in one building, with armed guards, and meet in the settlements meeting room. A couple of the soldiers ask us if we are going to execute them. I tell them that their fate depends on their commitment to El Presidente, and their willingness to cooperate with us. Naturally they all say that they are only doing what they were forced to do to prevent their families being killed.

We get as much information as we can from those that are willing to talk, and from Mary Elaina. She's the one who shot those two. Apparently, this guy that calls himself El Presidente moved into the settlement in Cuba a few months ago and just took over. He had a few men with him that were pretty vicious and sadistic, so the good people that built that settlement were afraid of them. Before they knew what hit them, he had recruited several of the local men that wanted to have power over the others, and now we are seeing the results of that.

The one said that they had scouted us, so now we are wondering if perhaps those people that tried to cause trouble a while back, may have been part of this plan. We discuss the best way to put a stop to this, but short of killing all of those in power, we are kind of at a loss. I volunteer to go down to Cuba, and try to talk some sense into this guy and his followers. Several of the soldiers ask if they could return with me, to get their families and return here, to either join this settlement or start another one near their friends here. This group collects boats the way our group collects cars and military equipment, so they have transportation for those of us who are going.

Naturally Dayna wants to go and so does Teddy, but I tell them I will have a better chance alone, at least for now. I tell them to give me a week, and if I'm not back, they can come and get me. Since this day is just about over, we decide to leave in the morning. There will be seven of us going, including Mary Elaina. She wants to get her family out of the country and have them move here. The rest of our group will be staying, until this is settled, rather than go home now. We discuss how I should handle the situation there, and come to the conclusion that I will not know what to do until I get on the ground, and see exactly what we are up against.

In the morning Tim tells me that he has faith in Zeus to take care of this mess, but if we have to wipe them out, to at least save him some action. I assure him that if these guys are as organized as we think they are, there will be plenty to go around. We check out the boat that we are going to take over, and it appears to be in very good condition. Of course Sara tells me she could take some of us over in the chopper, but that would definitely draw their attention to us. I would like to get the lay of the land, and scout it out before I meet with the leader.

I am happy when James and Jenna start talking to Roger and his group about the possibility of moving the location of their settlement. I personally can't see why anyone would want to stay here. Yes, it's beautiful here near the beaches and the ocean, but whenever there is a tropical storm they wind up rebuilding pretty much everything. James and Jenna are trying to talk them into moving to the other side of the peninsula that is Florida, or maybe even up to the area, that in our world was called the panhandle of Florida. That's in the area where Tallahassee was. Several of the people in their group are all for moving, especially after what happened today. They say they have had some close calls with other groups of men, but have been lucky enough to fight them off.

It's easy to see that they do not have a position here that is very defensible. This is one of the groups that since we didn't have much trouble for the past few years, thought we were safe from now on. We spend the rest of the day showing them where we are talking about on the map. We also point out that there is a pretty good sized settlement in Georgia that would not be very far off if they were needed. They are at least willing to look into it, plus they are excited about some of the new electric generating methods that James and Jenna want to show them. I am putting together a pack to take with me when Sara and Gary come over and hand me a ghillie suit to take with me.

A ghillie suit is something you wear when you want to remain unseen in your surroundings. They are very popular with snipers, and other people who wish to move around under cover. This one looks like it was made for jungle use, which is probably what I will need. I am starting to feel like I did before we left for an operation when I was with the Seal teams. I was not really looking forward to this trip, but the closer it gets to leaving, the more excited I am getting. Dayna must notice it because she asks me if I have missed being a soldier more than I realized.

I try to explain to her that I wouldn't trade my life here for all the treasure in the world. I know for a fact that I have not missed the war, and the fighting that the other world seemed to thrive on. But I always enjoyed the missions where we were just on a fact finding assignment, where we didn't have to engage the enemy. It was always exciting to infiltrate their lines, and get as close as you possibly can to them, without getting caught. That's how I am starting to look at this mission, if you would like to call it that. The last thing I want to do is go down there and start a war with those people. Unfortunately my experience has shown me that when most people experience a little power over others, they start craving more, and will do anything to get it.

We along with all the other settlements that we have talked to and visited want to keep our world free from people like that. Other societies have been successful for a period of time, but human nature and greed is a powerful thing. We will just have to see what we have to do to stop this threat to our relatively peaceful co-existence with our fellow man. Dayna, Teddy, and I talk for quite a while, discussing the strategy that I should use to approach those people. It all boils down to being able to get on the ground, talk to some of the people, and decide after that how to proceed.

I do not sleep well, I keep dreaming about other times that I had to go into places like this, on similar missions, but then it was as a team. Unfortunately my dreams are about a time when a team of six went into a South American country to extract the former President of the country, and several American diplomats that were there. When we got to the palace where they were supposed to be, we found out that all of the people we were there to help were already dead. From all appearances they died very long, painful, tortured deaths as well. We wound up having to fight our way out of there. All of us sustained at least one wound, and two of the guys had to be carried to the extraction point.

That experience is one of the main reasons why I will do anything I can to prevent someone, or several someone's, from becoming a ruler over our society. When we finally get up to get started, the sky is overcast and gray like it is going to rain. Hopefully we are not expecting a tropical storm that will cause large waves while we are going there. I have been there once before and the island is much closer to the US coastline than the Cuba in the world we left behind. Other than that, it is very similar to the other one as far as crops and climate. The language is Spanish, but a different dialect than the ones that those of us from the other world were used to. We can still communicate, but some of the words have different meanings.

We decide to take two boats, the one that the settlement is letting us use, and the one that the soldiers came over on. I am taking quite a bit of equipment to be traveling light and quick. One of the most important items I am taking is a satellite phone that actually works. That will be my way to communicate with the people here. We are hoping that it won't be necessary to call for help, but it's nice to know help is right here, if I need it. We figure that we could get a helicopter there in just a little over an hour if we have to. Let's hope we don't have to.

The biggest difference between this trip and the ones I made with the teams is that this time I have to say goodbye to Dayna and Teddy. After Ma and Gunny died I had no one who cared whether I ever came back or not. Teddy tells me he has a bad feeling about this trip. He wants to go with me, but that would just leave Nickie and Little Jon alone if something happens to us. In a situation like this it is easier to watch out for yourself, rather than have to worry about someone else.

The sea is a little rough, but the boats are big enough to take it easily. In fact, it only takes us about four and a half hours to get there. Of course we don't land near the settlement so that we don't attract attention from the wrong people. Mary Elaina has volunteered to show me around, and introduce me to the people that she knows are against the man calling himself El Presidente. She already told me that she is not sure how much we can trust some of the others that came back with us. They may use the information that I am here to gain favor with the leaders. I have already thought of that even before we left the mainland, but being as experienced as I am in situations like this, I do not even trust her completely. I have learned that in this world, everyone has pretty much their own agenda and that may or may not include anyone else.

We get off the boat as quickly as we can because there is no way of knowing if we have been seen. I would prefer not to be here if we were, and they are forming a welcoming committee for us. There are three settlements on the island, but they are fairly close to each other, and they, like us, consider it one larger settlement. The settlement we are going to first, is the one that Mary Elaina, and a couple of the others that came back with us, live with their families. George is one of those that said he just wants to come back long enough to get his family and return to the mainland. He has been a fisherman for as long as he can remember, but figures he can do that just as easily in one of the settlements over there as he can here.

It's a good thing we are being cautious, because as we get closer to the settlement, we start seeing armed men that look like they are patrolling the streets. We get as close as we dare in order to find out as much as we can from listening. From the conversation between the two guards, the guys that attacked the settlement on the mainland had a time limit to accomplish their task and report back. Apparently their President isn't a patient man, and has threatened to kill the guys in charge for not following orders. They mentioned that someone had the nerve to tell him that perhaps they were not able to defeat the Americans. Both men made the symbol of a cross when they said that the President shot that man for even thinking that.

I have no idea how people like that get followers. You would think that someone with half a brain would figure out that if he can shoot you like that, you can do the same to him. I know it's not that simple, because there is little if any trust among people like that. They must have to live worrying about being killed all the time. We watch the guards for about an hour, then I decide that I have learned all that we can from these guys, so I wait until they start making their rounds then sneak up behind first one, and knock him out, then do the same to the other. The second came looking for the first one, thinking that he may have found a woman to attack or something, by the questions he was asking as he came nearer.

The people that came back with me are impressed by the way I was able to knock out those two, but now they will either have to leave before these guys wake up, or answer some questions from El Presidente about why they failed their mission, and are still alive. They choose to get their families and their meager belonging and leave as soon as possible. Some of the people in the settlement are afraid to leave so those that are going head for the boat as quickly as they can. That includes Mary Elaina. She is worried about leaving before she has had a chance to show me the Presidents home and where the soldiers live. I tell her to get her family back to the mainland; I will have no trouble finding what I need.

The people of this settlement are worried about what will happen when the soldiers come to. I rig up what could be a section of a barn that just could have fallen and hit first the one on the head, and then the other one when he came to check on his partner. I wait to make sure they buy it before moving on. I don't want to leave the people to pay for something I did. If the soldiers start hurting these people, I will simply eliminate them. I am starting to think like a Navy Seal again. I had hoped that was all behind me long ago.

3

I must have hit those guards pretty hard because it takes a while for them to come to. They seem to buy the story that the people are telling them, but the fact that they were making a fuss over them, and trying to revive them helped sell the story. The settlement leader, who is a man that looks like he is in his early forties, shows them the dangerous loose boards on the side of the barn, and two of the settlement men take the time to remove the boards, so that no one else gets injured. I wait a while longer to see their reaction when they find out that some of the people have left. Watching these guys run around from house to house looking for them could be comical, if the situation wasn't so serious and volatile.

At one point I think I may have to intervene, because it looks like they are blaming the settlement leader, and are threatening to shoot him. Just when I am ready to use my bow to take them out, they get a call on their radio from their leader. They tell him that some of the people are missing, and whoever is on the other end of the line tells them to check other settlements for them. They will wait until tomorrow to do that, but for this evening one of them goes down to the docks to see if any boats are missing. The people took the boat that we came over on, and the other one was docked farther down the shoreline out of sight.

It looks like these people are going to be okay at least for tonight. The leader must not think that there is any threat after dark because as soon as it starts getting dark the guards jump into a jeep, that I don't remember seeing, and drive away telling some of the women that they will be back tomorrow, so they don't have to miss them too much. When the jeep is out of sight the women spit on the ground and curse the guards. I take this opportunity to go back into the settlement, and tell the people here that they may wish to consider leaving, or planning to fight El Presidente and his men. A couple of the young men say they are not afraid to fight, but they have no training, and only knives and farm tools for weapons. Against guns they would die very quickly.

I spend about an hour telling them about the settlements on the mainland, just to get them thinking. They offer to let me stay with them tonight, but if we get a surprise visit, it could get ugly real quick. I make my way back into the thick foliage and find a spot that I saw earlier to spend the night in. There is plenty of good water here, and in the light I recognized several edible plants that will help make my food last longer. Heck, I have been in worse conditions many times. Just as I am thinking this, an Anaconda about ten feet long, decides that he wants the same sleeping spot that I am using. If I dared light a fire here, I could cook him and have a feast.

At first light I go back to the settlement to make sure the people are going to be okay. There are more guards here today. They are questioning the people who live here. Everyone tells them that they didn't see those people yesterday, or that they saw them heading toward the shore in the afternoon. The one that appears to be in charge shrugs, and says that maybe they all went swimming and the sharks ate them, the rest of them all laugh and say it would not be the first time the sharks have tasted human meat. The two guards that were here yesterday remain, and the others leave to go somewhere else.

I decide that the people here are at least as safe as they were before I came, so I go looking for the second settlement. Many of the people from the settlement are heading down to the shore to go fishing as usual. If my memory serves me correctly, the next settlement is about a mile to the west of this one. It turns out to be about a mile and half, but having to go stealthily through what is actually a jungle, it takes quite a bit longer than it normally would. All the while I have been fighting my way through the foliage, I have been getting angrier by the minute at this guy who calls himself El Presidente. I could be back home being picked on by my family, instead of being a late breakfast for about fifty million mosquitoes and other insects that live off flesh.

I also run into a small group of wild pigs, and several other jungle animals that I don't even know the names of. I am thinking that if the pigs were as large as they are back home, I could possibly put a saddle on one and ride it everywhere I want to go. Luckily these are of a smaller breed. When I get close enough to the other settlement to hear voices, I stop and make my way slowly so not to be heard. If my memory serves me correctly this settlement survives by farming. They grow sugar cane, pineapples, and other fruits that we have traded for, but I don't know what they are called. They also grow all of the crops that they need to feed them-selves, and help the other settlements as well.

When I get close, I see a person that looks like they are hunting, so I hide behind a large tree to watch them for a while. They must be trailing something, because they keep looking down at the ground then like they are surveying the surrounding area to see if they can spot their prey. The person is working their way toward where I am hiding, when I hear a noise up in the tree that I am hiding behind. At the same time, I hear and see one of the wild pigs rooting around about ten yards away, between me and the person hunting. I look up into the tree, and finally make out a jungle cat that looks as large as a lion right now, staring at the hunter.

The hunter takes two more tentative steps and raises the bow and arrow they are using, and I can see that it is a young girl taking aim at the pig. I have my bow out with an arrow ready when she shoots at the pig and the large cat jumps at her. I aim and shoot at the moving target, and run to get to the cat before it can kill the girl. My arrow must have hit it somewhere, and scared the cat because it hits the ground, rolls once, and takes off running. The girl jumped out of its way and is now getting up and staring at me like I grew another head. The pig is thrashing around almost dead, so I walk over and put the poor thing out of its misery with my knife.

When I look back at the girl she has another arrow ready to shoot at me. I smile and tell her that I mean her no harm, and she at least lowers the bow and arrow. I take a chance and tell her why I am here and she acts like she knows exactly who I am. One of the men in her settlement came back yesterday from the mainland and talked to many of the older people in their group. Several of the people left during the night for the mainland to escape the people who took over. She is looking at my bow, which is a Special Forces bow, made mostly of aluminum. It screws together and has about a hundred pound pull.

The arrows I have are also aluminum, and are just a little shorter than normal, so that we can carry more. I have different tips for the arrows depending on what my needs are. The bow she has is homemade, but looks like it works very well, and like she knows exactly what she is doing with it. I help her field dress the pig and tell her what I am trying to do. She says that they have an old man in their settlement that survived the war, and he has already told them all that some men are like the jungle cats. Once they get the taste of blood in their mouths, they cannot go without it. He says that the men who took over are like that. He says that the only way to get rid of them is to kill them, before they kill you.

I tell her that I am going to try to talk some sense into them anyway, even if I agree whole heartedly with the old man. She says that she better get back, or the pigs that watch over their settlement will come looking for her. She has been eying my K-Bar knife like most kids look at sweet things. I have a couple extras in my pack so I give her one, but I warn her to keep it hidden and to be careful. That thing is razor sharp. She takes it like it is worth far more than it is, but then seeing the knife she was using to dress that pig, I can see why. She heads back to the settlement and I decide to circle around and see what there is to learn here.

From all I have seen these people have been living a good life here before this jerk came along and messed it up. Their homes are not as solid and well built as ours, but they may not have the expertise along those lines that we have been so blessed with. The crops they are growing look good and seem to be flourishing in this tropical climate. I run into a couple more snakes today, but I give them as much room as I can to go around me. I work my way up close enough to talk to a couple of the men of this group. They are not surprised to see me. Apparently the people who came back yesterday, and left already, told them what I am doing.

One of the men must be the old man that the young lady told me about. He says he is too old to leave his home for anyone. He also tells me that if he gets close enough to El Presidente, he will kill him with his bare hands. I assure him that I will do all I can do to help them. He tells me that I look like I can handle myself in a fight.

I may just be able to do something after all. He gives me a handful of fresh picked green beans, which makes an excellent lunch, while I head for the last settlement. On my way there I am pondering how a few mean, nasty, people can take over an entire settlement with over a hundred men in it.

It's not as surprising as many think. The mean, nasty guys are willing to kill and hurt people without conscience. Most good hard working people have trouble believing that there are people like that in the world, and by the time they realize it, the bad guys are in control. Often most of the good people are afraid to start something because of their families, so they live with the oppression, and hope it doesn't get too bad. Unfortunately, the more power the bad guys get, the more they want, until they take everything they can from the good people. They usually wind up raping and murdering everybody they have taken over. I did have some hope of appealing to these guys better nature, but from what I am seeing and hearing they don't have a good side.

I get to the third settlement around mid-afternoon. This is another farming group that looks about like the other one. Of course all the settlements fish and harvest some of their food from the sea. I wondered why I didn't see any electric lights in any of the settlements, and from where I am watching this group, I can see that their windmills have blown down. From the looks of them it happened quite a while ago. I'm sure that James and Jenna can help them overcome the problems that they face here with electricity. I am starting to formulate a plan on how I may be able to help these people take back their own settlements, with a little help from me. It's still too early to know for sure what will work.

In the two settlements I have observed today, it appears that the guards spend most of their time dozing in the sun, and bothering the women. I get to talk to two men and a woman in the field here. They have heard about the others leaving, but did not know the details. Now I am grateful that I kept up my Spanish, because these people don't speak any English. The woman that I talk to, tells me that a couple of days ago, she saw the men that are up at the mansion that the new leader took over, dragging two, what looked like

Americans, into the house over there. That sheds a new light on my mission here. I didn't think there were any Americans on this island except me. I will have to check it out.

I briefly outline my plan to the people I met and they say they will be happy to help me if I can do as I say. By the time we are through talking the sun is starting to set again. They offer me some of their meager food supplies, but I tell them I have my own for now, besides the jungle is full of very good food for those that know her secrets. I noticed today, that just before it started getting dark, the people had to take everything that they harvested today and the guards took the largest portion with them, leaving very little for the people to eat.

A couple of the fisherman in the group went back out into the jungle and retrieved some large fish that they had stashed there before coming into the settlement. It looks like they cook everything they have and divide it evenly amongst them. I watch until it is too dark and can see some of the men giving their portions to the women and children. I already found a comfortable place to spend the night and tonight I don't have to share it with a big snake. During the night I heard the screams of a woman, apparently being taken away from her home. The urge to try to find her and help was strong, but I realized that blundering around in the dark wouldn't help anybody, and may even get me and some others killed. I am going to have to move quickly though before this guy and his buddies ruin any more lives.

In the morning I call Dayna to tell her and the others what I am finding out. They ask if they should come right now, and we can wipe that jerk out, along with his friends. I ask for two more days before having them come down. Sara tells me that two days from today at seven o'clock in the morning, I can look for her to come flying in here with one of those Hueys we have. I work my way back to the second group to talk and outline my plan to them. I get to talk to some of the men and women in the fields and going toward the shore to do some fishing. They are willing to try anything, so I tell them I will be in touch again soon.

Today I go by the mansion that the leaders and his cronies are living in. There are several guards around the grounds, but it is obvious that they do not feel threatened at all. I see some women and men doing chores around the buildings, under the watchful eye of the guards. It's all I can do not to get close enough to pick them all off with my bow and arrows. The .308 I brought would take care of all of them even from here with no trouble, but that's not how civilized people do things. I continue on to the first settlement, and meet some of the fisherman down by the docks. I outline my plan to them and they agree that it will work, unless the bad guys decide to change their routine.

I spend the night in the same place I did the first night. Heck I can't remember how many nights I have been here, but I do know that I am getting very tired of sleeping in this stupid jungle, instead of in my bed back home with Dayna. Tonight I hear the screams of a wild animal that is being killed as food for a larger wild animal. It brings back memories of other nights that I have spent in jungles, very much like this one. I even spent several nights in the jungles of Cuba, back in our world. In my tortured dreams, I go over every detail of those missions, just like I am reliving them. Those missions were nightmares when we lived them, in my dreams they are just as bad. It's been a long time since I even thought about those days. Now I have something else to dislike these guys for even more.

In the morning it is raining. It started sometime during the night, but in my dreams it was rainy and miserable as well, so I didn't notice. There seems to be some sort of ruckus going on over at the mansion. I put on my ghillie suit, and see how close I can get to what is going on, and maybe learn something about the enemy. The suit weighs me down a little, but will definitely help me stay hidden in this jungle. I work my way close enough to listen to the conversation going on between the leader and one of his officers. The leader is not happy. Apparently someone told either the leader or one of the guards that there is an American on the island, looking to overthrow him.

He is literally screaming at his men to find that stinking American and they will make an example of him, to show these peasants who is in charge. This mission is bringing back so many memories that I may need that therapy that Sara has said I have needed for years. I am working my way closer while they are talking. The underbrush is very thick and goes almost right up to the area where they are standing and talking. It's kind of like a patio covered by ivy and other vine type plants. It is a much bigger area that I first thought it was until I got closer. I am literally only about fifty feet from them right now. I am tempted to shoot them both and get this over with, but I have no idea how many others there are.

The leader and his captain, I guess he is, head back toward the building when the leader starts yelling again for his men to bring him the two Americans that they captured the other day. He says that they will know where the other one is, and they will tell him or they will both die long very painful deaths. This is starting to get crazy. This is exactly what happened on one of those missions I was on way back when. Two of the members of a special fact finding mission were captured by rebels in Central America, and we were sent in to rescue them. We got them out, but the cost was high. My mind keeps flashing back to that mission. I have to forget that and concentrate on making this one end without so much bloodshed, although at this moment I can't see how.

I can hear scuffling at the other end of the patio, or whatever it is they are standing on. I can hear some shouting and some laughter, like the soldiers are laughing at someone. I am trying to work my way around so that I can see what is going on and possibly get into a position to help whoever is their prisoner. There are too many of them to move quickly, as it is I must make some rustling noise, because one of the soldiers turns and looks into the jungle right at me. I freeze, and stand perfectly still until he looks away. One of the other soldiers tells him it is probably a wild pig. He laughs and says if it wasn't so wet they could kill it and have it for dinner. He says better yet, have one of the peasants kill it for them. They all laugh at that comment, but at least they turn away from me.

It seems like it is taking forever to cover the distance to get into a position to see what is going on. I am afraid they are going to kill those two Americans before I can get into position to stop it.

Apparently they just got the prisoners out here, because I can hear the leader tell them that they will tell him everything he wants to know, or they will beg him to end their pitiful lives. I just need to get about twenty more feet to the left and I should have a good vantage point. The soldiers seem to be distracted by what is going on, and the wind picked this moment to blow heavier than it has been, so I can cover the distance quickly and unnoticed.

I can finally see what is happening. There are two people with their hands tied behind them, being more or less supported by the soldiers. I can't see their faces, but one looks kind of small like it may be a woman. One of the soldiers moves and I see that it is definitely a woman, by her hair and the shape of her body. The other is a man, I can't see his face, but he carries himself like an athlete or military type. He is continually pushing against his captors, I recognize that he is trying to get some room to possibly use his feet to kick his captors, to possibly get away. I feel sorry for the woman because I know what is coming unless I do something to stop it, and no matter what the odds I am going to try.

The leader is standing right in front of the man. I can see his face, I am trying to recall if I have ever seen him before, but he doesn't look familiar. He keeps yelling at the man for not answering his questions, but the man seems to be laughing at him which makes him even madder. I have both my Sig automatic and my bow ready to use. I also have my K-Bar in my waistband if it comes down to that. I am picking my targets to do the most damage, because once the shooting starts it will be too late. The leader is holding the man close to his face with a handful of his hair pulling him close.

He tells the man to tell him where the other American is hiding, or he will give the woman to his men and he can watch them take turns with her until she is dead. Naturally he is speaking Spanish with just enough broken English for anyone to understand. The soldiers are already starting to tear at the woman's clothes. The man tells the leader that he will tell him what he wants to know, but only if they leave the woman alone. The leader smiles a very wicked smile and tells his men to leave her alone, for the moment. The man tells the leader that the other American is close enough to hear their conversation, and he wouldn't be surprised if he has the leader in his sights as we speak. The leader was smiling, now he is totally enraged. He slaps the man's face spinning him around so that I can finally see his face. That shocks me as much as I can ever remember. I know him, but I can't put a name to the face yet.

4

Hello everyone this is Dayna. Jon has gone to Cuba to help some of our friends down there, so I thought I would bring you up to speed on what has been happening here, while he has been gone. First off James and Jenna talked the current leaders of the settlement down here, at kind of the tip of Florida, to check out some other areas of the state. There are areas that offer the same opportunities with the ocean, but may not be quite as exposed or difficult to maintain their electrical generating equipment. They have contacted us often to tell us that their windmills blew down, or the solar panels got torn off their stands and have to be replaced.

Actually just about the entire group is willing to check out some other areas. There is a good sized group up at the panhandle of Florida, where a city named Tallahassee, was before the war. That settlement is near the ocean, yet the people have less problems with their buildings and electric power. Gary, Sara, Tim, Rod, Steve, and Teddy decide to stay here in case Jon needs some help, while the rest of us go to check out a couple of other spots for a settlement. It takes a little more than a day to drive up there. We may have made it in a day, but we stopped several times to check out some interesting places, where we may be able to get a bunch of things that the settlements here will need.

We even find an air base that none of us knew was here. We will go back when we have the best people to get vehicles running, because whenever we visit a military base, we wind up bringing about half of it home with us. One of the things that we have found to be very useful are the Quonset huts and other steel buildings that the military used in abundance. The war did something to the steel that has made it harder and more wear resistant to the elements. This base looks like it will be a treasure trove for these people. There were also a couple of manufacturing facilities that James and Jenna want to come back and check out what may be in those.

When we get to the settlement we see that they are hurting as well from a couple of tropical storms that apparently hit the coast very hard about a month ago. They are without electrical power and appear to be stressed pretty badly. They are happy to see us though, because we at least have some people in our group that can get their electricity working again. They go to work almost immediately, while we meet with the leaders of both groups. They say they could use the numbers if the southern settlement wants to join them. They do not generally have to worry about attacks. They simply don't have enough people to do everything that needs doing.

The people from down south are impressed by the crops that they are growing, and by the fleet of boats they have for fishing. When we get to tour the settlement and get a closer look around, we can see that many of the houses need repairs. Some of them are in pretty bad shape. James is making a list of what will be needed to fix the homes, and to keep electricity being generated here. He spends the remainder of the first day here getting some electricity back for the settlement. Tomorrow morning he wants to look around the area for a place where the new technology will work best.

We refer to it as new technology. But according to the records on that base where we found the supplies to install it, the generation of electricity by the tides, was being tested with good results in several places around the United States and even on some of the island countries before the war. James and Jenna have read everything they could find on the subject, because it could help some of the settlements tremendously. I have trouble sleeping because I am so worried about Jon. I know that he is the most self sufficient man I have ever met, but he is still just a man, and he sometimes looks for the best in people, when some of them simply do not deserve it. It's not nice to say, but some people simply do not have a conscience when it comes to hurting others.

In the morning, I go with James and Jenna along with the current leaders of this settlement to look for a good place to put the tidal electrical equipment. We spend about an hour driving around the coastline, and according to James and Jenna we find several good possibilities. The biggest question will be, which of these will maintain the tidal movements to generate enough electricity to run the settlement. We spend the rest of the day working on the homes that have been damaged. The people in this settlement are very nice people, but they do not have a lot of experience with building and rebuilding.

Luckily for them all of us have helped in more building projects than I care to remember. Not that they were not fun, it's just that remembering them all reminds me of how much older I am than when Jon and I first met. When the work day is over we have a great meal of fish and shrimp that were just caught today. Some of the settlers from south of here went out on the fishing boats with the people from this settlement today, and they all say they really enjoyed the experience. Right after dinner James and Jenna take a ride back over the areas that we covered this morning, to see what the tidal patterns are in those areas.

When they get back they tell us that three of the areas we looked at this morning may actually be able to support the tidal electrical equipment. James tells us that based on the size of the equipment we have, and the number of dwellings that we want to hook up to the electricity, it may well take more than one setup. Some of us that they are explaining this to have either no idea what they are talking about, or have very limited knowledge about it. James explained it by asking if we know the principle of generating electricity by using a waterfall. Almost all of us have been told how that works, so we understand it somewhat. He tells us that the tidal generator works basically the same way, only instead of the power of a waterfall; we will use the power of the tides to turn the generators and generate the electricity.

Personally I am going to need to see it working before I will understand it more than just a little. I don't sleep much better tonight than I did last night. I keep having dreams that Jon is injured and alone somewhere in the jungle down there. I don't dare try to call him on the satellite phone, because he may be somewhere that he doesn't want others to know he is there. I get up in the morning and I help make breakfast for a bunch of us. We finish eating when the satellite phone rings, and I get to talk to Jon and find out he is okay. I wish I was there with him, or he was back here with me. I have decided that when we get together again, I am going to ask him if we can make a pact to never be separated again for more than a few hours.

At least our day is so filled with work that I don't have a lot of time to think about Jon. James wants to setup at least one generator using the tides, as a trial to see if it will even work. So far we are going on the research that they found. If the reports are accurate, then this way of generating electricity can be as effective as using a waterfall. This could be a huge finding, because two-thirds of the earth is covered by water, and there are thousands of miles of coastal shore line that can potentially be used. Some of the people from down south have decided to stay here, but some of them want to live closer to where they did before. We saw plenty of areas that did not look like it would take too much to make them habitable for a settlement.

James and Jenna spent most of the day with some of the people from the settlement that are good swimmers. The spot that James chose to put the trial generator is a secluded bay, only a couple hundred yards from the settlement. Some of us got to help in a different way, by helping basically rebuild a small cinderblock building between the settlement and the bay. Not far from the settlement, is what was once an electric transformer station that is obviously no longer used. According to James there are some transformers at this station, that if we get lucky enough could be used to capture the power being generated by the ocean currents. If I sound like I know what I am talking about, it is purely by accident, but now I am totally excited to see if this will work. I know we have used the power of the river, near our settlements, to run our flour mill for years and it works very well. If this is the same principle it should work just as well.

The rebuilding of the building to house the transformer went well today. The building looks like it originally had two rooms in it. James told us when we started that it would work using the larger of the two rooms with it being the size it is, but it would be better if we could take out the wall, and make it one larger room. The wall was already broken down, so it was easier to remove the rest of it, than it would have been to rebuild it. Some of us worked on removing the wall, while others worked on rebuilding the parts of the outside walls that were broken down. It never ceases to amaze me how talented our family members are when it comes to building or repairing something.

James was impressed also. First thing in the morning, he is going to check out the transformers and see if any of them are worth bringing over and hooking up. Jenna told me that she thinks James is being more than a little optimistic about finding anything useful there. The elements in this area are simply too harsh for something like that not to be affected by them. If they had been running recently she thinks they would have a better chance. She is sure that they will have to go back to that air base to find what they need. In the morning I have this terrible feeling that Jon is in trouble. I try to call the other part of our group again, and again I do not get an answer.

Nickie and a couple of the settlers that do not want to move here, say they will be happy to accompany me back to their settlement, if I would really like to go. I remember that Sara said she was going down today to help Jon settle that dispute down in Cuba this morning, so that may be why I am feeling like I do. We decide to wait until we hear something before running back to the other settlement. James checks out the transformers, and decides that none of them are usable without being rebuilt. Craig, who is one of the leaders of this settlement, mentions that he has seen things like these in some of the buildings in the city that is not far from here. James says that he should have thought to ask if there were any large manufacturing facilities in that city. Craig and the others laugh and tell him they still wouldn't have known what he is looking for.

We take the only good sized truck they have here, into town to see if there is a generator like we need there. We go directly to a place where a company once prospered, and find quite a few things that the settlement could use, including a generator with a transformer large enough to power this company. There are modifications to be made, and we will need to find and get ready the equipment we will need to move this, and possibly other generators. We go to a couple of home improvement stores, and find several smaller single house generators that run on gasoline, natural gas or propane. James wants to try to convert one of those generators to be run using the tidal currents. The good thing about those is that two men can handle them easily, and they only generate enough electricity for a house.

James spends the rest of the day working to get the generator changed over to work. Finally when the work day is over, and we are eating another great meal, Jon calls to tell me that they have overthrown the guy that called himself El Presidente, and everyone is doing well. We get to talk for a while then I can't help but start crying. Jon understands perfectly how I feel, which makes me feel much better. Then he tells me about all the attractive young ladies there, but Sara sets me and him straight on that topic as well, so I feel much better when we have to hang up. At least I sleep well tonight. I dream about Jon, and I hope I don't talk in my sleep or I will be very much embarrassed if anyone heard me. I am sharing a room with Nickie, who is Teddy's wife. She teases me about talking in my sleep, but says the only reason she knows what I was talking about, is because she was having the same kind of dream about Teddy. At least we can laugh about it together.

James says he is going to have to come back to finish the job of trying the tidal electricity generating. The people in this settlement don't mind, at least they have their windmills working again, plus they have several of the generators that run on propane or gas to help if a storm knocks out their power. Their electricians can finish hooking them up to as many buildings as they can. Plus they know what to look for to possibly get more of them just in case. I am in a hurry to start back to the southern settlement so that I can see Jon sooner. We get a fairly early start, but then everyone says we are going to stop at the military base we found on the way back. As much as I enjoy looking around those places, today it is just another delay in getting to be back with Jon.

We drive for what seems to be hours, and finally get to the base. Since I have to be here anyway, I decide to take the opportunity to see everything I can, so I can tell Jon all about it. Nickie and I know how much our husbands like new guns and other weapons so that's what we are looking for today. We are looking through what was the Base Exchange, when we hear quite a bit of noise coming from outside. It sounds somewhat familiar yet somehow strange, so we decide we better find out if we are being attacked. One lesson we all learned from Jon, is never go anywhere without a weapon, and if possible take more than one. We both have automatic hand guns and are both carrying a K-Bar knife, like just about all of our people do, when we get outside to see what is going on.

Whatever was making all that noise has stopped, but we still hear voices coming from around the building to our right, so we head that way with our guns drawn. We still can't see anything, so I have to look around the building and to do that I have to just about step all the way around it. Nickie is behind me when I step out, then I get grabbed around the waist by someone that is extremely strong. At first I am trying to get my gun around to shoot if necessary, but when I hear Nickie laughing, I know who grabbed me, so I drop my gun and wrap my arms around Jon's neck and pull him close for a welcome kiss.

5

The prisoner is still smiling, but the leader is pulling a gun to shoot him, so I do what I feel is the best thing I can do in this situation. I shoot at the leader with my handgun and miss, but I do hit the man next to him, which makes the leader turn tail and run into the house. The man I hit is only wounded, but it gives the prisoner a chance to strike out with his feet knocking his captors far enough way for him to kick at the men holding the woman. I have to hold my fire at this range or I could hit the captives as easily as their captors. I decide to use the bow, which I am pretty good with, if I do say so myself.

I put an arrow into the shoulder of one of the men trying to hold the woman, who is fighting as hard and the man is now. They are both kicking, trying to get away from the soldiers, and from where I am standing, it looks like the soldiers are more interested in getting clear of them than they are holding them. I shoot a second arrow at the soldiers, and it goes straight through one of their chests and sticks in the wall, near the door where the leader just stuck his head out of. He ducks back in quickly, and when I turn back to see where the prisoners are, they are just jumping off the patio into the small clearing between the jungle and the house.

I yell for them, and tell them that I will cover their escape. Actually I say, "Over here LT, I have your six covered. Your bad guys are running for cover." They run to where I am, and now I remember where I have seen them before. This is Lieutenant Mason, who was on the Seal team with Tim and I, and the lady is Nurse Kathy, from the hospital. They see me and ask who I am. Naturally I am wearing the ghillie suit and I have my face painted to blend into the jungle. Their hands are still tied behind them, and the lady has her blouse almost ripped totally off. I tell them I will explain later, but for now they should turn around so I can cut the ropes binding their hands, and we can get out of here.

They turn and I cut the ropes with my K-Bar, then as we are retreating I toss her a shirt to put on, and toss him a gun and a knife. When she is dressed again I toss her a gun while we are still moving through the jungle. We hear what sounds like pursuit, so I fire half a dozen rounds in that direction, and we hear someone shouting orders and what sounds like people retreating. When we are a couple miles away I tell them that we are probably safe for the moment. I take off the ghillie suit mainly because it is very hot with it on, and wipe at least some of the paint off my face. I can see that LT is trying to remember where he may have seen me before. When he sees the name on my tee shirt, he gets a look of total surprise on his face.

I may have forgotten to tell you, but Sara and Dayna decided one day to make some tags for our shirts with our nicknames on them. Tim had told them when we first came to this world what I was called by the other members of our Seal team. When we were on a mission I was often the one who took high ground with my fifty caliber rifle and snipers scope. I was also the one who decided which of the enemy died, so some of the guys started calling me God. I did not like being called that, primarily because of my upbringing by Ma and Gunny Horton. It just did not sound respectful, so the guys started calling me by the name of the leader of the Greek Gods, Zeus.

LT is looking at me like he can't believe it is really me, but Nurse Kathy looks at my face and getting very close she says "Jon Gorman", more like a question than a statement. LT says it can't be because I was killed in a subway accident fourteen or fifteen years ago. Then he says he'll be damned if I don't look a lot like Jon though. I am smiling now so LT starts looking to see if he is missing anything that may be funny. I ask him how they came to be here. He says first of all, neither of them is sure where here is. Then he explains what has happened up to this point.

"First, I am no longer Lieutenant Mason, it's Captain Mason, soon to be Major, if I survive this vacation. Kathy and I have been together for several years now, and the opportunity came up to take a vacation, and do a little diplomatic duty at the same time. Our relationship with Cuba has gotten much better than it used to be, so people from the US are spending more time here. Kathy and I were attending a party the other night, when we were invited to go deep sea fishing with some of the local leaders the next day, which was two days ago. Everything was going great until the worst fog I have ever seen rolled in, and we couldn't see past the bow of the boat."

I tell him that I bet the boats instruments all went dead as well, so the boat's captain had no idea which way to go. He looks at me and asks me how I know that. I tell them that I bet I can guess pretty close to what happened after that. He tells me to go ahead, so I tell him that he and Kathy went below to get out of the cold, damp, foggy air. He doesn't answer, but I can tell I am either right on, or at least very close. When you woke up you went back up on deck and it was still foggy, but there was no one else on the boat. He asks me how I could possibly know all this. I just smile and tell him to let me finish.

"Eventually the fog started to clear enough to at least see a little, and the boats instruments started working again. That wasn't very important though because you could just make out the shoreline, and were able to steer a course for the coast. As you got closer it didn't look like the area that you left, but you figured if you could just get back to shore you could make your way back to the city or village you left from. You may have even spent some time going up and down the coast looking for somewhere familiar. Finally you docked at an area that looks like it is used only by small fishing boats. When you came ashore, you were probably welcomed by a couple of your previous host's friends, and taken to him."

He asks me if I had anything to do with all that has happened, and I tell him yes I did. I made the fog roll in and did all the other things, just so I could get to see them. He says he knows that was a dumb question, but what the heck is going on around here, and who am I? I smile and tell him that I am the Jon Gorman that he knew back then, and that Tim and I, along with some others have come to this world. We feel it's to help the people that were living here survive. He looks like he doesn't believe a word that I am saying, but Kathy tells him as crazy as it sounds, it makes more sense than anything else has for the past few days. He says she has him there, but he is still not convinced.

I tell him I will take them to the area where the city they were staying in used to be. We walk through the jungle, avoiding other people, until we get to the city. It is almost totally destroyed, except for a few of the buildings that had walls about three feet thick. They recognize some of the landmarks that they noticed before the fishing trip. They ask what happened here that they need people from another world to help them survive. I explain about the war they had here, and how it almost wiped out the entire population, but left the cities and most of the other building pretty much the same. What we are seeing here is the effects of the hurricanes and tropical storms that hit this coast several times a year.

They ask how Tim and I came to be here, so I explain how our story is very similar to theirs, and how we have lived self sufficiently since then. I also tell them why I happen to be here at this time. Now LT tells me that the guy in charge has ten men that they were able to actually see, and they think that from the way they talked, there may be some that stay in the settlements most of the time. Kathy tells me that she knows that they have female prisoners that are used by them for pleasure. She says that this morning the leader told his men that they needed some fresh women. I hope that the events of this morning put that on hold, to give us time to stop these people.

I ask Kathy if she would like to find a safe place to stay until we can get back, and she tells me if I want to find a safe place I can, but she wants to teach those guys some manners. As we are walking through the jungle, to get to the settlements, I ask LT if he can still fight now that he is an officer and gentlemen. Kathy laughs and tells me he is not in the same shape he was in when we were on the team together. He tells me that when this little game of war we are playing is over, he will show me what kind of fighting shape he is in. Kathy asks me if anybody else they might know has come here. I ask her if she remembers a lady pilot that we brought in when we were in the Middle East.

They both say they do remember her, mainly because they found out a couple months after we were supposedly killed; she was killed in a plane crash back in the states. I tell them that she is here as well, and if we don't have this mess cleaned up in a couple days, she will come flying in here in a gun ship with rockets and bullets blazing. They both laugh and say it might be worth it to sit back and watch her do it. Unfortunately I am worried about what the leader may do to the people in the settlements now. We get to the first settlement and we get to talk to some of the people there. Apparently the leader pulled all of his guards back to the mansion to protect him. The people are happy to see that there are now three of us, instead of only me. I have to admit it should make the job easier.

We make it to the second settlement just before dark, and we get to talk to the same young lady that I met the other day. She is happy because she got another wild pig, and the guards went back to the mansion so they will not steal most of the meat. She loves her K-Bar and still eyes my bow and arrows fondly. She sees my rifle which is broken down in my pack, and likes that even more. I smile and tell her that when this is over I will trade her some boar tusks for the bow, or the gun, or maybe even both. We make sure she gets back to her group without incident and then find a spot to spend the night.

Tonight we get to sleep in an abandoned hunter's hut that Lillianne told us about. That's the young ladies name. Luckily I have a couple extra ponchos in my pack for Kathy and LT. It's not terrible cold at night, but it can be uncomfortable if you're not ready for it. We sleep well, and in the morning I decide to call Dayna to see what everyone there is doing. She tells me that she is with the group that is looking for a place to possibly move their settlement. Tim is back with some of the others at the original settlement. I tell her that I am afraid that the people that have taken over are not the type to listen to reason, so this will probably not end peacefully. I tell her about Kathy and LT, and she is excited to meet them. I tell her that we are going to try to bring this thing to an end as soon as possible and that I will call her later.

We discussed the way we think would be best to accomplish our task. If it wasn't for the prisoners in the mansion, we would simply set up a perimeter, and snipe at the bad guys whenever they show their heads. We're afraid they may kill all the prisoners if we do something like that. We decided to run this pretty much like we would back with the teams. The problem is we need at least two more people that know what they are doing to make it work right. We already know that there is no one at the first settlement that has the experience we need, so we are headed to the second settlement again, then the third.

At the second settlement, the only ones that will openly go against the leader are the old man and Lillianne. The others have little if any experience with fighting. We tell our volunteers that we will be back, hoping that we find some younger perhaps more experienced fighters in the third settlement. At the third settlement it appears that they have been hit the hardest as far as having their women taken by the soldiers. One of the men who is a fisherman tells us that he will help no matter what happens to him. Those people took his daughter and are holding her in the mansion. I know he means well, but we are not sure how much help he will be. Some of the others are willing, but they have no training in fighting or defending themselves.

LT asks me where Nolan is, and I have to think for a minute who he is talking about. I realize that the only way we can take these guys is by having at least two or three of my friends from the mainland come over to help us. I call on the satellite phone and Dayna answers on the other end. She is with James and Jenna at a settlement that is in the area where they were going to show the other people where it might be easier to sustain a good strong family. I ask her if she has any way to get in touch with Tim and Rob or possibly Teddy or Steve. She says she can call them on the short wave, but they may have to get lucky whether or not someone is listening at this time. She tells me she will try and have them call me back because they have a satellite phone as well, only she doesn't have the number.

This has got to be the most frustrating mission I have ever been on, mainly because it is too big to accomplish by myself, and I don't have enough help to do it right. I am not expecting too much to come from the phone call to Dayna. If Tim or any of the other guys knew we needed help, they would come in a minute. Actually I would hate to try to stop Sara from coming in with guns blazing. Hopefully she will come tomorrow morning with guns blazing as she said she would. Something tells me to go back to the second settlement and to assemble my rifle before I go. LT asks me why I am doing that, and I have to tell him that I have no idea, something just told me to do it so I am. Kathy just laughs and says that it must be something that all Navy Seals are born with, because her dad and LT are always telling her they just have a feeling about something.

We are going through the jungle when I hear, more than see, a ruckus going on in the jungle somewhere ahead of us. From the sounds that I am hearing I am pretty sure I know what is happening. I run to get close enough to see what is happening and it is exactly as I feared. Three guards have Lillianne, and they are not planning to be very nice to her. She is fighting for all she is worth, but they are simply too strong, and there are too many of them. She pulls the K-Bar I gave her and slashes at the men, but they block her arm and take the knife away from her. I see the one with the knife cut her blouse, then one of the others tears it off and knocks her to the ground. I was waiting for her to get out of the way because she was between a clear shot and her attackers.

I yell to get their attention and I fire as soon as they look to see who is coming. The one with the knife is knocked backward by the force of the blow. I am using soft tipped rounds that will mushroom big time when they hit. I jack a new round in the chamber and fire as soon as my sight is on his chest. He goes down like the first one did. The third one turns and is running, but Lillianne grabs his leg and trips him. He goes down, but he is frantically trying to get away. His biggest problem is the dense underbrush; if you try to go through this stuff too quickly it trips you up every time. I rush to get to him, but Lillianne found her knife on the ground and the third attacker is no longer trying to get away. If I had to guess, he is probably somewhere in the hereafter discussing what went wrong with their plans today.

Lilliannes blouse is in shreds, so I give her the last good tee shirt I have in my bag. Kathy is trying to console her, but that young lady is probably tougher than I am. She tells Kathy she is okay now, her friend Jon came to her rescue, as she knew I would. She wants to go kill the rest of those pigs now. To be honest I am not sure if the sound of the gunfire will bring the bad guys to us, or if they will hunker in deeper and make us come to them. Some of the other people in the settlement tell us that the bad guys do not have much food. They have been taking it from the workers here every day, and those men really are pigs. They eat all the food they take and still want more all the time.

That could work in our favor, but the problem of how to get the women out alive is still bothering me. I mention this to the people and Lillianne tells us that she played in the mansion all the time when she was a little girl. There is another girl, about the same age as she is, that says they both used to go there and pretend that they were grand ladies living in that house. They explored every room and every closet in the place. They tell us there is a way in from outside that is under the ground. The old man says that in the old days, before the war, the people who lived in the mansion were very wealthy. They made much of that wealth smuggling drugs, and many other things including people. At least that's what he heard from his father when he was a boy.

I ask them if they know where the underground passage starts on the outside. The two girls shake their heads yes excitedly. This could be the one bit of information we need to get the women out, then we can wait the bad guys out if we have too. I ask the girls to lead the way, and instead of going straight to the mansion, they head for the shore, about a half mile from the building itself. LT and Kathy are asking the girls questions about where the underground passage comes out inside, because they were inside, they are hoping to be able to remember where the opening is in conjunction with where the girls are being held.

We get to the seashore and the girls are talking about where the opening is. Apparently there is more than one, but they all lead to the same part of the house, they just lead to different rooms within the house. LT says that they were held on the first floor, in a room off the main great room. As far as they can tell, no one went into the basement while they were in the house. We will have to cross that bridge when we get to it. Getting into the house unseen will be a huge advantage. As we are looking for the openings, I am thinking about the series of tunnels we built into our settlements, for the purpose of being able to move around unseen in case of attack or even natural disaster. We have used those tunnels several times and are very glad that we decided to do that.

It is getting dark, which does not make it any easier to find what we are looking for. Finally the young ladies exclaim that they are sure they have found one of the openings. They say that there should be another one about a hundred meters farther down the shoreline. The openings look like caves in the rocks that make up the shoreline here. Unfortunately we are in high tide, so only the tops of the caves are visible above the water. We discuss the pros and cons of trying to get inside those caves at high tide. We are starting to think that maybe it would be better to wait until early morning, after the tide has gone out and then try.

6

I still do not have a good feeling about waiting. I know those women have been there for quite a while and odds are they will not kill them between now and morning, but they can sure make their lives a living hell between now and then. I ask the girls if they remember anything about the inside of the caves. They both tell me they only followed them out a couple of times, but they do remember thinking that they were very large, not far inside. I ask them if they mean that they open up once you get past the opening. One of the men in the group steps forward and apologizes for speaking without being asked. I tell him he is always welcome to speak to us, please tell us what is on his mind.

He tells us that he has heard that there are many very large lobsters and other good things from the sea to eat in those caves, so one time a few years ago; he took his small row boat right into one of them at low tide, to see if it is true. He goes on to say that when he got inside the cave, which was small on the outside, he was surprised at how large it was on the inside. He says he dropped his lobster traps and fished from his boat for a short time, when he started hearing what he thinks is the lost souls that were killed in the mansion. He pulled in his traps, which were full of some of the best lobsters he has ever eaten, and got out of there. He has never gone back. The girls say they remember hearing the moaning of souls as well.

The sea this evening is pretty calm, at least right here. It seems to be a quiet place out of the main coastline, where there are fairly good sized waves crashing into the wall that goes up to the cliffs above. As a Navy Seal we often had to swim miles at a time, and I have continued swimming, although not as much as I did back then. It appears that the current is going directly into the caves. I tell LT that he should wait here with the others, while I swim into the cave and see what there is in there. He argues, but he doesn't have a better plan, so I strip down to my tee shirt and shorts, strap my K-Bar and my handgun to my waist, and get ready to swim into the cave. I tell the others that I will come back out either way, to let them know if this is even a plan worth trying.

I dive in and the current starts carrying me into the cave immediately. At least I can swim on top of the water, except for the very outside opening on the cave, which is now almost under water. I get inside and I can see that it is lighter than I thought it would be. There must be an opening where the fading light of the day can still get in. it's not much, but it allows me to at least see shadows, and some of the inside of the cave. After going about a hundred yards or so, I get the feeling of being in a wide open space. I make my way to the side of the cave, and find a ledge that I can pull myself out of the water, and sit or stand on. It is about two and a half to three feet wide, and seems to run for quite a way along the wall.

I have a military flashlight that I can wind up to charge the battery. I light that and can see where this cave does open up quite a bit. The shelf I am standing on runs all the way to the far end of the cave. From here it looks like the water ends about thirty yards farther in than I am right now. Along the ledge there are places where boats could tie up and be secure. I also find at least two places where there are steps leading up to the ledge from underwater. I am surmising that boats used to come into the cave at low tide, and tie up here until their business with the people in the mansion was completed. Then they could climb back in their boats and go back out at low tide. I hear what I think the locals were calling souls moaning, it sounds like the wind in a tube or large pipe. I am betting they have some vents built into the roof of this place.

I walk to the far end, which is deeper into the cave. There are plenty of bird droppings on the ledge, but no indication that anyone has been in here for many years. When I get to the wall where the ledge ends, I am at a loss because I expected to find some kind of door, but there is nothing like that. The ledge runs about four more feet around a slight jutting area in the face of the wall. I follow the ledge and to my surprise, the wall opens up just about enough to slide through sideways. If Sara was here, she would tell me it's a good thing I don't have any bigger gut or I wouldn't fit. Once inside, it opens up to a decent sized passage way that leads back toward the mansion.

I figure that I better go out and let the others know, but while I am walking toward the front of the cave, I see LT swimming in to see if I am okay. I show him what I found, and we decide to let the others know what we are going to do, then go in to see if we can get the women out. When we get back outside the cave and tell the others, Kathy and Lillianne both want to come along in case we run into trouble. I don't bother to tell them that of course we are expecting to run into trouble. You don't usually take hostages away from people like that and not have at least some trouble. Both of them are better than average swimmers, but for this they don't really have to be. We get inside, then go through the opening in the wall to the other side. Lillianne says that she remembers that opening and that she also remembers a large room up ahead that looks like someone or many people stayed there.

As we make our way along the corridor, we come to the room that she was telling us about. She is right that it is a large room, and from the looks of it people did stay here and possibly for extended periods of time. At closer inspection, there is another smaller room off this one that has three skeletons in it. Lillianne makes the sign of the cross and says that it must be them that we hear moaning. I show her a hole in the ceiling that looks like it is some kind of a vent, and show her that when I cover it, the moaning stops. She smiles and says she likes that answer better than the ghost one anyway. We continue on toward we don't know what. I am counting my steps because I know the mansion is approximately a half mile from the shore. We pass an opening in the wall that appears to head back the way we came from, only at a different angle.

Lillianne tells me that we are getting close now. There should be a door up ahead that will lead to the cellar of the mansion. She is right; we come to a heavy wooden door with huge iron or steel hinges on it. I am expecting it to move with a lot of difficulty, but Lillianne pushes in the right place I guess, because it swings inward easily. It is dark on the other side, so I slowly poke my head around the door to see if there is anyone there. There are a couple more skeletons, but no one we have to be concerned with, so we all go into the large room and close the door behind us. It moves almost silently, it must be counterbalanced to move that easily. I can't wait to have James and Jenna see this. Mike and Morgan will definitely want to see this as well.

Lillianne whispers to me that there are many rooms in this basement. This is but one of them and some of the others also have doors like this one that also lead to the ocean. This room is impressive with the heavy oak furnishings. This looks like it may have been like a hideaway to get away from others, or a room for people to meet in. We look out into what looks like a large hall with rooms off it on both sides. There is a heavy layer of dust on everything, and cob webs hanging from the ceilings everywhere. It is obvious that no one has been down here in quite a while. Lillianne tells us that if we can discover what room the women are being held in, she may be able to help us get into it unseen. I tell her that if she shows us how we may be able to get the women out, it might help us locate which room they are in. She thinks about it for a few seconds then smiles, and says she sees what I mean.

She leads us into a room that is almost full of crates. We can't tell what's in them, but if I had to guess, I would say guns and munitions. We can check that out later, for now getting the women out is the primary objective. I ask Lillianne what she is looking for. She tells me in a whisper that there are passages that lead up to the rooms that are hidden from view in the rooms. She finds a place where the wall juts out a few inches farther than the rest of the wall and smiles. I am thinking that the farthest out section is the one that moves, but she is looking along the flatter wall beside it. Suddenly the wall slides to the side behind the jutting out portion. Behind it is a set of steps that has been carved right into the rock. It's a good thing we found some coal oil lamps that still work, plus a bunch of candles so we can save our flashlights.

I lead the way up the stairs, and at the top I find a landing that goes a ways farther along the wall. The wall on this side where the rooms are is made of wood, but the other wall is rock. I am looking along the wall when I see what looks like a small window in the wall. I carefully slide it to the side trying not to make any noise, and I can see into the room through what appears to be a tapestry hanging on the wall. The material is almost sheer where the opening is, but I bet you can't see that difference in the thickness from the other side. It doesn't really matter because there is no one in there to see us anyway. However the door to the room is ajar and we can hear some yelling and arguing going on somewhere fairly close to this part of the house.

Apparently the leader wants his men to go out and fight us, but they don't want any part of it. We hear footsteps coming toward the room, and a soldier drags a pretty young lady into the room and closing the door behind him, throws her on the bed and gets a wicked smile on his face. He tells her that if her friends want her, they can have her after he is done with her. It is very obvious that she is scared. She is pleading with him, asking him to please leave her alone. Lillianne is motioning me to keep going along the corridor until we are standing in front of a door in the wall. She motions that it leads into the room, but cannot be seen from inside. I misunderstand what she means and open the door and step into the room.

I thought she meant that there was something inside the room to keep me from being seen when I went in, but what she meant is that you cannot see the door from inside. Anyway, here I am standing in front of this soldier that is getting ready to assault this poor young lady. I'm not sure which of us is more surprised, the soldier, the young woman, or me. I am only a couple of steps from the soldier, who is turning to get a weapon from his clothing. I cover the distance in two quick steps, grab him around his mouth to prevent him from calling out, and he can now discuss where they went wrong with the other guys we ran into this evening. The young lady doesn't know whether to be afraid of me, or thank me until she sees Lillianne. She is not much older and knows her very well. We quickly lead her out of the room, and back down the stairs to get her where it's safe.

She tells us where the women are being held and Lillianne knows exactly where we can get into that room from. The room we have to go through to get there is a wine cellar with hundreds if not thousands of bottles of wine in it. It doesn't impress me, because I have never liked the taste of wine or any alcohol for that matter, but

LT says he will definitely be coming back here. We get up to the room where the women are being held and look in. Luckily there are several women in here and so far, no men. Again I go in the door, but Lillianne steps in right behind me and tells them they must hurry, so we can get them all out. She asks them if is all of them and they tell us that Isabella was taken earlier by one of the guards. We tell them that she is safe, so they have to hurry so that they will be as well.

Once all of the women are safe down in the basement, I tell LT that now may be the best time to hit them. We heard how afraid they are that we are going to come after them, so maybe we should go after them. We lay out a quick plan in the dust on the basement floor and decide we will attack from the room the women were in. Naturally Kathy and Lillianne want to go with us, because there are more soldiers than us. According to the women there are only five or six soldiers left. At least two of them deserted this afternoon after the guards that were attacking Lillianne were killed. Either way, we tell the girls that they need to stay here with the women. We sure could use a couple of automatic weapons besides our hand guns, but even with those we have at least thirty rounds of ammunition each, plus we have our K-Bar knives and I have the bow and arrows.

LT and I work our way back up the stairs to the room we just left. We were planning to surprise them by jumping out of the room with guns blazing. Sounds spectacular doesn't it? Well as usual something goes wrong, because just as we step into the room the door opens and there are two soldiers standing in the doorway. They are armed, but I don't think they remember that, because as soon as we raise our guns to fire, they raise their hands and surrender. We motion them back out into the big hall, where the rest of the soldiers are. They raise their hands as quickly as the two in the room. It's kind of disconcerting when you are primed for a battle. We yell down the stairs to the basement that the women can come up now. Naturally we checked all the rooms to make sure we didn't miss any.

When the women come up, Kathy walks over to one of the guards and kicks him where it hurts. The people keep coming up from the basement. These are the people that we left on the shoreline earlier this evening. I ask them how they got into the basement. They tell me the tide went out and they brought a boat into the cave, right up to the back door. I am thinking it can't be more than a couple of hours since we started this mission, but I look out the window and the sun is coming up. Kathy tells me it's true, time does fly when you are having fun. I have to admit in a warped kind of way, it has been fun. LT keeps eying the leader. He walks over to him and asks him if he would like to try smacking him around now that they are on even ground.

The leader says it does not look even to him. This time we hold the guns. LT tells him that there will be no guns; if the leader wins he walks away. If LT wins, we bury the leader. I know that sounds barbaric, but these guys have made the fine people of this settlement into slaves to do their bidding. I would like to think that they have learned their lesson, and will now be pillars of the community, and become the best workers here, but experience has shown that they will probably do the same thing to another weaker group of people. Besides he has a fifty/fifty chance of winning the fight.

We put our guns up and the leader rushes LT while he is turned away from him. LT wasn't born yesterday and we had to fight often using our hands or die. LT meets him coming in with a forearm to the face that knocks the leader flat. LT lets him get up before he wades in throwing punches and kicks that keep the leader backing up trying to cover up. He lashes out catching LT coming in and splits his lip causing it to bleed. LT just licks the blood away and smiles at him. They are both circling looking for an edge to put the other one down. They are exchanging punches and I know that this guy can't last against LT for very long. It doesn't take more than about another minute when he rushes LT trying to land on top and throw punches into LT's face. LT steps aside and punches the leader on the side of the head as he goes by. That puts the leader down and he lies there panting and gasping for breath.

It's obvious the fight is over. LT turns and starts to walk away when the leader jumps up, and goes after LT with a small knife he must have had hidden. I am ready to shoot, when the old man takes a step toward the leader and plunges the K-Bar I gave Lillianne into his chest. He tells him that's for stealing my daughters' innocence as the leader falls to the floor and lies motionless. We are just standing around, when LT says "that sounds like an old UH-1 helicopter." Now that he mentions it, I have been hearing it and not recognizing what I am hearing. We all go out to the patio where it looks like the entire settlement is waiting with every kind of weapon imaginable except guns. Sure enough the helicopter is coming right at us out of the sun.

It flies directly over our heads and we all duck even though Sara is flying far enough over us to miss hitting us. She flies past a couple hundred yards, then turns around and comes back much slower than she went past. She lands on the grounds, but not on the patio we are standing on. Teddy and Steve are manning the thirty caliber door guns. Tim and Rod jump out of the chopper carrying AK-47 military weapons, and I have to admit they look just like any good assault team I ever worked with. Sara and Gary get out and come over smiling. She asks me if I liked her entrance. They weren't sure whether or not we would need their help, but she didn't want to waste the opportunity.

She finally stops talking long enough to notice LT and Kathy. She tells them they look familiar, and ask if she has ever met them before. LT tells her they may have met, if she was ever a pilot in a previous life. Sara stops in her tracks and tells them it can't be. She says there is no way that this is the other Seal that helped pull her out of that crash, and Kathy can't be the nurse that helped her in that hospital. She asks them how they came to be here, then says, it's probably a good thing they are, or who knows how much trouble I would have gotten myself into. Tim comes up and smiles at LT, he asks him if we had a nice funeral. He says he would have liked a simple service, but nothing gaudy and pretentious.

LT gives him a hug and so does Kathy. With the formalities out of the way, we can concentrate on cleaning up this mess. The settlers ask us what they should do with the remaining soldiers. The people of the settlement, of which there are a whole lot more of them now than when we first came out here, say that they are welcome to leave, but if they are ever seen here again they will be killed on sight. The soldiers waste no time waiting around to see if the people will change their minds. The people are very happy to have their daughters and wives back. Many of them say they will catch enough lobster, shrimp, and fish for a huge fiesta this evening in honor of their guests.

7

Most of the people are very much interested in the helicopter, especially Lillianne. She is even more impressed that a woman flies it. She asks Sara if she thinks that Lillianne and Isabella could ever learn to fly one of those. She tells them that they may have to kick some man child butt to get the chance, but she is sure they could do it. Tim, LT, Rod, Steve, Teddy, Gary, and I decide to go back down to the basement to check out some of the treasures that are hidden there. One of the settlement men, named Miguel, asks if he may be allowed to accompany us. We tell him that he and anyone else that would like to see what they have is welcome. The first room we go to is the one that I am sure is full of crates full of weapons.

I am right, but they are mostly older military weapons that from the language written on the crates, they are from an Eastern European country, obviously before the war. Back in the world some of us left, these weapons would be worth quite a bit as collector's items. Miguel is speechless, because this is a great treasure for his people. We tell him we will help him and the others get the guns into proper working condition, and teach them how to use them safely and accurately. While we are looking at the guns, we hear the moaning sounds again. Miguel makes the sign of a cross, and says we have angered the spirits that live within the walls of this hacienda. I can't help but smile, and ask him if he would like to meet the spirits that are moaning. He gets a look of surprise on his face, and tells me that I should not mock the dead.

I take him by the arm and tell him I would never think about mocking the dead, or anyone else for that matter. I am sure there are more vents and that there are more than likely some right in the room we are in, but I show him the one that we found on the way in. When he realizes where the noise is coming from, he laughs and says he and the others have been superstitious fools. Steve and Rod both say that they were not so sure that it wasn't ghosts when they first heard it. Tim tells LT that it reminds him of some of the times LT had too much to drink. LT keeps reminding us that he is a captain now, not a lieutenant, but we tell him he will always be LT to us. Besides we are dead and are no longer in the military, so it doesn't matter anyway, because we're definitely not going to salute him.

We are going from room to room investigating what may be useful to the people living here. We find what appears to be a pantry full of jars of food that appear to still be sealed. Actually food here is not really a problem. The ocean is full of food and they can grow pretty much any crop that they want to. When we have finished with the basement, we go through the rooms upstairs. They are comfortably furnished and it looks like several families could coexist here with no problems at all. The grounds outside are in somewhat rougher shape, primarily due to neglect and tropical storms. There is a wall that runs around three sides of the main building. On the inside of the walls are homes that look like they were used by the people that worked on the mansion or hacienda before the war. I mention to Miguel that they could probably combine all three of the smaller settlements into one living here.

He says that they will discuss this option as soon as the groups can meet. He mentions that they are not very adept at making repairs to their homes and building new homes. They have been without electricity for a couple of months now, so some of us that have had experience with the windmills go to work getting them setup and producing again. We explain to the people here that this is just temporary, until James and Jenna and possibly Mike and Morgan can come down and possibly try some of the newer technology that may work better here than the windmills. By sundown we have power restored to two of the settlements. The people are having a big party to celebrate their independence from the man who called himself El Presidente.

I finally got to talk to Teddy alone today and asked him if Dayna had finally gotten through to them. He told me that they did not receive any messages from her. He says that he had a dream last night that Gunny came to him and told him I was in trouble, and that they should come down first thing in the morning, so they did. I tried to call Dayna today but could not get through. The people from all three settlements meet during the celebration to discuss how they may be better able to defend themselves in the future. I finally get through to Dayna just before I turn in for the night. She has been so busy today that she wasn't close to the phone. She definitely sounds happy to hear from me, and to learn that the leader here has been overthrown.

I ask her how she would like to spend some time down here with me, helping our friends rebuild, and she tells me as long as she is with me, she doesn't care where we are. Naturally I tell her we will be go back home, at least long enough to pick up any of our children that would like to come along, before we come back. She tells me that James is making some headway in getting the tidal electrical generator going. There is a lot to work out, so it will take longer than he at first thought, but then James tends to be just the tiniest bit optimistic. I get to talk to James for a few minutes and when I explain the lay of the land here, he thinks it may even be a better place to try than where they are currently.

I tell Dayna that hopefully I will be able to see her tomorrow. She starts crying, so I ask her if I said anything to make her upset. She tells me that she is just being silly and asks me to forgive her for acting so childish. I think I know why she is crying, so I tell her that I don't think it's childish to cry when you are away from the one person in the world that you love more than life itself. I miss her so much that I feel like crying too. Then I tell her that it's a good thing there are all these attractive young ladies running around in mini bathing suits, to take my mind off how much I miss her. She stops crying to tell me she is going to kick my butt when she sees me.

Naturally Sara sees me talking to Dayna on the phone and overheard what I said, so she has to get her two cents worth in. She takes the phone away and tells Dayna that even if there were attractive young ladies running around in bathing suits of any size, they wouldn't be interested in a fat old man like me anyway. Now Dayna is laughing and saying that sounds more likely than my story. I hate to hang up, but the call started to break up anyway. I can't wait to be with Dayna again soon. It seems kind of strange to sleep without having one eye open to watch for the enemy. Tonight I dream about some of the projects we have done that involved moving large metal buildings and putting them back up again.

You may think that would be a nightmare, but to me it is telling me that we are probably going to be doing that again, in the near future. We discussed before going to bed last night what we have planned for today. The people from this settlement are in agreement that they would like a couple of days to make some repairs, and to discuss how they would like to go forward. They realize that they were not ready for the kind of threat that they just faced. We make sure that they know we are willing to assist them in any way we can, to be ready next time, including helping them learn to fight better and show them how they can prepare their homes. That being agreed upon by us all, we are ready to head back to the mainland, for just long enough to put together a group to come here for an extended period of time to help the people here.

Our team brought enough fuel along to get us all safely back to the mainland, and once we get there we can refuel, and head for the military base that we were told about from the rest of our group. The people at the settlement in Florida are happy to hear that the bad guys have been overthrown and are no longer in charge. Those that escaped from there, say that they are in no hurry to go back. We explain what we are going to do to help them, and some say they will go back and try again, but others want to stay here, or at least they want to stay on the mainland, with a settlement here. Some of them, including Mary Elaina and her family, ask if it would be possible for them to join our settlement. We all tell them we have no problem with that, as long as they are willing to do their share of the work, and follow the rules which are basically to treat others the way you expect to be treated.

They all say they have no problems with living like that so we tell them they are welcome to join us when we go back home. We help get the vehicles loaded to go back to our settlement, then all of us going back home, except Teddy, me, LT, Kathy, Sara, and Gary get started on the drive back. We refuel the helicopter and head for the military base. When we get there we can see the vehicles that our group is driving, but no one is visible until we land. Jenna tells me and Teddy that our wives are at the BX, looking for new weapons for us war mongers, so we should probably head that way. That's when I got the idea to sneak up on Dayna and surprise her. I saw them coming toward where we landed cautiously, which makes me proud of our girls, because they are not taking anything for granted.

Teddy and I hide behind a door, then step out after they have gone past. We step out from behind the door and if we were the enemy Nickie would have shot us both, as it is she smiles and doesn't say anything so that I can sneak up and catch Dayna around her waist. When I grab her I realize that I could still get myself shot by her, but she must realize it is me, because she pulls me close and kisses me so hard my fillings would melt if I had any. Sara is laughing and telling us to knock it off, we have enough kids already. She tells LT and Kathy that I may have been innocent when they knew me in the other world, but in this world, I have had thirty or forty wives and so many kids they have lost count.

LT and Kathy along with everyone are laughing. I get to introduce them to everyone and everyone welcomes them to the family. Dayna, who is always the practical one, tells Kathy that she looks like she could use a change of clothes. She wraps her arm in mine and tells LT and Kathy that we will be happy to show them where they should be able to find some clothes that fit. She leads us to the BX, where LT, Kathy, and the rest of us find a bunch of good stuff that we along with the other settlements can use. The BX even has dressing rooms where LT and Kathy can change into some new clothes. The people that are along from both settlements are excited about the treasures that we are finding at this base.

Sara and Gary are already getting a couple of trucks running, with the help of Teddy and Nickie. They found a hangar that has several one and a half and two ton stake body trucks, plus some with boxes on them. They manage to get a nice two ton stake body truck running first. LT and Kathy are surprised at how well preserved everything seems to be, especially the rubber items and the steel. James starts to explain the technical terms that he and Mike use to describe all this, and LT tells him that just saying they last longer than usual will suffice for him. James tells him if he can fight as good as Tim and I can, he will be happy to skip the boring details in conversations from now on.

The tires seem to be holding air well enough for the trip back to the northern settlement, so we load the truck with the items that they say they can use the most right now, and they are on their way home. They are especially excited about the cases of K-Bar knives and the cases of chocolate candies in the sealed cans. We know from experience how tasty those are and we are sure that they will be a big hit with them as well. The second truck takes longer to get running the way it should, but we find out that LT is a pretty good backyard mechanic and has had a lot of experience with older military vehicles. We spend the night on the base, but we leave first thing in the morning for the southern settlement with a truck full of treasures for them.

The people from this settlement that went to the northern one explain about some of the places they saw on the way north. They tell them that they think moving to the other side of the state would be in their best interest. The climate is the same, but the ocean appears to be calmer on that side and they saw plenty of areas with plenty of homes for them all, plus there would be a lot of room to grow. All the new people from Cuba say that they will go wherever their new family wishes to live. Not everyone is convinced, but they are willing to go over and check it out. The worst that can happen is they decide they don't like it there and move back. One question that is asked is whether or not there are as many alligators, snakes, and other nasty beasts on the other side.

There is an area there that was known as the everglades in our world that is about as wild an area as you can get as far as wildlife goes. Some of the settlers here have expressed doubts about wanting to stay in an area where it can be so dangerous for their children. They have enough vehicles to take everyone on a trip, to see what the rest of the state has to offer; while we go back home and recruit some of the people that we will need to assist our friends here and in Cuba with the rebuilding process. We are flying home in the helicopter so it only takes us a couple of hours to get there and that includes a short stop for fuel. When we get there we are welcomed like conquering heroes. We actually beat the group that left before us, but they are driving, which will definitely take longer every time.

I am proud to show LT and Kathy around our settlement. They were thinking that all of the settlements in our world were as small as the ones we visited. When we get here it is a perfect time because just about all the crops that we plant are doing very well, as are the individual gardens that just about everybody has. We usually discuss what we want to grow with each other, so that we don't all grow the same vegetables at the same time. We also have the group crops where we grow enough tomatoes and other vegetables to can for everyone to have what they need. We have a few empty residences in each group, just in case we have people that wish to join us. LT and Kathy would like to stay with our group, while Mary Elaina's family would like to go to stay with Ryan's group, they have more Hispanic people in their group than we do.

There is not really much difference in the groups anymore, because we have pretty much grown together. Sara asked LT and Kathy if they are married or just living together. They are not sure how to answer, until I tell them that we prefer couples be married before they live together. We feel that it sets a better example for the young people if they see adults that they look up to are married before they engage in sexual activity. There have been a few exceptions, because people are individuals, and have their free agency, but at least so far it hasn't become the norm for our people to sleep around or to take the creation of other souls lightly. Kathy shows us a wedding ring and says she agrees with that practice totally.

In the morning, the others get back and we are all happy to see that our family is safe. All of us that were on that trip compare notes and decide that we need to hold a group counsel with all the groups present to determine who should go to help our friends down south. The young men that are our primary hunters ask me if it will be okay for them to take LT hunting for a wild pig. They are not quite as large as they were when we first moved here, but once in a while they run across one of the huge monsters. Normally now they only run between six and seven hundred pounds, instead of close to a thousand. Today they want to go almost fifty miles from home to hunt, because they have seen a couple of the larger hogs over that way.

We have always encouraged hunting away from home to save the game closer in, just in case it is needed some day. I tell them that I have no problems with it as long as LT wants to go, and they have at least one older hunter with them besides LT. When Teddy and the others find that the young men want to go hunting, they volunteer to go along. Thinking about hunting for wild pigs reminds me of Lillianne, I wonder what she would say if she could see one of the hogs that we get here. I told Dayna all about her and she can't wait to meet her. The way she talked she doesn't have any parents or any adult family members to help take care of her. Dayna mentioned inviting her to come to live with us here. We will be heading back within the week and there will be plenty of time to discuss where she wants to live at that time.

8

Dayna and I spend the day catching up the work that has not been done around the house since we have been gone. There's not that much to do because the kids pretty much take care of the house and each other. The house LT and Kathy are moving into is not far from our house. It's only two doors down as the kids would say. That house was lived in up until just about a month ago, when we brought back more of the Quonset huts from the military base. Our people love living in those. In fact we have several people waiting until we can bring more of them back to the settlement. When our house is back in order, the way Dayna likes it, we go over to help Kathy get her house setup the way she would like it.

When we get there, she is sitting in a chair kind of looking out over the settlement and the fields. We brought some fresh baked cookies, and some of the instant beverage kind of like coffee, only all natural that we make from toasted grains after we grind them up. With a little fresh honey it is not half bad. We are afraid that she doesn't like it here, but she tells us just the opposite. She tells us that she has never really had a place she could call home, other than the military and possibly the hospitals she has worked at. Her parents passed away in a car accident when she was thirteen, and from then until she was old enough to join the Navy, she was passed from foster home to foster home.

Usually either her foster father, or one or more of her foster brothers, would make sexual advances that she usually put an end to with whatever she could find that would stop them, several times it was a baseball bat. That's why she never stayed in one place very long. She says that this is the most beautiful place she has ever seen, and to think that she and Marion are going to be staying here, she is afraid that she is going to wake up and it will all be a dream. I understand how she feels, but I have to ask her who Marion is. She laughs and says that's LT's real name. He doesn't like it, but he would never change it because he was named after his father, who was also a Navy Seal, but he was killed in action when LT was twelve.

His mother passed away about two years after that from cancer. He lived with his grandmother until she passed away, and luckily he was old enough to enlist in the Navy. Dayna and I must be smiling a little because Kathy asks us if she said something funny. We apologize and tell her that we are not smiling about anything she said. It's just that all of us that have come to this world from the other world were pretty much alone there. Also all of us in this group that came from the other world, or whatever it was, wouldn't go back for all the money in the world. Kathy asks Dayna if there is some place where she might be able to find different curtains, or the material to make them.

Dayna smiles and points to some pretty good sized buildings that we have been using as warehouses for the extra items that we find and bring home. We take the time to explain that although we all have pretty much the same amount of worldly goods, we all have individual tastes and we all like certain things to make us comfortable, without going way overboard or wanting to own things just for the sake of owning them. We take her over to the warehouses and let her see what she can choose from. She finds some furniture that she likes much better than the furnishings in the house currently. We spend the next two hours swapping furniture, curtains, bedding, and she picked up a bunch of clothes for her and LT. She says she will wait until LT is here to pick out weapons besides the 9mm automatics that I already gave them and a K-Bar knife for each of them.

I draw another bow and arrows out of the arsenal because I gave the one I had to Lillianne. The draw is a little heavy for her, but I bet she is pulling it just fine when we go back. It can be adjusted down a little as well, that's one of the first things I showed her. I am relieved when the guys get back from their hunting trip because now LT can carry things and move the furniture around in his house. Teddy and Timmy are riding four wheelers and pull into the yard first. LT is riding in the truck, following them a few minutes behind. Teddy and Timmy come running up to tell me that LT was sure surprised when he saw the hog they found, and the bull just about blew his mind.

Teddy tells me this may well be the biggest pig yet. I have trouble believing that, but Teddy and Tim usually tell it like it is. The truck rumbles into the yard and as usual is the source of much curiosity. Just about everyone is interested to see what kind of meat the hunters are bringing home. LT jumps out and almost knocks Kathy down he is so excited about the hunt. He picks her up and swings her around he is so happy. He just about drags her over to where Dayna and I are talking to Teddy and Timmy, and tells me he thought I was pulling his leg about the size of some of the animals here. He tells Kathy that she has to see these two animals.

He tells me that he was sure we were pulling his leg when the young guys told him they need to take the truck with the small hoist on it when they go hunting. That's the truck we found in the lumber yard, with the lift that they used to use to load and unload lumber. We get to the back of the truck, along with at least fifty other members of our family, and I can hear the sharp intake of air when Kathy sees the steer and the pig that are loaded on the back. Both have been field dressed and both are extremely large even for here. Our hunters usually help butcher the meat they bring in, so our top butchers, Trevor and Bob, tell them to bring the truck around to the barn and they will get them quartered and hung so they can age properly.

Before the truck gets around to the barn, we have people from the other groups coming to see how our hunters made out. We have a lift in the barn that we can weigh the animal before we butcher it. The pig is a good fifty pounds heavier than any we have shot and the bull is seventy-three pounds heavier than the closest we have a record of. The hunters are reminded by several people that big does not necessarily mean good, when it comes to meat. Now we have some good natured joking about how tough the two animals are that were brought in today. Everyone is told that if they don't want to eat the meat, no one will twist their arms until they do. Everyone tells them they will give them the benefit of the doubt and eat some of the meat anyway.

LT is like a kid in a candy shop. He wants to help skin the animals and butcher the meat. The others are happy that he wants to get right into helping with the work. Tim tells LT that not just anybody can butcher a steer or a pig correctly. He tells LT that he will give him the benefit of all his years experience butchering meat for the family. Naturally Billy, Steve, Rod, Teddy, me, and several of the ladies in the group, tell Tim that if he is going to butcher those animals they won't be fit to eat. Tim just shakes his head and says that you make a little mistake by boiling a couple hundred pounds of spareribs, instead of barbequing them, and they never let you forget it. Everybody laughs and the real butchers show LT how to skin and quarter the game.

Our guys and girls have this down to a science and are very good and efficient at it. They have everything skinned out, quartered, and hung by the time dinner is ready. There are too many of us to take all of our meals in common, but we do have some meals this way, like this evening. We are having a cookout, with as luck would have it, spare ribs that are smoked and not boiled, hamburgers, and hot dogs along with several kinds of salads that were made by the ladies in the group. LT and Kathy are shocked by the food we are able to prepare here. We have our own hot sauce for the burgers and hot dogs as well as our own barbeque sauce for the ribs. If you remember we even make our own mayonnaise for the salads. We make the pasta and all the bread and rolls as well.

While we are eating, Sara along with Morgan, Lindsay, Jenna, and some of our more aggressive ladies in our family, come over and ask LT and Kathy if they would like to run the obstacle course in the morning. LT is excited to hear that we have an obstacle course, but doesn't really think it would be fair to run against the women, without at least giving them some kind of head start. I can see that Kathy is probably thinking the same thing I am. When we were back there in that jungle in Cuba, LT had all he could do to keep up. It is pretty obvious to me that he has been doing more diplomatic work than combat missions lately. Kathy tries to warn him, but he is the same as he was when we were on the team together. A good team player, but just arrogant enough to think he is better than he is at any kind of physical challenge.

LT winks at me and says that we will be happy to run the obstacle course against the ladies tomorrow morning at eight. I tell him I will be there and I will run, but as far as any bet he is making, he is on his own. Personally I have had to paint enough rooms and homes in this settlement because I lost a bet to those conniving females. Sara has been after Gary to paint their house for the past couple of months, something tells me that LT is going to be doing that pretty soon now. The evening ends and it feels so great to climb under the covers on our own bed tonight. I know there will not be many more nights at home before we have to go back to help our friends, but I am going to enjoy it while I can.

In the morning there is a big crowd at the obstacle course to watch the race. LT and I came over a little early so that we can go through it, just to give him an idea of what he is getting into. The longer we are going through it the more he is impressed with it. He sees the other obstacle course we have and asks about that one. I tell him that is for the children and those that just enjoy a challenge, but are not quite as crazy as some of us are. By the time we go through it at an easy pace he asks me how big Sara and Gary's house is anyway. I laugh and tell him it only took me about two weeks the last time I painted it.

The girls are waiting when we get to the start again. They ask how we want to do this, all at once, or run it for time and the best time wins. LT starts to say all at once and I tell them we will do it for time. I tell LT that if we all run it at once, they will block us in and we will not get past them until they have beaten us soundly. Lindsay smiles and looking all innocent tells me that I must be thinking of someone else, because these young women are far too ladylike to do anything like that. They all laugh and high five with each other and their daughters. My son Thomas is standing next to me and I ask him if he still likes Sara's daughter Misty. He tells me that they like each other very much. He says her competitive spirit is one of the things he really likes about her.

Dayna smacks me for asking Thomas that question. She really likes Misty as well and I have to admit he could do a lot worse. We draw numbers to see which order we will run in. When we run the course for a time, we usually have three or four people on the course at a time. We don't leave all at once. We usually wait somewhere around a minute apart. I personally don't care what my time is, but since the girls are as competitive as they are, I often let them win by a couple of seconds. I have to win sometimes or they will catch on that I am letting them win. That's not to say that every time they win that I let them. On the contrary, they have all beaten my times honestly and fairly several times. Today I drew number one and I really feel good today, so I think I will do my best and see if I can get an individual best time.

When we get timed there are at least three or four members of the family timing everyone. Today there are people from all the other groups to watch and even some to compete with us. It's a lot of fun and a great source of entertainment. It is time to start the course so Dayna gives me a nice kiss and tells me she will give me another kiss if I break my own personal best today. Sara asks Dayna whose side she is on anyway. Perverts like me will do most anything to get a kiss from a good looking woman like her. Dayna just smiles and asks her if there was ever any doubt whose side she is on. She is just as big a pervert as I am.

Our obstacle course is as challenging as any I ever had the pleasure of running when I was in the service. If you take off too fast right at the start, you will be extremely tired by the time you get to the end. I tried to explain all this to LT when we walked the course earlier, now we will have to see if he paid any attention to me or not. I have run this course so many times it is like second nature for me. I know exactly what pace to start off and when I can turn it up and where I have to be extra careful. This course can bite back if you are not careful. Not that you will get hurt badly, but your pride may take a pretty good beating if you have to finish soaking wet from falling into one of the water hazards.

Believe me I am well aware of what that is like. Today I am going along well and I feel like I can probably do a personal best time. About two minutes in I am starting to feel the last couple of weeks catching up with me a little, but not enough to slow me down. I can hear someone on the course behind me, but I am a full minute ahead if not a little more by this time. We have walls that we have to climb over, as well as towers that we have to climb, and then rappel down the other side. We also have four bridges that have to be crossed and a swing over a pretty good sized stream. That one, if you do not get a good swing you will wind up not getting to the other side without getting at least your feet and legs wet.

Today I navigate every obstacle cleanly and finish with a personal best by almost a full minute. Lindsay was the one directly behind me and she finishes almost three whole minutes after I do. She is wet from the waist down and laughs when we ask her which water hazard gave her the most trouble. She says pick one, because they all managed to pull her in today. Sara finishes next and she has a personal best time as well that is not that far off my time. She is gasping for breath when she comes in, which shows how difficult this course is. When she can talk she says that LT left a minute ahead of her and two minutes ahead of Morgan. Morgan comes in and between gasping for breath; she tells us LT should be here soon.

When Jenna comes in ahead of him we figure we better go looking for him. He is sitting on the fourth obstacle from the end holding his side when we find him. We ask him if he is okay and he laughs and tells us that everything is fine except his pride. We help him up and we all walk back to the beginning of the course. Everyone tells him that at least he tried, but maybe he should use the smaller course until he gets into better shape. My sons ask me what my time was. I tell them it was a personal best, but I will not tell them the time. Now that the challenge race has been run, the younger members of the family want to see if they can beat our times.

I tell Timmy and Tommy that I really want them to run the course as fast as they can and not be concerned with beating my times. They decide to run it together as a race which gets most of the people excited. Our sons are very popular in all of the groups that make up our settlement, and they are known for their athletic prowess, as well as their knowledge of different topics. The boys are talking about how they are going to kick each other's butts. Dayna tells them that if they don't play nicely together, she will be the one kicking butts. They laugh like they always do and give their mom a kiss. They both have to bend over quite a ways to give their mom a hug and a kiss. They both come over and tell me they need a hug for good luck. I start to hug them when they keep walking to give Bobbi and Misty a hug. Naturally that gets a laugh from everyone that is here.

The boys line up and just as they are about to start the race, Tommy steps aside and Bobbi takes his place. Something tells me this was planned from the beginning, because Timmy just smiles and wishes her luck. She tells him that it is going to take more than luck for him to beat her. The starter fires the starting gun, which just shoots blanks, and both runners are on their way. They both set a pace that would probably kill me before the course was completed. Tommy and Misty wait two minutes before starting after them. Today I am timing my sons because I can see how fast they are running, and every time they run the course they tell me that I just beat their times. LT and Kathy come over to talk while we are waiting for the young people to finish.

Every two minutes another pair takes off. LT keeps saying he can't believe that he couldn't even finish. I tell him that this is the toughest obstacle course that I have ever run. We have refined and improved it for the past ten years. I am getting ready to tell him that we are thinking of changing a couple of the obstacles, when Timmy comes across the finish line a full thirty seconds faster than my best ever finish. Bobbi is only about fifteen seconds behind him, which means she beat my best time as well. Timmy tells us that we should really change those obstacles because everyone can pretty much run right over or through them. I tell him to get with the other young people and present a couple of suggestions, and the council will discuss them and we can vote on the changes.

By this time Tommy comes running in, followed closely by Misty. I managed to beat their times today, but only by a couple of seconds. Naturally Timmy and Bobbi tell them that they have had time enough to eat lunch and take a nap waiting for them. We head back to the house to shower and have a meeting to discuss how we are going to help our friends in the southern settlements. Tim was on the short wave radio last evening and they are wondering when we will come back as we promised. LT and Kathy want to be involved in whatever we do at those settlements. James and Jenna have had the time to discuss the possibilities with Mike and Morgan. They all want to be involved with setting up the tidal electrical generation. They all feel that the location in Cuba would be the best place to start, unless they can find something similar on the coast of Florida.

We have to hold our meeting in one of the larger meeting rooms because of the concern and support for these projects. We have no shortage of volunteers to help with the work and with teaching our friends how to defend themselves. Gary, Sara, and I remember that there were a couple of helicopters at that base in Kentucky that were outfitted to carry cargo instead of armament and passengers. James and Mike say that we could really use another one of those hangars that we left there. We know how long a project like moving a hangar takes because we have done it, but we feel that we have learned enough that it will go much smoother this time. The biggest problem is that we can't wait until the project to get more helicopters and another hangar is complete.

Tim says that he probably has no business putting in his two cents worth, but maybe we can send one team to our friends down south and send another team to Kentucky. We have plenty of people to cover both projects; beside we can be back in a couple of days if we have to. Tim and I are not on the council this time. If you remember we hold elections and have a rule that no one can be on the leadership committee more than one term consecutively. They can be on it several times, but there has to be a break in their position. We feel that prevents anyone from having more of a voice than everyone else. Our group has asked Tim and me to be the leaders of our group on a permanent basis. We are the ones who asked that we change leaders periodically so that everyone gets an opportunity to be on the council.

We all think that is an excellent idea, but we agree to adjourn for the day and to meet again in the morning and be prepared to set the teams and when we will be leaving to complete them. LT and Kathy come home with us, along with Tim and Charity, Gary and Sara, James and Jenna, and Mike and Morgan. LT says that he would be happy to help out anywhere we feel he is needed the most. It doesn't take long and we know who we will recommend as the two teams.

9

Dayna and I spend the evening visiting with the children and making sure everyone knows what they have to do, to keep up the house while Dayna and I are gone. Not that it takes much planning; the children did a great job taking care of the house while we were gone before. We are also visited by some of the family members that have said that they would like to go on the trip down south. Teddy stops by with Nickie and asks me if we could manage without him this time. He has quite a bit of work to do on their house, and it really needs to be gotten done. I tell them that I was counting on him to keep a watch over our group, and the other groups that make up our settlement.

I do not expect to have to do any fighting while we are there. I expect to be training them to fight and to notice when someone may be trying to cause trouble. The training, the rebuilding and helping them setup a new electrical generation method, are the main reasons for going. It should not take a large group to accomplish these tasks. In the morning we meet and let the committee know what our suggestions are. Not surprisingly we are all in agreement of who should be on each team, and approximately how long we should be needed. It is decided to leave in two days, when we should be ready with everything we will need. Dayna and I spend the rest of the day getting ready.

We decide to leave tomorrow because we are ready and we may as well get started. James, Jenna, Mike, and Morgan will not be leaving until the planned time, but we can be getting started while we wait for them. We load our truck with the supplies that we will need before we turn in for the night. In the morning it is dark and wet out to start our adventure. LT says he always hated missions that started out this way. It seems like the worse the weather, the larger the opportunity for unforeseen trouble. I on the other hand do not mind the weather to start a mission. I found that most of the time if the team had problems; they were caused by our lack of planning. This adventure, or mission if you would prefer, is very well planned and we know pretty much what to expect, so I for one am not expecting any problems other than small ones.

Last night we received word that the group that wants to stay in the original settlement on the east side of the state, found a very large mansion or hacienda that is very much like the one in Cuba, with passages out to the shoreline of a fairly peaceful bay. We know what to look for so we will be going to that settlement first, to investigate the area and start teaching the groups how to be more self-sufficient. We make good time the first day and get there around noon of the second day. The people in this group are very excited about their find, so we don't even unload and setup camp before we are being shown the mansion.

It sits on the shoreline of a bay that runs off the ocean here. The mansion has underground passages that lead to the bay by way of caves like the one in Cuba. We are not experts, but we think it should be a good place to try the new technology. We unload our trucks and setup our camp here with our friends. When that is done, we go looking for a pretty long list of items that James and Mike gave us to find before they get here. Actually they just said it would be great if all these items are available when they get here so that they don't have to waste time looking for them. After doing as much scavenging as we have, we know what kinds of places to look in to find certain items.

That's the case today, when we find the wire that will be needed for this project. We find a whole roll of the right wire in a warehouse, for a store that sold electrical supplies for industrial applications. LT proves his value on this project by helping me get a fork lift running, so that we can put the wire on the truck we brought with us. We are able to drive the fork lift onto the flatbed truck from the loading docks here at the supply store. There are also several large industrial generators in the warehouse, as well as a lot of other supplies that look like they will be useful either here, or somewhere else. We take the wire back to the mansion, and spend the rest of the day unrolling the wire out from one of the rooms beneath the mansion, through to one of the underground caves.

The caves under this mansion are very similar to the ones under the mansion in Cuba. There is always water in them that is always flowing into and out of the caves. Since LT and I are expert swimmers, we decide to jump in and see what kind of a floor we will have to secure the generator paddles to. Knowing how dangerous tidal currents can be, we make sure we are secured to a safety line and that someone is tending that line all the time. The water in the cave was just about five feet deep at low tide. Right now it is not quite high tide, and the water is over nine feet deep. There are two other caves similar to this one under the mansion, so we check all of them to make sure we will have the information for James and Mike tomorrow when they get here.

All three caves have a serious undertow, which means the water flows in on the top few feet, and then runs back out a few feet below the surface. It is too strong for either LT or me to swim against it. I'm not sure, but I think that is going to be a good thing for what we have in mind. That is except for having to be in the water to secure the generator paddles. The bottoms of all the caves are pretty much corral that is teaming with ocean life. I am not sure how James and Mike will want to fasten these down, but having worked with them on a couple of projects in rivers and lakes; it was usually easier to secure the brackets that will hold the paddles in place to the walls. At least we could drill into the stone and use masonry anchors.

While we were at the electrical supply place today I saw some brackets that look like they will work nicely. That is if I understand how we are planning to position the paddles. We have done just about everything we can for today, so we call it a day and see what else we might be able to help our friends with. They are in the process of installing a windmill, to generate electricity until we can get the tidal generators working. Those non-believers keep adding "If we ever do" whenever they talk about it. They always laugh and say they hope it will work because they get tired of having to replace the windmills and the solar panels pretty much every time they have a tropical storm down here.

I am watching while they set the windmill in place on a tri-pod type stand near the building where they want to use the power. They have already run the wire to the generator in the building. This is an old two story apartment complex, with about twenty apartments in it. We saw them earlier in the day and they are not in bad shape after our friends cleaned them up. The building is a couple hundred yards from the mansion, and about an equal distance beyond the mansion, is a nice little housing development that looks to have possibly two dozen houses in it. It is built so that it forms three sides with a nice dock and a great area in between the two sides of the open ended rectangle. From here it looks like all these homes are made of brick or cinderblock.

I am watching a piece of cloth that seems to have gotten caught up on a line of some kind, and it looks like a flag waving in the breeze. The funny thing is where we are standing there is very little breeze. Dayna is looking the same direction I am, she asks me if I am thinking what she is thinking. I tell her if she is thinking that those houses over there look promising I am. I ask one of the members of the council if they have looked at those houses over there. They tell me that Marty, who is kind of the guy in charge of housing, prefers buildings with room to house several families under one roof. He says they are easier to defend and people can take care of each other more easily.

I agree that can be true in some cases, but they have too many families to fit into the apartments. Marty comes up and tells me that's what the mansion is for, to hold those that won't fit into the other building. The mansion already looks like it has been broken up into what appear to be apartments, but most of them are not equipped with kitchens and there is only one door in and one door out of the mansion right now. Actually it looks like it was converted into a place where people could come down here and stay in luxury, but they would have to go out for their meals. Like the mansion in Cuba there is a large stone or brick fence around it, with several small houses built around the fence that look like they may have been housing for servants. They only run from about halfway back of the house and around back to the same place on the other side.

Dayna, LT, Kathy, and I decide to go look at the houses beyond the mansion. We go from house to house and they are not in great shape, but they are in no worse shape than the ones we moved into. With some hard work these could be great houses. The biggest thing that I can see, is that the area in between the rows of houses could be protected from the worst weather by building a stone wall across the open end. The houses don't run all the way down to the water, there is a couple hundred feet of beach, shoreline and even some docks that ran out into the water a ways. I am thinking that we could build the windmills so that they can be protected from the worst of the wind during a storm, and we could build the solar panels so that when a storm comes they could be covered and protected.

Like I always do back home I start to sketch my ideas on paper, to show them to the committee and see what the rest of our group that is here think about them. It is getting dark so we call it a night and go to our areas for sleeping. I have another idea while I am trying to fall asleep, but I will have to wait until morning to check it out. In the morning, Dayna and I go looking to see what we might find. We find several more housing developments that are only a short distance from the ocean, but even this far away the difference of the wear on some of the houses is evident. It looks like most of this area was built in squares. We find one development that is less than a half mile from the ocean, there are more than thirty houses in this part of it, and they run around a couple of square blocks.

It looks like this area was just developing when the war hit. These houses are in better shape than the ones closer to the ocean. I tell Dayna if we were looking to move here, I know where I would want to be. She agrees with me, now to see if the people who live here will agree with us. We are talking to some of the others in this settlement when our people get here. Our conversations about the other housing areas gets put on the back burner until after we show the team what we are working with. James, Jenna, Mike, and Morgan are very excited to see what we have to work with. As usual they want to get right to work.

LT and I tell them about the underwater current at least at high tide. They both say that they have done some studies of tides and if there is a strong undertow at high tide, there is probably one all the time. The biggest reason to identify this is to be safe when we are working in the water. They agree that the best way to secure the paddles will be against the walls of the cave. They ask if we have any wetsuits to wear while we are working in the cold water. Even at seventy degree water your body core temperature will lower if you are in the water long enough, and this water is nowhere near seventy degrees.

This time we were able to surprise them, because being experienced swimmers and having been subjected to ocean water for long periods of time, we stopped at a store yesterday and found all the gear we will need. They brought the paddle wheels with them. While we were at the military base, where we found most of this technology, we also found a large warehouse full of the materials we will need to get started with it. For this first experiment, they are planning to put four paddles here in the cave to generate the electricity. We make a discovery that could make this experiment easier than we ever anticipated. This entire building is hooked up to an emergency generator that must have been used when the weather knocked out power to this part of the suburbs.

We are happy to see that this particular generator is powered by propane. We decide to try to get the generator running, while James and Mike work on getting the paddles set in place, and getting them hooked up to the wire. The propane tank is empty, so we go looking for a truck that may still have propane in it. We do not have to go far to find an almost full truck. Getting it running good enough to get it back to the mansion takes the rest of the day. I am happy to have LT with us. He is a pretty fair mechanic when it comes to even these older vehicles. I mention that to him and he tells me that if these engines were much newer he would not be as successful as we are being. He grew up helping a neighbor, who was a farmer, keep his equipment running. Most of that equipment was the older vintage, so he learned a lot about it.

However he learned it the skill will help us immeasurably here. It is dark by the time we get the truck back to the mansion. We fill the tank and James asks us if we feel lucky enough to have the generator start. I tell him I have been here longer than most of them have and I have never seen one start first time over. We did however find a few that didn’t take much to get them to work. We figure we have nothing to lose, so we decide to try to turn it over. Surprisingly it actually coughs a few times and almost starts on the first try. Tim came down with James and Mike, he says it sounds like it isn't getting enough fuel, so he makes an adjustment and it starts, but it dies after just a few seconds. He makes another small adjustment and the generator fires right up and starts running.

It's running rough, but it is running. Naturally it isn't generating electricity yet, but we take care of that and within an hour we actually have electric lights in the mansion again. Not many because most of the bulbs are blown, but enough to know that our generator will work. We take a walk around the mansion to see what the generator covers and are pleasantly surprised to see that it even covers the houses along the fence. They are going to have to find a store with a bunch of light bulbs, or they will be in the dark anyway. We turn the generator off while we are sleeping, because propane is one of those things that we cannot make. Every time I say that to someone, James and Mike always add yet, to my statement. To be honest I will not be surprised if they figure out how to separate the propane from the natural gas.

In the morning, the ladies go looking for bulbs and other treasures in the stores in this area, with our friends from this settlement. Dayna shows the houses we looked at yesterday to some of the women and they like the idea of being at least a short distance from the ocean. They also like the houses and the possibilities. There is quite a bit of open farm land right across the road from that development, all the way around it. We suggest that they learn to grow crops even if they decide not to live there. There is quite a bit of room for growing several fairly large gardens inside the wall around the mansion as well. We brought some of the hybrid seeds of vegetables that we have grown in our gardens. It's nothing earth shattering, but we have been successful in growing some different hybrids of tomatoes, corn, bell peppers, some squashes, and even green beans.

In most cases the newer varieties are larger and have more flavor than the ones we started out with. The ladies that care for our chickens have worked with Jenna and Morgan and have been able to breed some chickens that are much bigger than the ones we found running wild here, and have increased the output of eggs substantially. Jenna and Morgan both say that it was more the efforts of Jenny, Jessica, Rachel, and Samantha reading about how to do those things, then having the patience and perseverance to follow through with it. These are some of the things we want to share with our friends. It seems like they have not grasped the importance of continuously improving their living conditions. That may be part of why they have not grown as much as most of the other settlements have.

We work hard all day, getting the paddle sections secured so that they can still turn freely. We do use the brackets that we found in the electrical store. When I tell them that I found them, James tells me that even a blind squirrel finds an acorn every now and again. Naturally I tell him that if I wanted to be harassed and picked on, I would have stayed home with Sara and the others. He laughs and tells me that they made him and the others that came on this trip promise to make sure I don't get a swelled head. At least we can all laugh at ourselves. Today we were able to install two paddlewheels I guess they could be called. We are planning to put two more in tomorrow, and then they will start wiring everything together.

They have diagrams explaining the process down to the finest details of it. They are optimistic, but cautious, because we have all had enough experience in new ideas and technology to know that making it work after hooking everything up correctly isn't always easy. The ladies found a large supply of light bulbs of every description today. We run the generator for a while during dinner and long enough to have a meeting with the leadership of this settlement. We wanted to get their permission to teach the others in this settlement about farming and raising livestock. At first I thought they may be against it, but they explained that they have been afraid to start because they have no one with any experience in those areas.

We are going to meet with the rest of the settlement tomorrow, after the paddles are installed. It took most of the day today because we did not know what we were doing. Now we are experienced, so we should be able to knock off at least an hour or more. I am not sure why, but today we knock a full two hours off the time it took yesterday. The rest of us address the settlement while James, Jenna, Mike, and Morgan work on the electrical installation now. One thing for sure, the paddle wheels are turning constantly at a pretty good pace. I let the ladies do the talking at the meeting we have, but as soon as they are done with their presentation that guy Marty asks me why I didn't tell them about everything. He asks if I am too important to do the manual labor required to do the farming and the taking care of the livestock.

I start to say something, but Dayna beats me to it, when she tells them that I have done every job on our settlement and have done all of them many times. She also tells them that if they are not interested in helping themselves, it is their prerogative, but we will not waste any more time trying to help them. The ones working on the electricity can stay, but the rest of us will go to Cuba to try to help them. If they are not interested either we will go home and spend our time with our families. Several of the people listening tell us that whether Marty is or not, they are and they appreciate the sacrifices we are making to help them. The people that are here from Cuba say that they may be able to help these people with their farming because they have some experience growing crops as well. They are polite to say that they are sure we know more about that subject than they do and are excited to be learning all we can teach them. We tell them that we will be happy to start the lessons tomorrow morning.

10

In the morning, a bunch of us from our group goes running. LT kind of started it by telling me he knows he has to start working out more or he will just get further out of shape. I tell him I know how he feels, but not to let the other day tell him what kind of shape he is in. Both Tim and I experienced some fatigue and feeling weaker than usual when we first came here. It took a week or so to go away then we felt fine and were as strong as always. He smiles and tells me that he wishes that was the problem, but he knows he has done far too many diplomatic missions the last four or five months to be good for anybody. He just got used to eating the rich foods and drinking more than he should. Now he is paying for it, but its nothing hard work won't take care of.

We do about three miles at a pretty good pace and LT even manages to keep up. He is tired and winded pretty good, but he does keep up. When we get back to the local group, there are more people than we thought there would be for us to work with. The people from Cuba are very knowledgeable in farming and are very much interested in trying the newer hybrid varieties of crops. The way we are doing this is the way we trained our own groups. Those that have a particular interest or knowledge in farming go with the people teaching farming, and those who have an interest in building are learning to build, and more importantly, to rebuild and to make repairs.

There are also some of the group members working with the electrical group, which is probably one of the most important things, but they are all important. This is a brand new area for these people and it's important that they get started right. We are also planning to teach self defense, but that will be taught to everyone after the day's work is done. For those learning to grow crops, the first thing we did is go looking for the equipment they will need to plow the fields and cultivate the crops. We found the equipment we will need on the other side of the fields that I saw earlier. One of the Cuban gentlemen volunteers to see if he can get the tractor running.

It is kind of funny to watch him work with it. He tries to start it and when it starts coughing and sputtering he is telling it that it is a good girl and just needs to run a little bit to feel better. When it stops doing that he yells at it and smacks the side of it. He is speaking Spanish so some of the people don't know what he is saying, but his expressions and the way he is talking, they can guess pretty much what he is saying. After yelling at it for the second time, LT who is laughing like the rest of us, including Pepe, which is our new friend's name, asks him if he can try something. Pepe tells him to be his guest; this tractor is as stubborn as his wife and the tractor he left back in Cuba. That gets all of us laughing and gets him smacked by his wife.

She is laughing so we all know she is not really angry. LT fiddles around with the carburetor a little. He takes the fuel filter off and blows through it really hard then replaces it. He tells Pepe to try it again and miraculously the tractor starts. Pepe's wife tells him that if LT had been in Cuba with them, they may have been able to plant a crop. The tires on the tractor are low, but we can at least drive it over to the compressor, which we got running before we started on the tractor. The tires hold air and we are ready to start learning how to plow a field. I have had a lot of experience since that first time I drove one and was only able to plow about an acre for the entire day. I am still not as good as Frank, Eric, Rod, Dan, or Don, but I can do a reasonable days work. Pepe and LT hook up the plow, after greasing it good, and show everyone how to set the depth that they want to plow the dirt up. Then they all take turns trying their hands at plowing a field.

Even I get a turn and I don't do too badly if I say so myself. LT is a good teacher, he even points out a stand of trees at the far end of the field and tells the people driving the tractor to pick out one tree and use that as a reference to keep their lines straight. The lines are not very straight today, but we do plow up a pretty good chunk of ground. Tomorrow we will learn how to disc it and smooth it out for planting. I forgot to mention that we had to use a brush hog to cut the grass down enough so that we could plow it. Back at our settlement, we would bail the grass for either bedding for our dairy cows or use it for feed. The area we are using for practice is not the one we want to plant crops in. We want everyone that wants to learn to have that chance where it won't hurt anything.

Pepe and Craig, who is one of the original members of this group, decide to stay behind and cut the grass on a larger section of field closer to the homes I looked at the other day. When they get back to the group for supper, they along with their wives asked us if we can show them how to catch some cows for milk and possibly some chickens for eggs and meat. I know this group used to have all this and it looks like they simply got lazy, or just didn't understand how important it is to be self sufficient. I talk to some of the long time members of this group and they say that the people who took care of the cows and the chickens left the group, and no one else knew what to do with them, so they kind of let them go wherever they wanted to.

Plus they have moved around some trying to find just the right place for a settlement. I ask them if they are planning to move from this location. They say that this is by far the best location they have ever had, so they are planning to stay here. Dayna and I discuss this new information with the rest of our group and we decide to continue teaching them and with the new people from Cuba they may be able to build this settlement into a small city like our group. In the morning we call a meeting and tell them that in order to be self sufficient there are certain things that must be done. We outline that to them and they all agree to make it work for them. There is one question after our conversation. Pepe and Craig asked us if they can't make it work here, can they come and join our group.

We all tell them absolutely. We have plenty of room for anyone that doesn't mind working for a living. When we go to get the tractor, we see that Pepe and Craig mowed at least a couple of acres of the fields closest to the homes I told you about. They ask the group with us how many of them would like to live right here. They will be close enough to the others, but also close enough to the fields, and hopefully some farm animals to take care of them properly. Since everybody has had an opportunity to drive the tractor, most of the people here pick out homes for them and their families. There is a very nice little cul-de-sac that has enough houses for everyone here, plus some extras in case anyone wants to join them.

The area is excellent for defense and all the houses are within yelling distance, and they are all right up against the fields we are planning to use. The grass that was cut yesterday is piled high in the back yards of a couple of the homes. We start laying out the area for a couple of barns and sheds for the animals. We are sure that we can find the cows and chickens the same way we did. They were running wild and all we had to do is feed them and give them a place to get in out of the weather, and they were happy to stay. While the fields are being plowed, we go looking for a couple of barns. We find exactly what we need less than two miles from where we are settling. There is a farm here that reminds me of the one we settled on. There are eight or nine houses laid out in kind of a circle around a farm yard, with several large barns and a couple of smaller barns or sheds near them. It's hard to tell exactly how many barns there are because some of them are kind of in the woods that have grown up around them.

There are several acres of land around the homes just like where we settled. Pepe and Craig and their wives take one look around and say they are going no further; this is where they will live. I can't blame them, this place has everything they will need to survive and live a good life. After looking through the houses several of the others say that this is perfect for them as well. While we are standing on the porch of the last house we look in, we see cows in the woods around us staring at us. Dayna says she wouldn't be the least bit surprised if there are hundreds of chickens running wild in the woods. We go back to the others and report what we have found. There are others that would like to see the houses and the location.

We get there and several other families say they would like to live here as well. The coast is great for those that enjoy fishing for a living, but not all of them do. Some want the option to go fishing sometimes, but they would prefer to grow crops and livestock for their living. That way they can be helping feed the entire group. The fishermen can as well, but not everybody wants to eat fish for almost every meal. We are discussing these things when that guy Marty drives into the yard. For one thing he has a driver that he tells to wait for him, he will be back in a moment, and another thing, we have not seen him in two or three days. He comes walking up and asks us what the heck we think we're doing so far from the rest of the group and who gave us permission to even come over here. He doesn't use the word heck, but Dayna will smack me if I use what she considers bad language.

Some of the people start to head back to the rest of the group, back at the mansion. I ask Marty who the heck he thinks he is that we have to get permission from him to do anything. He tells me that I may be a big shot in my own settlement, but here he is the big shot, and people will do what he says. I tell him that we just overthrew one dictator down in Cuba that tried to take over this settlement.

"The people in this group better decide if they want to trade one dictator for another, because we will not waste our time here, if that's the way they want to live. Our settlement has several groups that make up one large group, but each individual group is lead by a committee that changes every six months, to give everyone a chance to have a say in how things will be done. Everyone, whether on the committee or not, has a job to do, plus we all fill in when someone is ill or having a baby so that everything runs smooth. We set up our settlement that way because we do not believe in people who think they are better or more important than everybody else. It appears that that is not the case here, again that's up to you, but we will not waste our time doing your jobs for you."

I tell the people that are still here that we better go back to the rest of the leadership, and decide once and for all how this settlement will be lead. Pepe, Craig, and their families tell us that if Marty is running this settlement then they will go with us. When we get back to the mansion, which is kind of like the main living area at the moment, I ask who else is on the leadership team here. Two guys raise their hands and say that they appointed Marty to be in charge because of his leadership experience. I ask him what experience he has in leading a settlement like this one. He starts naming other settlements that we know very well. When he is done I ask Tim to call each of the settlements and ask them about our new friend here.

Everyone we contact tells us that he was with their groups for a short time. He always left when they told him he either had to carry his own weight or get out. They say they had problems with him bothering some of the women as well. Two of the women that came over from Cuba tell us that he has already told them that they will be working for him personally when he is the leader of this settlement. Jenna and Morgan tell the people gathered that if this guy came to our settlement he would be welcomed if he is willing to do his share of the work. If not he would be asked to leave. If he assaulted any of the women in the settlement he would probably be killed to make sure he doesn't do it again.

We explain that we realize that our ways are harsh and may seem to be barbaric, but how barbaric is it to force your desires onto an innocent woman or girl. This group used to be led by Roger and several other good people, but apparently they all chose to move to one of the settlements farther north. Some of the people here were members of their leadership committee at one time or another. We tell them we will leave them alone to discuss how they want their settlement to be run. We also tell them that if they choose to have a dictator or what amounts to the same thing, we will not support them in any way. Some of the people tell us that we are not being fair.

Dayna, Jenna, and Morgan point out that we are using the bible and other books on religion to base how we want to live our lives.

"All the books we have read show explicitly that when societies are governed by an individual, they are destined to fail; societies where people live together working for the good of all prosper. We stress the family as our most important asset. Everything we do in our groups is for the betterment of all, not for certain individuals. When we find treasures at a military base or in a city where something we need is manufactured everyone in the settlement benefits. Every settlement we have visited in our travels is run in the same manner. This one was, up until a short time ago. It's up to you; we will wait to hear your decision."

We go outside to a beautiful warm evening. All this talk about families makes Dayna and me wonder what our family is up to. Dayna says they are probably having a good time playing miniature golf or any one of a dozen things they can do for fun back home. We can hear the discussions that are going on when they get heated, which is happening quite often now. We are lucky that we did not have this kind of trouble when we settled our groups. Dayna reminds me that the rules were already in place when the others came, so they either agreed to live that way or were asked to leave. LT and Kathy ask if we had to force anyone to change the way they wanted to live.

We tell them that we can honestly say that everyone that came to us wanted to live the way we are. They were all living similar lives somewhere else, but without the structure or the support of a large group to help take care of them. We told LT and Kathy pretty much how we started our group or settlement originally, but now Dayna and Charity go into detail how we started with basically their family and invited other small groups to join ours for safety against the predators. They explain that they didn't even know how to do the simplest things for survival like using a can opener, but they learned. They tell them that the greatest thing that they learned is how to read. That gave them the opportunity to know if what Tim and I was teaching them was correct.

They tell them that not one of them ever doubted that Tim and I knew what we were doing and that if they followed us and did what they were asked to do that everything would be fine and it has been. There have been others that tried to change their way of life, but it was always for the betterment of a few individuals. It wasn't Tim and I that drove those people away. It was the entire settlement because they know what is right and what is wrong. They don't need anyone to tell them. History has shown them the way they need to live to be happy and prosperous. LT and Kathy tell them that they don't have to convince them. They are sold and wouldn't want to live anywhere other than with our extended family.

There has been some heated discussion going on inside, but now it is pretty quiet in there. James says at least we haven't heard any gunfire yet, so odds are they are still all alive. We all laugh then the door to the room they are meeting in opens and they start coming out. From the looks on their faces we can't tell what they decided, until Marty and his two buddies come out and head for the car he was in earlier. Marty starts yelling at them that they will regret this and they will be begging him to come back and lead them. The rest of the people in the group tell him that they will take their chances.

Marty looks over at us and starts yelling at the women that they should keep their mouths shut if they know what's good for them. He is using some pretty foul language so I tell him to please keep the filth in his mouth and just leave before he says something that may get him hurt. I guess he considers that a threat because he comes toward me asking who is going to hurt him. James tells him to choose whoever he feels that he may be able to take in a fight and we will be happy to oblige him and his two henchmen as well. Marty points at me and says he is going to teach me a lesson before he leaves. I shouldn't be, but I was hoping he would choose me.

LT just shakes his head and tells Marty even he wouldn't choose to fight me because he has seen me in hand to hand combat too many times. Marty tells us that he has fought bigger men than me and stomped them to death. He adds that now it is my turn. I won't go into details, but I don't get stomped to death, but neither does he. His friends do have to help him into the car so that they can get out of here. When they have gone I tell Craig, Pepe, and the others that odds are they are going to wind up killing those three to protect their settlement. They say they already know that and if that's what it takes to live as free men, then that's what they will do whether they want to or not.

11

Our friends ask us to help them get started the way we did. We tell them the first thing they need to do is elect some committee members to represent the different groups, so that they don't have twenty or thirty families trying to be heard at meetings. The committee members will do the talking for the entire group. We help them do this, to at least get started, then they discuss the benefits of having their settlement broken up into two sections to start with. They all agree that if some of the people would like to farm then they should do that. The ones that want to fish can do that and they can grow gardens as individuals, or a couple or several families can get together and have a garden in common.

We are finally seeing some enthusiasm in most of the people here. Personally I think they were afraid of Marty and his friends, so they didn't have their hearts into making this work. The work continues on the electrical and those of us who are interested in farming, start fresh in the morning getting the houses cleaned out, while others work on getting the equipment in the barns running. When they have a tractor running fairly well, they work on cutting the grass and luckily the people that worked this farm before the war, had a machine to make bales of hay out of the cut grass. Several cows seem to be interested in what is going on, so we leave the corral gates open after we fix the gates to open and close the way they should.

The women and younger girls went out into the woods to see if they can find some chickens running wild. They are really surprised to find as many as they did, but getting them back to the farm is another problem. Dayna tells them how Jessica and Jenny enticed the chickens into the barn where the chicken coop was. They find some grain marked chicken feed and they leave a trail of it from close to the woods to one of the barns that has a good sized coop attached. Naturally they are impatient to get the chickens coming, but we know from experience that they will probably come into the barn, but it will be on their terms, not ours.

Once the houses that are going to be lived in first are cleaned out and the electricity is restored by use of windmills, we go into the nearest town to look for furnishing for the homes. We also get new carpeting and appliances while we are at it. It takes almost a week to get everything the way the people who are going to live here want it. That's not perfect, but at least livable. Don't worry; they are doing most of the work. We are here more or less to help and advise them. We do help with the work, but only if they can't do it themselves. The same type of work is going on at the mansion. The people that want to live there are doing exactly the same things as the people here are.

The people here have managed to entice a couple dozen chickens into the barn with the coop, and the other night three cows with calves came into the barnyard, and started eating the grass there. The people led them through the barn and into the fenced in portion of the yard there. Luckily some of them know something about cows because I don't. Just like we did, several of the people that are going to live here want to plant individual gardens. They discussed it and some are going to plant certain vegetables and others will plant other vegetables and they will share the crops. Some of them have had gardens where they settled before and have some favorite types of plant seeds.

We give them some of the hybrid seeds that we have developed and some of them want to do tests by growing two or three different types of tomatoes, corn, bell peppers, green beans, lettuce, and cabbage and even some other types of plants, and compare the growth and taste of them. Finally our electrical experts say they are ready to flip the switch and see if the tidal paddles will generate electricity. They have done some successful preliminary tests, but have not tested it on a large scale yet. We are all standing in the mansion to see if the lights will work when the switch is thrown. I guess the ladies in the group like Jenna and Morgan had no small part in making this possible. They are going to do the honors of turning it on.

They throw the switch and we hear the sound of the generator running, then the lights start glowing low at first, but they pick up intensity quickly and in less than a minute are glowing brightly. Now time will tell if it will last for very long. We are planning to stay here for a couple more days then go to Cuba to help them. They will be farther ahead when we get there because our team has been in touch with them and has told them how to get started. The last time we talked to them they told us jokingly that if we don't hurry they will have it done without us. They are starting to sound more like the settlement that we have known right along.

We spend the next couple of days wrapping up loose ends and helping our friends learn more about surviving. We have had some excellent classes on self defense as well as taking them into the city and showing them how to find guns and other weapons. We also show them how to shoot the guns they found. We show them how in an emergency where their lives are in danger, everyone should not necessarily come running at the same time. It is usually better to have a couple of designated people to hang back and make sure that it is safe before they join the others. We also show them that if there is trouble, like being invaded, how important it is for each member of the team to pick a target and be ready to shoot if it becomes necessary.

Some of them have already had this training once, but some of them say since they haven't used it yet they kind of forgot about it. We assure them that doing practice drills is a big help in staying sharp. We remind them that they were attacked a short time ago and when we got there to help there was basically no resistance by them. They assure us that it will not happen again. For some reason I believe them, the people in this group remind me of the people in our original group. Most of them are pretty much at the end of their tolerance for not living as they know they can with a little work. We also keep reminding them that the more they work together, the easier it will be for everyone.

I get smacked by Dayna when I tell the men in the group that they already have it easier than I did when we settled our group. The houses here are single story so they will be easier to paint, plus most of the houses are constructed of cinderblock or brick, so they will only have a little bit of trim. I exaggerate just the tiniest bit when I tell them that our house is bigger than the mansion with many floors that had to be scraped and painted. The painting itself took me over a year. Then there were several hundred shutters that I painted once, then had to do them again because some people didn't like the color. I was pointing at Dayna on the side when I said that last part.

Dayna threatens to hit me again if I don't tell them the truth. I tell them that maybe I exaggerated a little bit, but it seemed to take a year to paint it. Our friends take it in the manner it was meant which is in fun. One of the biggest things we have tried to stress to our friends is that if you can make the jobs fun, you have it beaten. By doing projects together it is much easier to have fun doing them. We told them about several of the great projects that we have worked on and now they want to do most of the same ones to make their lives easier. One project we told them about that they show great interest in is when we found the grindstones for grinding our wheat in bulk, rather than using hand grinders that it took most of the day to grind enough wheat to make bread.

They also liked the idea of having much larger ovens to bake the bread in. We agree to help them at least get started on those two projects before we leave for Cuba. Again we go to the nearest city to look for what we need. We are looking for signs that say something to the effect that they ground wheat there. Dayna sees a sign that says "Tortillas made fresh daily, using only fresh in store ground wheat." We figure that is as good a place to start as any. We go into the store and the others start to walk to the back of the store, but I stop at the counter. LT asks me what I am doing so I tell them I want to get some fresh tortillas. Dayna grabs me by the shirt and tells me she will make me some tortillas if we find a wheat grinder here.

We do find a wheat grinder and it is much bigger than a small hand turned one, but nowhere near as large as the ones we found. For our Cuban friends this is a treasure trove of the items they need to cook their native cuisine. There are several kinds of tortilla presses and cookers, as well as several rice cookers and dozens of other cooking utensils and dishes along with all the pots and pans they could ever need. Our friends are ready to start moving everything back to the settlement right now. I ask them if they know what building they want to use for the grinder and if they intend to distribute the bounty that they have found here with the rest of the people.

Everyone says of course they will share the bounty and they want to put the grind stone in the kitchen of one of the empty houses in their settlement. They have all been cleaned, but for the preparation of food they want to clean it even better. As they talk they decide that they can keep some of the cooking equipment at that house as well and the women can take turns going there to make tortillas and bread for the entire settlement. That's what I was waiting to hear. We take a couple of hours disconnecting the wheat grinder and packing everything that the people want to take with us, then loading it on the truck. We go down a couple more new streets on the way out of town and see a sign very similar to the last one on the side of a building. Naturally everyone wants to stop to check this place out as well.

Except for how things are organized it is very similar to the place we just left. The biggest difference is that this place used to bake bread as well as tortillas and the grinder they have is almost twice the size of the other one. Plus, in the back room is a very nice baking oven that will hold what looks like ten to twelve loaves of bread at a time. We gather everything we can load on the truck and agree to come back later today if there is time or wait until tomorrow to pick up the rest of the treasures. The second place also had a couple of large freezers that they must have stored meat or vegetables in. Our friends ask us if we can move them to the settlement so that they have a place to keep meat fresh.

I have been waiting for someone to mention a large freezer for a couple of days now. When we get home I take everybody around to the largest barn, which is behind the house that Craig and his wife, along with another couple are living in. There is a large double door in the barn that leads to the inside of the barn. Now if you go straight through the main open area inside the barn you will find another door that leads to a large room in the back of the barn that not only has a large freezer in it, but all the equipment they should ever need to butcher their own meat. While we were in town I found several cans of Freon, which is used to charge cooling systems. We have to do the same thing to this freezer that we did to the ones on our settlement.

We take care of that then set the temperature to see if it will hold the charge and if the thermostat is accurate. We will check it again tomorrow to see how it is holding. We decide to look closely through the other barns to see if any of them have a freezer in them as well. We find one more on the other side of the compound I guess we can call it. We do not have power to all of these houses yet, even though we cleaned them some. I showed Craig and Pepe how to recharge the system if it needs it when they get electricity to those other homes. The house they want to designate as kind of a bread making place is right at the middle of the group. It has a huge kitchen and will work out very well for what they want to do.

The two wheat grinders we found will work well on electricity so we don't have to worry about water power, at least for now. Their electricians get to work getting a windmill in place and working to that building. We have been working with windmills that we can take the blades off in case of high winds that could destroy them otherwise. They do not complete the job today, but by tomorrow evening that building should have electricity. One of the grinders will be going to the group that will be living in the mansion or hacienda, depending on what member of the group you are talking to. They are going to continue looking for another commercial oven for the other group.

So far the paddles in the cave are working without a hitch, but then we didn't really anticipate any. If we had installed them where the waves could pound them, they would probably not stand up very well. Where they are is about as good a condition as you can possibly find for this type of power generation. We will be going to Cuba in a couple days to help them get settled in and get the power hooked up. In the morning we check the temperature in the freezer and find that it is holding very well. We ask our friends that live here if they would like to do some hunting to fill that freezer. There has been plenty of fish and other seafood that most people consider great, but I will always prefer a nice steak to any kind of fish no matter how you cook it.

We take one of the jeeps and a pickup truck to drive to an area about twenty miles away to keep the game close to the settlement there and untouched in case it is needed later. I bring my bow so that we don't frighten the animals any more than necessary. One of the guys in the group tells us that he has been in this area before and that he knows of a nice little lake about a half mile through the woods from the road. We decide to walk in and see if there is any game here. Personally I can't see how there couldn't be game here, but maybe these guys know something I don't. Walking through the woods we see plenty of sign for deer, cattle, and hogs as well as many smaller animals. There is also some sign that I don't recognize, so I am being extra careful today.

I check my sidearm to make sure it's loaded because I have had too many close calls with the very large animals that are running wild. Soon we hear the sounds of at least two animals that do not seem to agree on something. We hurry and break into a clearing where a very large alligator is between a large hog and where it wants to go. What the large hog doesn't see is the second alligator coming up behind it, while the first one keeps its attention. I have never heard of alligators hunting in pairs like this and it is possible that the one coming up from the rear is just taking advantage of the situation to get a meal. From the size of the tusks on that hog both of those gators better watch out or they will be impaled by them, they have to be eight or nine inches long.

I do not usually take sides when two creatures are fighting it out, but I hate alligators and I am hungry for some good pork. I already have an arrow ready, so I draw and let it fly at the one blocking the path of the hog. I hit it right behind the head and the shot definitely doesn't kill it right off. The twelve foot beast starts twisting and turning all over with its jaws opening and shutting as fast as they can like the animal is trying desperately to kill whatever it is that attacked it. While this is going on, the one behind the hog decided to make its move now. It moves surprisingly fast for a large animal and it looks like it will get to the hogs back legs before it notices what is happening. Surprisingly the hog turns quickly and takes the gator right under the head.

Those huge tusks go right through the bottom jaw and would go through the top as well if the gator had its mouth shut. The hog lifts and acts like it is trying to throw the gator. Instead it is whipping that large body back and forth and trying to trample the gator at the same time. The one I shot with the arrow is still moving, but not as much as it was a few seconds ago. The gator snaps its mouth shut which drives the tusks up into the brain killing the gator almost instantly. The hog throws it around a few more times to make sure it is dead I guess, then shakes its head to dislodge the gator from its tusks.

We are still watching when the angry hog turns and sees us standing here. It snorts several times and starts to paw the ground in its anger. I tell LT and Tim that if we don't want to have to kill this hog then we better get out of here quick and it might already be too late. Actually we take a step back and the hog charges at us. I let fly an arrow that strikes it in the neck, but does not even slow it down. Tim and LT both fire at the same time striking it in the head, but it is still coming at us. Craig, one of the guys from the group here steps to get a side shot at the pig and fires at the same time that Tim and LT shoot again. The pig finally falls forward and comes to rest about eight feet away from us.

LT is sweating profusely from the excitement. He tells Tim and me that we should hunt these things the way we hunted the enemy when we were Seals. He says I should be using my old fifty and taking high ground. I never really thought about our missions as hunting the enemy, but looking at it totally unbiased that's exactly what we were doing. We get to work field dressing the hog and the gators. No sense leaving meat out here in the sun to rot. I have eaten gator in the other world and didn't care much for it. Pepe and Craig both say they like the gator tails when they are cooked properly. Pepe says his wife knows how to cook the meat just right.

We have to drive the pickup we are using as close to the kill as we can get it and we still have to quarter the hog to get it into the back of the truck. The gators are no picnic to load either. With all that meat on the truck there is no room for anyone to sit in the back of the truck, but we manage to squeeze into the cab and the jeep to get back. When we get back the young people want to know if they can have the teeth from the two gators. Craig and Pepe ask us if we will be offended if they would like to keep the tusks from the pig. They want to give them to their sons who are ten years old. We have no problems with that at all, besides if we wanted pig tusks we have plenty of them back home.

Luckily we can drive the pickup right into the barn to unload the meat. At least a couple of the guys and ladies from the local group know how to cut up the meat correctly, but if they didn't there are plenty of charts on the walls. While they are doing that, Tim and I go looking for a smoke house. From the size of the freezer and the area they have for preparing the meat they must have at least one smoke house. We find it not far from the barn almost covered by underbrush. It takes some help, but we get the brush away from around it and get it cleaned out and ready for smoking meat. By the time this is done they have the parts of the pig that they want to smoke ready, so we show them how to build their fire for maximum smoke and put the bacon and some cuts of the hams in the smoke house.

One of the guys and his wife were in charge of smoking meats when they were with their settlement in Cuba, but they mainly smoked fish and much smaller pigs. They don't see why they can't learn to do the same thing here and we agree wholeheartedly with them.

We get to taste alligator tail cooked over a bed of red hot coals, but even if they would have smothered it in barbecue sauce, it wouldn't make it taste good to me. Most of the others seemed to at least not mind eating it, I don't know, maybe it's just the thought of eating an alligator. But then I have eaten snake and I don't mind that. I'm not going to worry about it though because there are too many good things to eat to worry about one that isn't. Tonight those of us that are going to Cuba in the morning, turn in a little earlier than usual, so we can get an early start.

At least that's the plan, but as usual it doesn't work out quite that way. The guys that are in charge of the electricity here have a bunch of questions for James and Jenna, and Mike and Morgan. Finally they get them all answered and we can board our boat and start our journey. It wasn't a total waste of time though, because we were able to talk to Sara and Gary back at our home group. They are excited. They had very good luck taking down another of the hangars and are getting ready to start hauling it back to the settlement. We already marked off a place for it, kind of between Doc McEvoys group and ours. We want to make sure we can defend the hangar in case of attack.

The boat we are using today must be more powerful than the ones we came down in the last time. This trip only takes about four hours, but maybe a little longer than that, because I didn't exactly check the time when we left. It feels good to be able to just walk into the settlements when we get here. They already look much better than they did the last time I was here. We even notice armed men hidden in the jungle that watch us almost all the way to the first settlement. They come out when they are told to do so by their current leader. He tells me proudly that no one will ever get the drop on them again.

We check out this group and they are doing much better than before. The houses are better cared for and are much neater in appearance than the last time I was here. Everyone we see is excited to meet Dayna and they are all excited to show us how much they have done since we left. This always was a great group of people that worked very hard to start their groups and to maintain them. Dayna is impressed with the gardens they have and the variety of fresh fruit that they grow here. We are treated to some very fresh pineapple that several of the members of this group grow. There are large patches of sugar cane that grows wild here. James and Jenna were here before and since then have investigated how to make sugar out of it. The local people assured them that they know where a factory is that used to refine sugar before the war. We may wind up being here longer than we anticipated at first.

When we get near the second settlement, I hear my name and look up just in time to catch Lillianne before she almost knocks me down, running into me to get a hug. I introduce her to Dayna who is looking a little perturbed that Lillianne is as friendly as she is. When I introduce her as that little girl I told her about she says that Lillianne is no little girl. She may be a young girl, but she is no little girl. I don't think Lillianne understands what Dayna is saying, but she throws her arms around Dayna and tells her she is just like she has imagined her in her dreams. She asks me if the offer to come to our settlement, and live with us as a daughter, is still open. She looks so afraid that I am going to tell her no.

I tell Dayna what Lillianne is asking, she smacks me and tells me that she speaks Spanish enough to know what she said. She holds her arms out to Lillianne and welcomes her to the family. Lillianne is about as happy as anyone I have ever seen then she looks serious and asks if her friend Isabella can come with us. She tells us that she has no family to take care of her either. Dayna tells them both that we have a big house, with many children already, a couple more won't matter. LT tells Lillianne about the pig he shot back home. She motions that he is loco if he thinks she will believe that. I tell him that I am planning a small hunting trip for the girls when we get back home. She will never believe it, until she sees it for herself.

We get to see how much this group has done since we were last here. The houses look much better and the gardens are definitely doing better than they were doing. After talking to pretty much everyone in the group that is not out on the ocean fishing, we head for the mansion. There has already been quite a bit of work done toward getting the houses along the perimeter fence livable, and they are currently using some of the solar panels and windmills to generate electricity to these buildings around the main building. The people here are just as excited about everything they have been able to accomplish. We notice some of the people who are in the first and second groups helping out up here.

The people explain that they had new elections to pick the council of leaders. They chose two from each group to represent them when they have meetings. They want to keep it simple, but they have others that are well respected in each group to call on if something comes up that they don't feel comfortable with. The gentleman that is talking to us, Felipe tells us, that has happened already and they hope that they made the correct choice. I ask him what choice is that and he tells us it will be better to show us. He leads us through the main house, which is looking much better than it did, now that it is being fixed up for several families to live in it. He tells us that many of the families do not feel comfortable living in the big house, because the people who lived here before the war were very wealthy and had much political power.

I joke with them and tell them they are even wealthier than they were and have more political power as well. At first they think I am being sarcastic with them and are a little offended, but I explain that they live very well and they don't have to hurt anyone or take advantage of any of their family members. Plus each of them will get the chance to be on the council that helps make the rules and enforce them. When they look at it like that they say they are just as good as the people who lived here before. Like many people that have lived in smaller countries like this one, the social levels are present in their thinking even today. We have had some instances where we have had to work with members of our groups that didn't feel equal to the rest of us. As far as we are concerned everyone on the face of, wherever we are, is equal and will be treated with respect as long as they show they deserve it.

We head down to the lower level, where we found all of the rooms and the way in from the ocean. We hear a humming noise just before we come to the room that I knew James would be the most interested in. Felipe opens the door and apologizes for having the generator running, using propane that they found in a large storage tank on the property. Felipe tells us that they have used it very sparingly, but in some areas of the house it is difficult to see and to work without electric lights. James tells him that this is the best thing they could have done to get ready for what we want to try here. Felipe looks down at the ground and says that's the other thing they want to show us.

We go toward where the cave ends and the house begins. He shows us some large rolls of wire that they found in the city that is not far away. When we get to the door leading to the cave, Felipe tells us that if we would prefer, they can take everything they have done apart and start over. We tell him we can't imagine them doing anything that would make us do something like that. He opens the door and we can see what appear to be three men and two women working on fastening the paddles to the sides of the cave. We are about as surprised as we can be, in a good way. James asks Felipe where they found these paddles because these are exactly the kind we need.

Felipe tells him that when we were here before, James showed them the plans for the generating system and left a picture with them. There is a former military base about one and one half hours from here, so they went there to look for what they will need. That's where they found the wire and the paddles, along with more papers that tell about the tidal generators, so they brought them all back with them. Of course it took a couple of days to get a large truck running, then get it loaded and bring everything back. The very heavy things, like the rolls of wire, they loaded into one of their boats and floated them into here then they widened the door enough to get the rolls through it. I thought it looked bigger than the first time I went through it, but I thought it probably just looked that way because it was newly painted.

All the people here are waiting to hear if they have done good, or not so good. James and Jenna and Mike and Morgan tell them that they have done fantastic. They tell them in fact we couldn't have done any better, if as good. That makes them very happy and proud that they were able to accomplish so much. Now they want to show us how they are anchoring the paddle wheels. Actually they are doing something that I thought about at the first sight, but didn't mention because I thought if it was a good idea, one of the smart people would think of it. That is to run a large diameter steel bar across the width of the cave, fastening it to the wall, or in this case, to the ledge that runs along the wall.

Then they slid the paddle wheels onto the large shaft with solid bronze bearings at each end of the paddle, with a spacer in the middle, to hold the paddles apart so that they can turn independently. There are some weaknesses to doing it this way, but it should be good enough for the startup. If the generator works the way we think it will, we are going to build some concrete pilings under the water to fasten the paddles to. That will be the permanent fix. Our experts decide to get to work right away, so those of us who are not particularly needed right now decide to help the people working on the houses and gardens. Dayna and I work with LT and Kathy, helping some of our friends with their gardens.

They do plant some crops that are for everyone and like us; they grow their own gardens to have some fruits and vegetables that they particularly like. We brought some of the hybrid seeds along for them as well. Naturally we don't try to tell them how to grow their crops, but we let them know that we have done some experimenting to come up with the results we have. They all seem to be happy to try at least a couple of each of the plant seeds we brought with us. When the work is done for today, we all change into some clothes that are appropriate for swimming. Dayna loves the beach that is not far from the first settlement. The settlers here tell us we must be careful about swimming out too far, because of the strong currents and there are large fish that will eat you, if they catch you in the water.

The old man that I met on my last trip here tells us that they are talking about sharks. He says he doesn't see them often, but sometimes when he is in his boat fishing he sees them. He says that they usually swim near his boat, but then swim away, probably looking for fish to eat. He laughs and says that the sharks take one look at how skinny he is and decide that he wouldn't be a good enough meal, so they move on. Everyone laughs and tells him they can't blame the sharks for that, his hide is tougher than leather. One of the young girls in the group tells us that she loves it when she sees the dolphins come close to shore.

She says it's like they are trying to talk to her and the others and they even let the people pet them, in the water of course. One of the other settlers tells us that about ten years ago one of their people lost his boat on the rocks farther down the shoreline in a bad storm. They were all worried about him because he was the last one out on the ocean and everyone was looking for him along the shoreline. She says she heard the dolphins screeching at them, like they were trying to tell them something, then they saw a body being pushed through the water toward them. The waves were a little high for the dolphins to get too close, but they pushed the body as close as they dared, then the people ran out into the water to see who it was.

It turned out to be the fisherman and when he could talk again, he told them that he was sure he would drown when the dolphins pushed him to the surface and held him up until they got him to the people looking for him. One of the men in the group tells us that he is that fisherman and whenever he sees a dolphin when he is fishing, he always throws them some fish to eat. He also says that sometimes when the fishing isn't good, the dolphins show him where to fish. He continues saying that we may not believe it, but one day when he had no luck catching fish and he knew his family would have nothing to eat, the dolphins pushed a very large Marlin that looked like it had been bitten by a shark, but it was still alive, just barely, but enough to show him how it had died so he could eat the fish. He says his family and many other families ate well for several days on that fish. We all get invited to go fishing with our friends tomorrow. Some of them fish with nets and some fish with a rod and reel. Some of them fish for lobsters, crabs and shrimp. I don't know if they fish for all three at the same time or not. I figure I will go out with some of them and that way I can find out without sounding too ignorant.

We turn in early so that we can be up at dawn to go fishing with our friends. Dayna and I go with some of our friends that use rods when they fish. LT and Kathy love the crabs and the other shell fish, so they go on one of the boats fishing for those. Tim and Charity go on one of the boats that use small nets to catch fish. As usual we make it into a competition to see which group catches the most today. Our hosts tell us that they don't fish everyday because they don't need that much fish. They say if they catch too many fish, some of it will go to waste because they can only eat so much.

Being the person I am, I ask them if they have ever smoked the fish to preserve it. Apparently they have not, because our friends smile and say that they are not familiar with that term. I try to explain it with no luck, so I tell them I will show them what I mean when we get back to the docks this afternoon or evening. It's about as beautiful a day as anyone could ask for. The sun is shining brightly and the ocean is just kind of rising and falling in shallow swales. Our friends tell us this should be a good day to catch fish. Apparently when the ocean is flat and smooth, the fish do not bite as well.

Actually, as relaxing as this is, I couldn't care less if I catch anything or not. There are six lines in the water on what our captain told us are downriggers at different depths, to catch the fish wherever they may be today. This is really a nice boat. The captain says that they found the boats they all use at a marina a few kilometers from the settlement. One of the guys in their settlement is a pretty good mechanic and was able to get enough boats running for everyone that wanted one. The boat we are on is about thirty feet long and was made for this kind of fishing. Each of us is assigned to one of the rods, so that is what we are watching.

I must doze off or something because one minute I am sitting here watching my line and the next the line is being pulled out at a rapid rate, by what appears to be a large fish. The captain is laughing when he comes over and tells me to grab my pole, or the fish will take it with him. I am not a very experienced fisherman, but I know enough to pick the rod up and set the hook. Then I increase the drag on the reel to make it harder for the fish to pull the line out. I can feel the fish on the other end fighting, but I can tell it is not a monster anyway. I sit down in one of the chairs and lock the rod in place in one of the fixtures for that purpose and start fighting the fish.

It doesn't take long when I can tell the fish is getting tired and not long after that I am reeling it in. I get it close to the boat and one of the crewmen reaches down with a large gaff, and hooking the fish, pulls it up into the boat. As I said it is not a monster, but it is the biggest fish I have ever caught. The crewman smiles when he tells us it is a very nice tuna. Dayna smacks me when I tell him it can't be tuna because there is no can. Apparently they don't know about canned tuna fish because they smile politely, but they have no idea what I am talking about. They really laugh when Dayna tells them not to be embarrassed, because most people have no idea what I am talking about half the time.

I act like I am hurt and Dayna tells me and them that she loves me whether anyone understands me or not. Now that I have caught my fish I step back and let someone else watch the rods. It seems like just a few minutes and another fish is on a line. Our friends tell Dayna to take this one. She has done quite a bit of fishing in the lakes and rivers up near our settlement and has caught some pretty good sized fish. This one is obviously larger than any of those, but she sits in her chair with the rod locked in and fights the fish perfectly. Finally she can reel it in and the same crewman reaches overboard and hauls in another tuna that is bigger than the one I caught. All of our friends are excited for her. They say that if we can catch one or two more like this we will have plenty of fish for today.

As luck would have it another fish strikes just about as he finishes talking. They smile and tell me to take that one because they get to do this whenever they want to. I take the rod and start to play the fish which feels bigger than the first one. While I am doing this, Dayna is reeling in one of the lines to keep us from getting tangled, and a fish takes that line and is off and running. It almost takes the rod right out of her hands, catching her by surprise like that. Luckily that fish takes off toward the other side of the boat so there is no immediate danger of getting the lines crossed. I fight my fish until we can finally get it into the boat and this one is a little bigger than the one Dayna caught.

I am feeling pretty good about that when she pulls her fish alongside the boat where it is gaffed and brought on board. Our friends start laughing because her fish is bigger than mine again. The captain tells me that if I can live with my shame, at least until tomorrow, we can go in now because we have more than enough fish for the settlement. He is laughing when he says it just teasing me. I tell him I will never live it down, but it is never shameful to be bested by a beautiful woman. Dayna comes over and gives me a kiss just for being me. The captain smiles and says sometimes the one who finishes last wins the best prize. I agree with him fully.

13

When we get back to the dock the others are just getting back as well. It looks like everybody had a good day because they are off loading quite a bit of seafood from all the boats. The second fish Dayna caught is the biggest fish of the day. Everybody tells us we must have cheated somehow, but it's all in fun and no one really cares who caught the biggest fish; we all had a great day. I ask the others if they have ever smoked fish and to my surprise they all tell me they don't know anything about that. I look around the settlement and I don't see any smoke houses, so I decide to teach them how to smoke fish, then they can either use this method or not.

There is a small storage shack at the edge of the settlement that looks like it may just work for what I want to do. I explain it to James and Mike and they think it's a great idea. That way the settlers can also smoke some of the pork that they get from hunting. With James and Mike helping, we wind up with a much more deluxe model smoke house than I was envisioning when I started this project. The other groups that went fishing today had pretty good luck as well, so we take some of the fish they caught, which is what they called Sea Bass and some of the tuna and put some of the fillets in the smoke house. If nothing else the people are curious and excited about trying something new.

We have a feast on the fish and other sea food that was harvested today. I even eat some of the tuna dipped in wheat flour and deep fried. We talk about our experience today and our friends laugh about the colorful stories we tell about our fishing success. It's all in fun and helps us all feel more like family, than friends. Just about all of the people in the settlements here are trying to learn to speak English. They are very self conscious about it, but we encourage them not to be and to keep trying. Lillianne and Isabella are trying as hard as anybody, and probably more than most. Just before we turn in James and Mike say that they would love to be able to go out on a boat to just study the shoreline.

All the fishermen in the group tell us that it is not good to stay too close to the shoreline. That is where the rocks and other dangers are. James and Mike assure them that they are more than willing to listen to our hosts and would like very much to have at least a couple of them show us the safest way to study the shoreline. They agree with that, but it is going to have to wait a couple of days until the bad weather that is coming passes. The weather looks great to us, but our friends assure us there will be wind and rain tomorrow, around mid-morning. They smile and tell us even the children know how to tell when the weather will not be good.

We turn in still not knowing how they can tell that the weather will be bad tomorrow. In the morning the skies are looking overcast and the wind is picking up. In the cave they have almost all of the paddle wheels fastened down, but in there you can't tell that the weather is changing outside. They are planning to continue working, unless something interrupts them. Those of us not working on the electricity decide that today would be a good day to teach our friends how to can vegetables and even the smoked fish. We went over much of this when we came down here a couple years ago, but the settlers here say that they don't need to can foods because food is always readily available.

I really have no answer to that. When people have never had to go hungry for a while, they don't realize how important it can be to have a supply of good food on hand. I am about to quit trying, when Dayna asks the women if they had plenty to eat when those people took over their settlement. They admit that they didn't, but that those guys would have taken it if they would have had canned food for an emergency. We are meeting in a building that was obviously once a school because the room we are in and most of the other rooms still have blackboards in them. Dayna tells the people they may be right, but what if they did something like this, and starts drawing something on the blackboard.

What she is drawing is the tunnel system we put in under our homes and out to a safe place where we can go if we are attacked. We also put in storage for emergency rations and food to last several weeks if needed. One of the girls in the room says that it looks like the caves under the hacienda. Dayna tells her that is a very good example. She goes on to ask what would keep them from storing a couple months worth of food and other supplies under the hacienda, or maybe even right under their own homes. She tells them that they could even get away from men like that if they planned well and prepared ahead of time like we did. There are some men in the group as well and one of those tells us that the soil here is not easy to dig in, so it would be very difficult to do something like that here.

I ask them if they know what a backhoe is. They are not sure, so Dayna draws one on the board; it looks just like a backhoe too. The same man says that he has seen them, but has never used or driven one. LT tells them that when the weather gets better, we will find a backhoe and see just how difficult it is to dig in this ground. Dayna doesn't give up yet though. She tells the ladies that everyone should know how to preserve fruits, vegetables and meats, because we never know what Mother Nature or other people may throw at us. For today's lessons we have several different types of fruit and vegetables and even a couple different kinds of meat.

Up until now they have frozen some food, but the power is not all that dependable, so they have had to eat a lot of food sometimes to keep it from going to waste. We have four women from our settlement to teach our friends today, so each one takes a topic and we split up into groups to get some experience at all of them. They are teaching how to can using a couple different methods, we are teaching them how to make jerky and how to smoke other meats to preserve them, but also just to make them taste better. We are also showing them how to dehydrate fruits and vegetables for great snacks and to preserve them. Some of them have been taught before, but have simply not used the knowledge in a long time.

We go through a lot of fruits, vegetables, and meat, but when the day is over I think we have convinced at least some of them that it is not that difficult to preserve food, and it even gives you more options on using it. Just before we finished for the day, we went and got some of the smoked fish that we are making and let everyone that wants to taste it, do so. Then we showed them how to can the smoked fish, which will make it last a couple of years if need be, and they really liked that idea. Personally I do not care for smoked fish, but the dehydrated mangos, pineapple, bananas, and other tropical fruits turned out great. Even if they do not do a lot of canning, they will definitely dehydrate more fruit. Our people are going to spend a couple days dehydrating some of the fresh fruits that grow wild down here.

The electrical people tell us that they completed the job of fastening down the paddle wheels today and have started running the wire to the generator. I know there is a lot more to it than I am saying, but when they talk about it, they lose me very quickly. I try to learn pretty much everything I can, but electricity has always scared me. People can lose their lives if you make a big enough mistake when you are working with electricity. James and Mike always tell me that if I don't want to work with electricity then they will do that and I can do everything else I don't mind doing. I think that's what makes our groups so successful, we all know our strengths and weaknesses and we work together to take advantage of each of our strengths, and in some cases even our weaknesses. Those often show us what we need to work on the most.

After dinner, the people that live here go for a walk outside and come back with the news that tomorrow will be more of the same. I ask Lillianne if she knows how they can predict the weather so accurately. She says it is very easy and volunteers to show us. Some of the others want to tag along just to make sure she tells us correctly. We go to a small building on the outskirts of the village, where she shows us a barometer and a couple of other weather gauges. Jenna and Morgan guess that they check these gauges after seeing certain signs from the birds and other wildlife and probably even from the color of the sky at sunset. The readings on the gauges confirm what the other signs are telling them.

Our friends tell us they are correct. Usually just watching the birds and other animals tells them all they need to know. We spend some time just sitting and watching the ocean wave's crash into the rocks on the shoreline. I ask them if they are worried about their boats and they tell me that this is just a little bad weather, when the tropical storms hit the coast, then they have to worry about their boats. Then they say they do not worry so much because there are plenty of boats around the island if they lose one. Several of us decide that if the weather isn't too bad tomorrow, we will take a trip around the area to see if there is anything that could make our friends lives better or easier.

When we go back to the quarters we are using while here, LT asks me if we really have a series of tunnels under our homes that goes out into the woods over a mile. I tell him we do, I also tell him how we have had to use those tunnels to defend ourselves a couple of times. He and Kathy can't wait to get back so they can see them. I have to tell them that not all the houses have the tunnels now because we have grown so much, but the tunnels are strategically located so that they will still be very useful. In the morning the weather is not good for going out on a boat, but it is not bad for taking a look around the area. Some of the local people want to go along to show us what we want to see, so we take a couple of cars to hold us all.

Dayna and I are amazed at how beautiful it is here. There are so many colorful birds, lizards, and other animals, and plants that are just so beautiful. We go to a city that is about fifteen miles away from the settlement. The houses are kind of rundown, but there are a lot of stores that we are sure have at least some things our friends can use. If there's one thing we all like to do it's rummaging through stores and even houses to find treasures that can make our lives better. The women are looking for pots, pans, ovens, and pretty much anything that helps in a kitchen. We men are looking for stores that sold firearms. Some of our friends say that as far as they know, before the war the people in this country were not allowed to own guns.

I agree that may be so, but that doesn't mean people didn't sell guns under the table. I am looking in a store that sold all kinds of fishing equipment and even some hunting equipment like bows and arrows, slingshots, and their supplies. The fishermen that are with us are gathering up an impressive collection of new rods, tackle, and pretty much anything they can find. LT says we are going to have to find a truck to get everything back to the settlement. I am checking the building over carefully because something just does not look right to me. I go into the stockroom and call the others to come and check out all the stuff in here. LT is right about needing a truck, all that needs to be decided now is how many trips we are going to make.

The stockroom shows me what I am looking for. The building doesn't look right because it has a hidden area behind a wall. It isn't much, but it is there. LT keeps asking me what I am looking for. When I see what I need to know, it's just a matter of finding the trigger or switch that will open the wall to the hidden area. Dayna is the one who finds it. She remembers all the places we have looked in since we met. This wall has a double latch and then you have to push a section of the wall to the left to open it. I do that then point into the room and tell him, "that". He looks into the opening and we can see even more guns than are under the hacienda and there is a bigger and better selection. Several of the guns here are from the United States military as well as some from pretty much every country with a military.

From the records we find, this guy must have been selling to a fairly high class clientele because these guns are more expensive than the average person could afford. LT and Tim are like kids in a candy store. Most of our friends from here say that they have never fired a gun before, but they would like to learn how, if we would be so kind to teach them. LT tells them that if Zeus can't teach them how to shoot, then no one can. That just confuses them until Dayna explains it to them. We now know that we are going to need a decent sized truck, so we go searching for one that we can get running again. We find a large building that has a sign that says that it was once a company that moved freight for businesses.

We can't believe that we could get lucky enough to find several trucks that have been inside since the war. The lock presents no problem and when we go inside the building, there are six very nice trucks that look like they range from a pickup up, to what looks like a nice two and a half ton truck, all with boxes except the pickup. LT tells us that even though the trucks are in good shape, the gas will not be any good after this many years. We explain that none of us know exactly why, but for some reason the fallout from the neutron war caused just about everything to stop, or at least slow down the aging process. That doesn't seem to be true with people, but all the materials we have found here are in much better shape than they should be, based on their age.

We go to work trying to get at least two of the larger trucks running, plus one of our friends says he would love to have the pickup truck. He also says that we would have to teach him how to drive it, but he would love to have either this one or one like it. We tell him as soon as we get the others running that one will be next. Surprisingly it takes less than an hour to get all three trucks running. They are skipping some, but the longer they run the better they are sounding. The warehouse these trucks are in is a metal building that looks like brand new. We tell our friends that they may want to move this warehouse to their settlement, to store their new trucks and other equipment we find in.

They are excited about the prospect of having not only the trucks, but the building as well. Our friends are wonderful people, but I think they lack imagination in some ways. We take the pickup truck and one of the other trucks back to the store to load our treasures. The ladies have just about an equal amount of treasures to take back as well. Tim's wife Charity tells us that if we are still in the market for a backhoe, she knows where there are at least a couple of them. She shows us to a store that sold farm and industrial equipment. There is more equipment here than four settlements the size of our friends will ever need. There is even a flatbed truck that is made for hauling equipment like this.

That is a project for another day. We better get our treasures home before it gets too late. When we get to the settlement, everyone is excited about everything that was found. Charity has a surprise for our friends that she found in the city today. Actually she has a couple of surprises and so do we men. Actually Dayna found it in the stockroom of the store we were in, but she was with us men, so it counts for us too. After dinner we are talking with our friends about what they do for entertainment. They say that they tell stories and some of them have books that they read out loud sometimes, but other than that they don't have much along what most people consider entertainment.

Charity asks Tim and me if we would be kind enough to get the surprise out of the truck and bring it in. I was thinking about something like this, Dayna and I talked about it, but forgot to look for one when we were in town. It's a good thing Charity didn't. Oh, I almost forgot to mention that she found a record player and several large boxes of records in town today. We help her set it up, so that in some cases the people can hear their first music. It's as big a hit as when Tim and I introduced our family to music. When the women and girls hear the music they start moving to the beat, so naturally the women from our group, grab us men and insist that we show them how to dance.

At first many of them are self conscious, but before long they are dancing just as badly as we do and they are enjoying it. The hacienda has a very large room that will work perfectly for when the settlements want to get together for some relaxation and fun. Dayna tells me that we have to find a movie theater somewhere, so we can introduce our friends to movies. That is the next thing on the agenda. Our friends told us this evening that the weather will be better tomorrow, but it is best not to go out on the boats yet. The guys working on the electrical are making great headway toward getting everything functional. We figure about two more weeks here and they should be pretty well on their way again.

Before everyone breaks up for the evening, we surprise them with another treasure. We found hundreds of sealed cans of candy in town today, so we pass out the cans to the families. This is only the second, or maybe the third time that most of them have ever tasted candy. There is plenty just from what we found today to last quite a while, if they ration it carefully. They will probably find a lot more before they are done. We get a surprise from our friends this evening as well. They show us how many jars of vegetables, fruit, and fish they canned today. It is a very impressive amount, plus they told us how much they enjoy doing it. The weather tomorrow is supposed to be better, but not really good enough to go out on the boats yet, so we plan to go back to town.

We leave early and head to town. We spend more time looking in more stores today and find a lot of great things that they can use. We also get the truck and a backhoe running, so that we can start digging if they even want to do something like that. Dayna is always reminding me that just because we feel that it is necessary to protect ourselves as much as we do, doesn't mean that everyone feels the same way. I already know that, it's just that I have seen so many terrible things happen when they could have been avoided. Even Gunny and my dad have come to me in dreams and told me that you cannot protect people from their own ignorance. Often it takes a tragedy to make people aware of what they should be doing. The trouble with that is it is often too late by then.

While we were in town today I checked and found some of the same type of conduit that we used to make our tunnels. I hate to admit it but after thinking about it in detail it may be very difficult to keep the critters like snakes, lizards, alligators, and who knows how many varieties of bugs, and other things that can either kill you, or maybe make you wish you were dead, out of the tunnels. It may actually be more feasible to bury some supplies in bunkers that they make for use in case of an emergency. They could be built out of cinderblock and concrete with steel doors and secure locks on them. We will see when we get the chance to try digging with the backhoe.

14

Just like yesterday everyone is excited about the treasures that we keep bringing back from town. There are several more cities on this island that are much bigger than the one we are finding everything in. There should be more than they will ever need in those other cities. I knew there had to be more than one military base and one of the older gentlemen confirms that, telling us that there are two large military bases on the island, as well as an American military base. We would like to visit all of them before we leave. When things finally quiet down we are told that if we would like to take one of the boats to check out the shoreline, tomorrow should be a great day for it. When I hear that I get a very strong feeling of dread in my stomach. You know, like when you feel like something is wrong, but you don't know what it is.

Dayna must notice as soon as it hits me because when we are alone she asks me if I would prefer not to go out on the boat tomorrow with the other guys. I shrug it off telling her that it's probably just being away from her for several hours that is bothering me. She kisses me and tells me I'm telling stories, but she likes hearing that kind of story. The more I think about it the more I think the feeling must just be something I ate. Seafood can do that to you and I have been eating more lately than ever before. I don't sleep well and lay awake for about half the night trying to will that feeling away. It must work some because in the morning I don't feel near as bad as I did last night.

The others going today ask me if I'm going to be okay or if we should postpone the trip again. I tell them it must have been that fish we had for supper last night, because a trip to the little boys room this morning and I feel better already. I get smacked by everybody that is going and told that's more information than they wanted. I thought some of our local friends would be going, but apparently they are going to be busy catching fish, but they did tell us to stay out at least a half mile because of the rocks and to make sure we take compass readings before we leave the dock. That will help us find our way back. James and Mike are both experienced boaters and Tim, LT, and I have been on enough missions where we had to keep our bearings to find where we had to be and how to get out of there, so we should have no problems at all.

The boat we are on is beautiful and handles the almost calm sea very well. We head out the half mile we were counseled to maintain and then head clockwise around the island. Our goal is not to circle the island, but to go along the coast a couple hours and then turn around and come back. The coastline is fascinating and looks very rugged with the waves washing up on the rocks that can be seen. Our boat has a depth finder, so we are keeping an eye on that as we watch the shoreline. We are out about three hours when we spot some docks and what looks like a nice little bay to go through to get to the docks. We can't see if there is a city beyond the docks, but according to the map we have, there is supposed to be.

We watch the depth finder and some of us keep watch off the side of the boat, looking for rocks or anything that could poke a hole in the bottom of our boat. We get docked fine then go ashore to see if there is indeed a town or city here. We go inland for about two hundred yards and sure enough there is a small city or town looking like people could be living here today. That is of course except for the lack of people to live here. We walk around town looking in stores and shops, finding a few treasures that we take back with us. We can see how to get here by car or truck because there is a huge amount of things that our friends can use. We even carry a couple cases of cans of what the label calls, Special Dark European chocolate, back to the boat with us.

When we get back to the boat, we notice that somehow a couple of hours must have gotten away from us because it is past the time that we wanted to turn around and head back to the settlement. It shouldn't be any big deal. It will just be a little later when we get there than we had anticipated. James is the one steering the boat and when we start to go back he tells us the compass is not working properly. Mike looks at it and says that we may be in an area with a lot of magnetism in the rocks. That sounds logical to us and we know which way we came to get here so we don't think anything of it.

We are moving along well for about an hour, when James tells us the compass still is not working and now the depth finder has quit. Again we tell him that the shoreline looks familiar, so all we have to do is stay out about this far and follow the shoreline home. I forgot to mention that even the compasses that each of us are carrying, are not working either. We go what we feel is about another mile when the shore is getting more and more difficult to see. The sun is still shining, but starting to set on the ocean side of the boat and it looks like some fog is starting to roll in toward the shore.

We go maybe another half mile, and now the boat is enveloped by the fog, and we can barely make out the coastline. Mike suggests that we go a little farther out because we can hear the waves crashing on the rocks on our left side. I am getting that sick feeling in my stomach again. By our calculations we should be about two hours from the settlement. We can't believe that we took that much time in that city. We go out to deeper water for five minutes, which at our current speed we figure is about a mile off shore, which should be safe. We are going along mostly by listening for the waves crashing on the shore, until James and Mike tell us that we should probably drop the anchor here and wait out the fog.

It's thick, but we can still see a little ways in every direction, just not enough to see the shoreline. We open a can of the chocolate we found and Tim, LT, and I start telling stories about some of the times we had to wait out fog or other elements that Mother Nature tends to throw at people. The hours go by slowly. We are straining to hear if someone is calling our names from the shore or possibly from a rescue boat. James tells us that he doubts very much that anyone would venture out on the water in this fog. It would be far too dangerous and the odds of finding anyone in it are far too low to even think about.

We pretty much run out of stories to tell, so we all kind of sit around with our thoughts. We are all glad that we brought along jackets as well as rain gear, in case we ran into a squall of some kind. The fog is cold and very damp, but none of us want to go below deck, even if we are uncomfortable. I look at my watch and even that has quit working. Tim is looking at his, then he looks at me and says it can't be. LT starts to say that this is what the fog was like that night he and Kathy came into our world, but stops when he realizes what Tim and I were thinking. All of us came into this world in some kind of dense fog. I think I am speaking for all of us in this boat when I say a prayer to Heavenly Father, praying that he is not sending us back where we came from.

We sit quietly with our own thoughts for what seems like a long time then James tells us that he and Jenna were always loners before they came here. Coming to this world is the greatest thing that ever happened to them. They know that this is where they belong and they would not want to live anywhere else, but here with all of us. We all feel the same way and we all express our love for the lives that we live. I tell them that if I was sent back to the world we came from, I could probably adapt somehow if Dayna was with me. Without her, I don't even want to think about what my life would be like. The others all agree that without our wives, the will to live would be gone.

I must doze a little because I dream that Dayna is standing on the dock watching for our boat with the tears running down her cheeks. Lillianne and Isabella are with her as well as Charity, Morgan, Jenna, and Kathy. I see Gunny and Ma Horton, but when I ask them if I will get back to Dayna they just shrug and say they don't know. My dream drifts back to Dayna and the others standing on the dock when a dolphin swims up and starts chattering to them. Lillianne kneels down and pets the dolphin who continues talking to her. She tells the dolphin that her papa is out on a boat somewhere and they are afraid that we may not make it home. The dolphin makes some excited noises like it is talking to them, and then swims away quickly. I wake up disappointed that the fog is still heavy, cold, and wet, but the sky does appear to be getting lighter off to what must be the east.

At least our boat is headed the right direction, even if we are not moving. The others are asleep as well, so I am trying to decipher my dream when Tim wakes up LT then the other two. We all must have had a similar dream except that theirs were more about their wives than mine. The sun must be burning the fog off at least a little because we are starting to see at least twenty or thirty feet off the boat. I say another prayer that we are not back in our old world. I even tell Heavenly Father that if that is what he has in mind for me, then to take my life now and get it over with. I do not want to live without Dayna and the rest of our family. That is probably the most heartfelt prayer I have ever said. Actually I haven't said anywhere near as many as I should, even if I am just thanking him for all I have.

The others all say amen to that and we strain to see if we can find even enough coastline to stay clear of. When visibility gets up to a cloudy hundred yards, James says he is going to start the boat and just creep along for a while. We agree that we must still be at least a couple of hours from the settlement. We can't see any reason not to at least try it for a while. We are going very slowly watching the ocean, listening for the waves on the rocks and looking for shoreline. All of a sudden I see a dorsal fin sticking out of the water off to our left, which is toward the shore, but we are at least a mile off shore anyway, so this could be anything. My first thought is that it is a shark, but Mike sees it too and says shark fins just don't look like that.

When he says that, the dolphin that belongs to that fin, jumps out of the water startling all of us and splashing us with water as well. The dolphin is acting like he or she knows us, chattering away and swimming all around the boat. Finally she takes off swimming fast then comes back and starts chattering at us again. Tim says what we are all thinking, that she wants us to follow her. I am calling it a her now, because there is a little one swimming right along side of her. The fog is lifting slowly, but we can see her staying a safe distance ahead and to the side of us. We are not moving very fast, but at least we feel like we may be on our way home now.

I didn't say anything about the part of my dream that had the dolphin in it, but I am hoping harder than I ever have before that this is the miracle we needed. Finally we can start to see the shoreline and even though we didn't know it, we must have been getting closer to the shore all the while. We are still a safe distance, but close enough to see details. Up ahead of us is what we think we recognize as the last large jutting out portion of the coastline before it tapers back a couple hundred yards to the small cove where the settlement is located. Right now there are five men praying for all they are worth that we see our friends and families standing on the dock or the shore waiting for us.

Our dolphin friend swims ahead of us and takes off, just as we get around that peninsula and it takes a couple of minutes to get close enough, but we see several people running on the beach toward the docks where there are even more people starting to wave and shout. When we finally get the boat to the dock, all of us except James, who is driving, jump off the boat and into the arms of our wives. Jenna jumps into the boat and doesn't even wait for him to stop the engines when she starts hugging him. Our dolphin friend is swimming around just off the dock having fun spraying water at the young people standing around watching. Apparently they are used to the dolphins because some of them jump into the water and start petting the mama and baby dolphin.

Dayna and I along with Lillianne and Isabella jump in to play with them as well. The little one is so cute and shy, but when the mama lets us pet her, it comes over and wants to be petted too. I ask Dayna and the others if they sent the dolphin to find us. They say that they wish they had, but they didn't. Dayna says this is the first time she has seen them. We have all heard tales of dolphins helping stranded sailors, I'm not sure if I believed them or not before, but I definitely do now. Odds are when the fog lifted we would have found our way home, but the dolphins were like an insurance policy today. I wish there was some way that we could take them home with us. They are such beautiful and loving creatures. After a little while they swim away to wherever they spend their time.

Our wives fix us a nice breakfast and we tell them all about our adventure, while we are eating. We don't say much about our fears until we are alone. Dayna tells me when the fog rolled in as heavy as it was, all the wives feared the same thing we did. She says they all prayed harder than they ever had before that we would all return. They wouldn't want to go on without us either. Dayna tells me that when we were apart the last time, when I came down here alone, she vowed to be with me all the time after that. She says she lets me out of her sight for one day and I get into trouble again. This time she is not letting me go anywhere without her.

She tells me the other wives made the same vow last night, so we men better plan on taking all of our wives if we go anywhere farther than the latrine. I laugh and ask her what if I want to take a shower. She just smiles and says we will work something out. As much as I would like to go to bed for a few hours the time we have to spend here is getting shorter by the day. We still have a bunch of places to see and things to do to help our friends here. James and Mike are planning to help with the electricity again today, so the rest of us, that's Tim, LT, and me, along with our wives of course, decide to go into town again, only this time we are looking for a vehicle big enough for all of us plus a couple of our friends to go looking around the island.

As luck would have it we find a place that apparently provided guided tours of the island and had several small busses in a really nice metal building that our friends are planning to come into town and take it back with them. That's a big project, but once the crops are in the farmers will not have all that much to keep them busy. Projects like moving those buildings are great to keep people out of mischief. I never knew that LT is such an experienced mechanic and Kathy is just as good as he is. I mentioned this to them and they both said in this world they are probably better than the average, but in the world we left, they are almost as useful as an anvil would be to a drowning man. Naturally Tim has to tell me to remember that analogy because it fits how useful I am in most cases.

Some of our friends are confused at what Tim said. He tells them like he is whispering that I am really not all that inept, but if they tell me how good I really am, I will be very difficult to live with. He makes a sign like someone with a big head and they all laugh and wink at him like they have a secret. We get the small bus running quickly enough that we go looking farther east on the island. We come to what is the largest city we have seen on the island so far. We see something that shows a lot of promise so Dayna and I ask Tim and Charity if they would like to check it out or should we. They tell us they would like to if we don't mind. We noticed or should I say the ladies noticed that many of our friends clothing is showing signs of wear so we go looking for places that sell clothing and find a store that must have thousands of clothing items of all sizes and styles.

While the ladies are checking that out, LT and I are getting another nice sized truck running. By the time we leave they will have quite a variety of vehicles to use. There are literally hundreds of military style jeeps or at least jeep style vehicles that we would love to have several of at home. We get the truck running and air in the tires and it actually works. We fill the tank from a pump at the business where we found the truck. We see another large building around the corner from where we found the truck, so we decide to check it out. It turns out to be what in our world would have been like an armory for Military reserve units. Talk about kids in a candy shop. LT and I are checking out the vehicles when we find one almost just like the one Ryan back home has with a thirty caliber machine gun mounted on the back. LT wants very badly to get it running, so we can take it back with us.

He stays to do that while I take the truck back to the store to load the treasures there. We fill the truck up about halfway, leaving room for other treasures. We are driving back toward Tim and Charity when Dayna notices a sign that says it was a candy store when there were people living here. That is just too much to pass up, so we have to explore that one. The display case is full of what was once candy, but none of us are interested in tasting any of it. The shelves are almost full of cans of different kinds of candy that are still sealed, so those we will try. We load several boxes full from the shelves then go into the stockroom to see what is there. There we find hundreds of cases of canned candy and the ingredients for making candy along with recipes and the equipment that is required to make different kinds of candy.

The items we take from this store almost fill up the rest of the truck. By the time we get back to Tim and Charity they have enough to finish it off and just as we are getting ready to go looking for LT, he comes driving up in that military vehicle with the thirty. Two of our friends that came along want to ride in that vehicle on the way home. They are more like kids playing soldier than grown men, but there is a little child in all of us, at least those of us who are lucky. When we get back, we find out that they actually hooked the wire up to the generator and it is working as we speak. That's a huge step forward for these people.

The items we brought back today go over big as well. Tim and Charity hold their surprise until after supper tonight. They ask everyone to please step out of the big room that we have been meeting in, then they hook up their surprise and call us all back in again. When everybody is back and seated, they start the movie projector, showing an old movie on the large white wall in the front. Most of our friends cannot believe that they are actually watching a movie. Only a couple of them saw one before the war. We have all of the movies back home that they were able to find today except these are done in their native language.

Lillianne and Isabella, who want to be called Lillie and Izzie, now that they are moving to live with us, were disappointed at first because the settlement is getting all this neat stuff when they are getting ready to leave. Dayna tells them that we have had these things for years now and tells them about the other things the young people in our settlement can do and now they don't feel bad anymore. Its fun to show the other settlements what is out there for them to be able to use to enhance their own lives a little.

15

Our days are filled with traveling around the island and helping our friends realize that their lives can be more than just living and working. The only thing that holds them back is their imaginations. The new clothes were a big hit with just about everybody. The tidal generators are working better than we had even hoped they would. I finally got invited to see how the generator is setup and it's totally different than I thought it was. The generator had to be moved so that the drive shaft from the paddle wheels is turning the generator. Actually it is turning a turbine, which in turn is turning the generator, which is generating electricity. They assure me that it is being done the same way back on the mainland.

Morgan and Jenna tell me that they will not tell Sara that I am not an expert on everything. They say they wouldn't want to have her hero come crashing down. Then they laugh like a couple of ninnies. Don't ask me what a ninny is, but Gunny and Ma Horton were always saying that. James and Mike, along with Jenna and Morgan thought that they would have to babysit the new generator for weeks, if not months, to make sure they keep running, but they must have planned it well enough that they took care of the potential problems up front. They are talking about installing another one in one of the caves near the other two settlements and running the wire up through the ground to cover both of them.

I will leave that up to them, but if they need equipment I know I can find that for them. We are planning to leave the island in a couple of days, but before we do we want to go all the way to the far end of the island. We had thought about making the trip by boat, but after that fog, we are going to drive. The roads on the island are not in very good shape, so it's difficult to make good time when we go somewhere, but we are expecting to spend the night somewhere on our route. We are taking the tour bus and the pickup truck, mainly for supplies and in case we find something small we can't live without.

The trip to the other end of the island is beautiful. There are so many multi colored birds and the vegetation is beautiful as well. We pass several very beautiful waterfalls and the coastline has some of the most fascinating views of the ocean we have ever seen. Lillie and Izzie decided to come with Dayna and I on this trip. LT and Kathy, and Tim and Charity came with us as well as Philippe and his wife Maria. They are some of the leaders of their settlement. We are getting close to the end of the island when Lillie tells me we are being watched from the jungle. I already saw at least three men watching us as we drove past. I ask Tim to stop and as luck would have it, we stop where two men and two women are watching us from behind some trees.

I speak in their direction, in Spanish of course, that we mean them no harm and that we are from a settlement on the other end of the island. The men step out first and ask me my name. I tell them and they say they have heard my name on the radio, but they thought I lived on the mainland. Tim tells them that he is usually the one on the radio and introduces himself along with the rest of our group. Now the women come out and the people we passed catch up to us as well. It makes me feel good to see that they are armed and cautious. We go with them to their settlement, which is not as big as the three on the other end, but it looks like it is well maintained and the people look healthy and strong.

I do notice the lack of vehicles and electricity, but other than that they look like they are doing well. They show us their radio, it's an old hand crank kind, but they tell us it will only receive, they can't send any messages. They also tell us that they listen and try to do some of the things they hear us talking about, but they are limited on how much they can do because they have no one that knows about cars or electricity. We tell them they are in luck then, because we can help them with both of those items and pretty much anything else they may be in need of. It is almost dark by the time we get to meet everyone, but we tell them first thing in the morning we will get them started.

We spend a pleasant evening getting to know our hosts. LT, Tim, and I take turns making sure no one tries anything. Don't worry we are discreet about it, we pretend to be sleeping, but we are keeping an open eye on our surroundings. In the morning they show us the nearest city, which is only about a couple miles away. LT asks them if they see any particular car or truck that they might like to have. They point to a nice pickup truck and a small bus similar to the one we are using. While LT and I are trying to get them running, Tim takes their radio guy, whose name is Juan, and they go looking for a decent radio. By the time we have the truck running; they have found enough electrical equipment to build a couple of windmills and at least two very nice new radios. They also found some very nice generators that will run on propane and we know there has to be at least one propane truck around here.

We find one a block away that is almost full and another one a couple of blocks away from that one. While the others take the bus and truck home, LT and I stay to get the propane truck running. When we get the first one running, we drive it back to the settlement. This is fun for us to be helping our new friends like this. Dayna and Charity both commented that it feels like when we were doing these same things to get our own settlement going. We have enjoyed doing this every time we have had the privilege of helping others. The size of the homes they have is small enough for one of the generators that we brought back, to supply electricity for two or three easily. They are not even sure how to use it, so they will use even less than most, at least for a while.

The number one project is to get the radio working, so we can contact the other settlement and let them know they are not alone here. We are sure that they are going to be happy to come here and help these people progress in all ways. At least Tim and I know how to do that much. Tim contacts the other settlement as well as the one in Florida and our group back home. Actually he gets Ryan, from the group next to ours, who tells us we should stay here for a couple of years because things are running so smooth back there. He is only kidding; we have been harassing each other for years. We all get to talk to some of our children and grandchildren who all tell us they miss us terribly. Hearing their voices makes us miss them even more.

The settlement at the other end of the island is pleasantly surprised to hear that there is another settlement here. They will be happy to send some electrical people and a couple of mechanics to teach them about cars, trucks, generators, windmills, and pretty much everything they know. These people use row boats for fishing because they do not know anything about motors. For what they do know they are doing a great job. They have nice gardens that they turned the soil over by hand to plant and they know about smoking meat and fish and they preserve some fish using salt or a brine solution.

We do notice that they do not have very many guns to defend themselves with. I decide to go back into town with Tim, LT, and a couple of our new friends to see if we can do something about that. If this Cuba was anything like the Cuba in our world it was under military rule and the people were not allowed to own firearms. We find two very nice caches of firearms, again mostly military weapons, but there is plenty of ammunition, along with some very nice military uniforms and other military items like knives. Naturally they are not as good as the K-Bar, but they are not bad.

Now our friends have enough weapons for everyone to have one and enough ammunition to practice with. We would like to be able to stay and help them for several weeks, but the other settlement on the island is looking forward to helping them and learning from them. When we are getting ready to leave, we get a call on the radio telling us that if we would like to spend a couple more days here we can. They are having some minor problems with one of the generators, so James and Mike want to get it worked out before we leave. We don't mind at all, that will give us time to help them get a boat or two running and maybe even teach them some self defense techniques.

At dinner Dayna tells me that Lillie and Izzie spent most of the day teaching the girls, their age and a little older, how to use the bow and arrows to hunt with. I ask her if she remembers that I have a couple more of the Special Forces bow and arrow sets in my pack. She tells me that I did have a couple sets in my pack. The young ladies love them, even though they are a little harder to pull back then they would like. I start to tell her they can be adjusted and she tells me that they already did that as well. I tell her that I know I saw a bunch of re-curve and compound bows in town today at the place we found the guns. Dayna tells me that Tim loaded a bunch of them while I was loading the guns and ammunition. Now all the girls have their own bow and enough arrows to practice with and for hunting.

Our new friends are really enjoying the electricity that they are getting from the generators we found and helped them hook up. We are enjoying getting to know them better and helping them understand and speak a little English. A couple of their group members are fairly fluent in English, which is how they were able to understand what we were telling the other groups on the radio. Tonight we get to talk to Teddy and our other sons for a while. Tommy tells me, that Misty told him, that her mom wants us to stay until she can fly one of the big helicopters down here and pick up enough fresh sea food for a big party back home. Misty came on the radio and tells me that her mom said that I should get off my big behind and at least help our friends here catch some of the sea food we will want.

Misty is quick to tell me that she is just passing on a message from her mom. Actually we can hear her mom laughing in the background. Thomas asks Dayna and me again how old he and Misty have to be before they can get married. I tell them that personally, I think thirty-five or forty would be a good age. He and Misty are laughing and Dayna smacks me. She tells them they should wait at least a couple of years and they tell her they aren't ready yet, but they are just gathering information now. I hear Sara again, so I ask her if she has a shopping list for the seafood that she wants me to gather for her. She rattles off enough food to feed our entire settlement, including the outlying ones.

When she finishes I tell her that list will barely feed her and Lindsay. Lindsay is listening and tells Dayna that her husband is going to get his butt kicked when we get home. Dayna tells her that if I'm not careful I won't have to wait until then. Everyone is laughing and it's almost like being back home with our family again. I ask Sara what credit card she wants us to put the cost of all that seafood on. Our friends here have no idea what we are talking about. Many of our friends here are asking what we are talking about a helicopter. Lillie and Izzie explain what a helicopter is and are very animated about it. Now all of our new friends want to see one, they are not sure whether or not to believe that something that big can fly.

Sara tells me that our hunters are going to get a large steer and butcher it to trade for the seafood. She tells us that she has already talked it over with the other settlement. That makes me think that there should be cows or steers on this island as well, but I have never seen one. We talk for a while longer, and then we have to go. I ask Lillie if she has ever seen cows in the jungle. She is not sure what I mean so we look through a couple of books and finally find a picture of one. She tells us that she has seen animals like this, but they are too big to bring down with her bow. She tells me that I could probably kill one with my bow, but she is afraid to even try. One of the ladies in the group says that when she was a girl, her family had a milk cow and they loved the fresh milk.

I tell them that we can probably teach them how to catch a couple of cows, but I do not know how to tell a milk cow from any other. The lady tells me that if I can get them some cows, they will know what to do. A couple of the kids in the group are anxious to show us where they have seen the cows not far from here. We will go to check it out first thing in the morning. In the morning our new friends tell us that they would like to help us get some of that seafood that Sara wants. They tell us that they already owe us more than they can ever repay for helping them get a radio and electricity. We tell them that we will be happy to help them, but we don't want to take food that their families need.

One of the fishermen asks me if I can swim and dive below the surface of the water. I tell him I can and so can Tim and LT. He says that after we find a cow for his wife, he will take us to a place he knows, where there are more lobsters and crabs than they could ever eat. He also says if we like shrimp, he can show us where we can catch more than we can eat. I tell him that won't be difficult for me because I don't care for seafood that much. He laughs and says then he can show me where I can catch enough for all my friends and family. Looking for those cows is turning into a pretty big event. I can't blame these people, they have been living here alone for many years and now they are getting to meet people just like them.

The young people who told us they could show us where they have seen cows before are right on the money. We don't see any cows right off, but there is plenty of sign all around this area. We also hear what we believe to be several chickens not far off as well. We decide to go into town for a quick trip then work on getting a cow or two and maybe even some chickens. The woman, who told us that she knows about cows, also says she knows how to raise chickens, but she has never been able to catch any. Part of the reason for that is that being in the jungle alone can be very dangerous. There are many animals that will kill you quickly if they get the chance and sometimes there are animals on two legs, who are worse than the other animals.

In town we go directly to a store where we saw plenty of grain and animal feeds in large plastic bags. We also find a large cooler that must be six feet long and about thirty inches high and wide. That should work well to keep some of that seafood fresh in. Our friends are not sure why we are getting these items, but they see soon enough and they are amused and embarrassed that they never thought of it. We take a couple bags of grain out to the area where the cow sign is and start leaving a trail of grain leading right up to the barn of one of the settlers. When they see what we are doing they cut several stacks of deep grass from around the settlement and stack it up for feed and bedding if the cows follow the grain.

There is also a place that looks like it was once a chicken coop in that same barn. We fix the hinges on the gate so that it will close when we get some chickens in there. When that is done it is just past noon, so we decide to go fishing to at least see all them lobsters and crabs our friend is talking about. We go down to the docks and see that there was once a very large marina here and there are still many large boats that have been inside since the war. Most of them are decked out for fishing and some for lobster or shrimp fishing. Our guide Juan, looks at those boats longingly, but he doesn't know how to fix the engines in them. We tell him we will help him and the others get some of these boats running again. He tells us that God must have sent us here because they have all prayed to him for as long as he can remember to help them to be able to use some of the great things around them.

16

We tell our friends to pick out which boats they would like then we go to work getting them to run. It takes a few hours to get the first two boats running. We get those back in the water and by the time we take them for a spin, it is getting dark so we do not get to do any fishing today. That's okay with us. The excitement on our friend's faces is priceless. In the morning we get three more boats running and our friends tell us that is more than enough for them to use. It will at least get them started, until the mechanics from the other settlement can come over and help them. We finally get to go fishing with them and they take us to their secret spot for lobsters and crabs. LT, Tim, and I are better than average swimmers, so when they ask if we can swim we tell them a little.

They tell us to try to stay up with them and they will show us where they get the bounty from the sea. They jump in with facemasks and snorkels on so we do the same. The water is beautiful for swimming and the coral reef is breathtaking. We swim along the top of the water looking toward the bottom and it is easy to see that there are thousands of lobsters on the bottom here. While we are swimming a school of shrimp swims right below us. There must be thousands of them in the school. I think everybody in our group except me loves almost any kind of seafood you can name, so we dive down to the bottom and gather up enough large lobsters for dinner.

We go back to the boat and our host takes us to the place he catches crabs. We pretty much repeat what we did diving for lobsters, only this time with large crabs. When we finish gathering seafood, our host takes us for a tour of the coastline here. He points to an area where the water seems to be churning a little and heads toward it. He dips a small net into the disturbance in the water and pulls it up overflowing with shrimp. He does this twice and we should have enough shrimp for at least twice as many people as we have in this group. Our hosts love the boat they now have. The one they have been using is slightly larger than a rowboat that had one sail that they could use when the wind is right.

We get back to the settlement in time for the very capable ladies in the settlement to cook the seafood feast. They also show us that four cows, with calves, found their way into the barnyard and are eating the straw grass that the ladies collected for them. There are also several chickens in the barn that the young ladies in the settlement are trying to get to know. They remind Dayna and me so much of the young ladies in our settlement. We think they are well on their way to being totally self-reliant. We have been spending some time each evening teaching our new friends self-defense. They seem to enjoy learning anything we will teach them and are doing very well. The young girls are picking the self-defense up very quickly and just like the girls in our settlements, they enjoy practicing at the expense of the young men in the group.

Just before bed time we get a call on the radio, telling us that Sara called them and told them she would be coming down in three days. That will give them time to make sure everything is working the way it should, then they can turn it over to the local electricians. We tell them that we are planning to come back tomorrow and they say that will work out well. We turn in planning to head back to the other settlement tomorrow. I am awakened by one of our new friends saying that one of my amigos says they need to talk to me. That starts me worrying; unless it is very important they wouldn't call in the middle of the night.

I answer the radio and I hear James voice speaking low, telling me that they are sure that they are going to be attacked soon. He says that a large boat was going up and down the coastline just after dark. They could see men on board checking out the shore with binoculars. He says they would have called earlier, but they were hoping that they would go away, however it doesn't look they are going to. One of the settlers has been watching the boat since it was spotted and he says that they landed a mile or so down the coast, and that several men were preparing to come ashore, and they are armed with guns. He asks if we can come back as quickly as possible because none of them know how to fight well enough to stop men like these.

I tell him to hide everybody and we will be there as soon as we can. I wake up the others and explain the situation while I am packing. I start to go to our bus, when several of our new friends tell me they can get us to the other end of the island more quickly in one of their new boats, than we can drive it at night. Besides they would like to try out their new rifles and other weapons. I can't argue with that, I grab one of the guns we found in town. It's a really nice .308 rifle with a variable scope on it, a very nice weapon for the time when these were made. Actually it's a good gun for what I may need it for, no matter when it was made. LT and Tim say it's just like old times. LT starts barking orders like he did in the Seal team, so Tim and I stop and look at him. He sees us looking at him, and says please in a conversational tone, and we all laugh including the girls.

Our friend Juan tells us he will accompany the ladies back to the other settlement as soon as the sun comes up and they can travel safely. He says he will also bring a group to help clean up the garbage that may be left lying around after the fight. Personally I hope there is no fight, I have never enjoyed taking a life, but unfortunately I have had to defend those I love and it always seems to come down to us or them surviving. We load the boat with everything we absolutely need and as many men as we can and head for the other end of the island. Our boat captain knows exactly where to go, he says it is easy with the instruments in his magnificent new boat. He can go quite a bit faster in the water than we can go on those roads in the dark.

The sun is coming up when he tells us we are getting close to the coordinates we gave him to find the other settlement. We dock the boat about a quarter mile before the settlements themselves and walk in. As we get closer to the settlement, we can hear men's voices arguing, saying that they don't know where everybody went. Then a familiar voice tells them that they better find him some women or he will shoot them. Tim mouths the name Marty, LT, and I shake our heads in the affirmative. It is getting light now, so we start to look for ways to see what they are going to do. Just when it sounds like they are going to give up and leave someone from down near the beach yells that he has found some women.

I get a sick feeling in my stomach because now this is not going to end peacefully. I know as sure as I am standing here that we will eliminate every one of these men if they harm those women. I am not surprised to see the two guys that were kicked out of this group when El Presidente was overthrown, dragging two young ladies about fifteen or sixteen years old. Marty, who appears to be the leader of this group, is smiling when he shouts that they have two lovely ladies that have volunteered to entertain them, is there anyone else with guts enough to try to stop them. James and Mike come out of the hacienda and tell Marty to let the girls go and they can leave. Marty asks him what they think they are going to do against all of his men with the people of this settlement.

James tells him that his men are surrounded right now and all it will take is a signal from him for them to open fire. The men with us have already been taught to pick a target and wait for my signal. Our men are spreading out to just about surround the bad guys. They are stopping almost right behind the one they have picked to shoot. I tell Tim and LT that I have high ground and that Marty is mine. They can have the two that were kicked out earlier. LT and Tim are making their way very quietly towards the clearing. The plan is to have them step out at the last second then I will shoot Marty. The way he is fondling the girls it will be my pleasure to shoot him.

I whistle a signal that we used on the teams. LT answers with the same whistle and we can see some of the guys getting nervous. One of the guys says that they should just kill the men and take the girls. Marty has his eyes glued on the opening where he thinks someone may come through. That would be too obvious. LT and Tim are moving to come out on his side, where he will have to turn to cover them. Marty must be getting nervous because he is shouting at James and Mike that he is going to kill them, unless they bring him more women. Just as he finishes, Jenna and Morgan step out from behind the fence where James and Mike are standing. They are holding K-Bar knives in their hands and tell Marty if he wants them come and get them.

He turns part way around to face them head on, when LT and Tim step out of the jungle and tell him to throw down the gun and let the girls go. He cusses at them shouting that he is going to kill them all. LT catches the eye of one of the girls and I see him signal for her to drop as we taught the girls in case they ever become hostages. Tim tells Marty he has until the count of three before he dies. Tim says one and Marty laughs at him. He says two and Marty raises his gun to bear on either James or Mike. Tim starts to say three when Marty and I fire at just about the same time. The young lady being held by Marty dropped the way she was taught which gave me a clear shot at his upper body.

As soon as I shoot the rest of our men open fire on the bad guys who are raising their guns to shoot anyone not part of their gang. Luckily James and Mike grab Jenna and Morgan and push them behind the wall for protection. It's over as quickly as it started. There are a couple of superficial wounds because some of the bad guys got shots off. One of those is Mike, who must have been grazed on his side by the shot that Marty took. Unfortunately we have ten men to bury today, what a waste. I will never understand why some men feel that it's their right to take whatever they want from others or those that will kill someone just to use their body for pleasure. It's a good thing our friends here have that backhoe that we got running for them.

We only know the apparent leader, but apparently some of our friends know who at least a few of these men were. A couple of the men from the settlement ask if they can find their boat and see if maybe it can be used for a good purpose. We tell them to go ahead and it doesn't take long before they drive the boat up to the docks where their boats are kept. It really is a beautiful boat. Actually I think this one would be called a yacht rather than a boat. Our guys blow the horn until we look to see what they want. They point out that there are three young women on the boat that came from an island farther to the east. They tell us that they were, kidnapped yesterday and brought here by those men.

They are worried that they may come back until they see the new graves and are told that their captors cannot hurt them anymore. Naturally we are all excited to hear that there are more people on the islands east of here. The young ladies tell us that there are about fifty people in the group they lived with. They don't have electricity or boats with motors and a lot of the things that the people here have. Those of us who got here this morning get a tour of everything that they have done while we were on the other end of the island. Some of the people that came with us from the other settlement know some of the people in this group. Apparently they all thought the others had been lost at sea or had perished in the jungle. We all know only too well that there are many ways to lose your life around here.

It is early afternoon before the rest of our group gets here. They ask what happened and our friends from that group point to the new graves on the hill overlooking the sea. The boat they came in draws a lot of interest and so do the young ladies that were freed. It doesn't take much discussion to decide to take the new boat along with the young ladies and go looking for their settlement. Since it as late as it is, we decide to wait until morning. The young ladies don't seem to mind too much. This is the first time they have seen electric lights, besides the ones on the boat, plus our friends are showing a movie that they found in a theater in town.

In the morning we get up before dawn and head for the island to the east. Our friends from the other end of the island are taking their boats back along with a couple of the men from this group. The young ladies tell us that their people will be happy to move to this island if the people here will allow them too. We are taking the ladies home and most likely invite the rest of their group to join the groups on this island. The big boat makes really great time along the coast and we are back at the other settlement. We figure we are about two hours away from the other island by boat. We are going to take the big boat and two of the fishermen with new boats are coming along, in case they do want to move here. We keep the number of people going to a minimum so that we will have more room to bring people back. The trip to the island is nice and smooth. When we get within twenty miles of the island we see sailing boats coming our way.

These are not big sailing boats, more like small fishing boats with sails. When they see the large boat they head right toward us. These may be simple people, but they do not lack for courage when it comes to defending their families. When they get close enough to see them we can see that each boat has at least three men in them and it looks like at least two of the men in each boat are armed with a rifle, or some other weapon. The two smaller fishing boats that are with us move ahead of us to intercept the sail boats. We are all flying a white flag to signify that we want no trouble with them. The guys on the fishing boats pull up alongside the smaller boats and we can hear their conversation, but can't make out all the words.

As soon as we get close enough to recognize faces, the young ladies with us start yelling to their families and friends that came to rescue them. The excited guys in the small boats come as close as they can get safely and talk to the three girls as we head toward their island. They cannot keep up, so we toss them all lines from our boats and tow them to the island. When we get docked safely, all the people in the group come running to see if their family members are safe. The girls tell them all about their ordeal and how we found them on the boat. Their families ask where the men are that took their daughters. We start to tell them when the girls tell them we killed them all. The people here make the sign of the cross, but say that they were very bad men and the only way to stop men like that is to kill them.

Now that the important business is out of the way, they want to see the boats we came in up close. They are very much impressed with all the boats. Our friends tell them that they have only had these boats for a few days and that they only have them now because of us. They want to hear all about how we live, even though we can see that they don't really believe half of what we are telling them. These people are living very primitively, even more so than our friends that are with us. Our friends invite them to come to their island and see all that they have, and then they can make a decision whether to stay here or join them. The girls keep telling them about everything they experienced in the one day they were with us. These people have never seen electricity and simply cannot fathom lights without fire and being able to listen to music or watch a movie.

We assure them that if they come with us and don't like what they see, we will bring them right back. In fact, we will make sure they have boats of their own to come back in. It's a good thing there are not very many people in this group because we just about have room for all of them on the boats. Dayna is as happy as she can be because one of the couples in the group has a two year old little girl and Dayna gets to hold her for most of the trip back. We get to the first settlement just a little before sunset, so the people get to look around a little before it gets dark. Our friends are waiting to turn on the lights until it is dark, to impress our new friends even more. As it is getting darker some of the new people are talking among themselves, saying that they don't see any special lights yet.

We are walking up the main street in their settlement when the lights are turned on. Most of the people run to the nearest light bulb to see how the light was coming out of it. The people from this settlement are proud to show our new friends the vehicles they have and especially the cows and the chickens. The new group proudly tells them that they have two cows and calves as well and that they have twenty chickens and a rooster back on their island. We try to stay out of the conversations as much as they will let us. We want them to make their decision based on what they see and are told by the people that live here. It is quite a bit later than usual when we finally hit our beds for the night. Dayna is excited and thinks that they will move here soon. In the morning they ask us about the boats we promised to help them get. We take them to a marina in the town that has a large selection of boats indoors in a huge warehouse.

We tell them to pick a couple of the boats and we will do our best to get them running for them. The two they pick out are in great shape and it takes almost no time to get them running and loaded on trailers to haul them down to the ocean on. Naturally we have to fill them with gas and make sure they have plenty of good oil in the motors. When we put them in the water, you would think it is Christmas, as excited as the fishermen get. A couple of the people from the settlement here show them how to drive the boats and in no time they are having a great time driving along the coast. When we get back to the settlement in the afternoon we get a call from the other settlement, telling us that Sara and the others arrived earlier today and want to know where all that seafood we promised them is.

Everyone that can hear the conversation between me and Sara are laughing. When we hang up the radio, one of our good friends tells Dayna and I that Sara sounds more like a wife than a friend. Dayna laughs and tells him that we are more like brother and sister and he says he knows exactly what she means. His sisters are always telling him what to do as well. As if to prove him right, as soon as we walk out of the building with the radio a woman tells him that he should quit wasting time and help us get the seafood that we want. He just rolls his eyes and asks if we can see what he means. Dayna tells him exactly and we all laugh including his sister. Our friends help us gather up the lobsters, crabs, and one of the boats goes looking for shrimp for us.

Our new friends help us and gather enough for all of them as well. That's their way of telling us that they have to celebrate finding a new home and new friends. Several of them already know a couple of the people from the new group, so it is like coming home for some of them. We were going to wait until morning to go back to the other end of the island, but Sara flies over in the helicopter to pick us up. She is flying a personnel carrier that will hold all of us and the seafood that we collected to take back. We are planning to fly back to our settlement with a stop to get fuel tonight. Now that we are finally leaving, Dayna and I realize how much these friends have come to mean to us. We promise to come back and take some of them back with us to visit our settlement.

Lillie and Izzie are excited to be going, but sad that they are leaving friends they have known all their lives. They are especially excited to be flying in the helicopter and all of our friends here are excited to be seeing one. Sara and Gary must have really missed us because they spend almost the entire trip home talking about the adventures they have had, getting this helicopter and a couple of others in flying condition and getting another hangar back home and setup. Mike's wound is healing well, but is still painful. We stop at the settlement in northern Florida to take on fuel. Naturally James and Mike have to check out how the new generators are working. All is well so we can get on with the trip home and hear more about what a time Sara, Gary and their team had getting that hangar home.

17

When we finally get home, it is the middle of the night, but we still have a large welcoming committee to greet us when we land. There are about fifty or sixty people to welcome us, but Sara tells Lillie and Izzie that all those people are Dayna and my children. They are not sure whether to believe her or not, especially when Teddy, Nickie, Timmy, and Tommy all yell welcome home mom and dad as soon as we open the door to the helicopter. Nickie grabs Lillie and Izzie and tells them she has a room all fixed up for them, if they don't mind sharing a room at least for tonight. Sara, Lindsay, Jenna, and Morgan are supervising the unloading of the seafood that we brought back.

Everything is in tanks to keep them alive until they are to be cooked and consumed. Even I am impressed with how much food we brought back with us and I helped gather it. There are even several large fish that have been cut into fillets and packed on ice to keep them fresh, that I will probably eat some of simply because our friends prepared them so well for us. That idea goes out the window when Timmy tells me that the beef from that steer they killed is cured now just about perfectly. My sons don't care much for fish and seafood either. We spend a little while introducing everybody to each other then I can't wait to climb into my own bed for the first time in what seems like months.

When Lillie and Izzie see the room that the girls fixed up for them, they say they have never even dreamed of having a room so beautiful and beds so comfortable. I tell them that no matter how comfortable the beds are, they are expected to be up at the crack of dawn to go to work. Even they don't believe me, but my loving children tell me that if I am up at that time, I should call them around nine or ten. As tired as I am I still have trouble sleeping. I keep wondering how many of the other settlements are having trouble that we don't know about. We have our problems here, but we have so many people with advanced knowledge about pretty much everything that no problem slows us down for long.

In the morning I talk to Tim, James, Mike, Gary, LT, and Ryan. He just happened to come over to see if they are invited to the seafood feast this evening. I even get to talk to Doc McEvoy, Doc Betty, Josh, Barb, and Karl. They all heard that we have come into a fairly large amount of seafood and they want to make sure none of it to goes to waste. Naturally I have to act like them being here is the worst thing that could possibly happen or they will be disappointed. We made sure we had enough for everyone when we picked up the food. I didn't mention it before, but Sara and Gary brought a bunch of beef jerky, canned beef, several bushels of vegetables from our gardens, and the meat from a whole hog that has been smoked. The hog was cut up before it was smoked but, we smoked all of that meat for them.

We all have a meeting to discuss how we can make sure that all of our friends in the different settlements are doing well. It's great to have Colonel Bob, Blake, and Trevor included in our meeting because they travel around a lot and they can report on the settlements that they have visited. They report that they have been as far west as the coast and the settlements over there are doing very well. They say they told them about our helicopters and now they are looking for some. The Arizona settlements are doing well. They are also looking for a helicopter. Sara laughs and says that next time we talk to those people on the radio, we should tell them to quit trying to keep up with Joneses.

The only ones who understand what she means are those of us from the other world. Doc McEvoy asks his wife if they know anybody named Jones that has a helicopter. Doc is such a great guy that we do not want to laugh and embarrass him, so Sara explains that it's just a way of saying that someone is trying to keep up with their neighbors. Like if their neighbors get a new car, they want one. When he finally understands it he laughs, so we all laugh with him. The reports that they have on all the settlements to the west of us are very good, so that leaves the settlements north of us, east, and south. Bob, Blake, and Trevor, along with their wives volunteer to check out the settlements to the north. Dayna and I along with LT and Kathy volunteer to go to the east and check on the settlements in Florida again.

We all agree that we will at least call the settlements on the radio first and if they would like some help we will go and help them. Everybody says that we will get on that first thing tomorrow, after they make sure all that seafood doesn't go to waste. Dayna and I spend the rest of the day catching up on what our children are up to in their lives and introducing Lillie and Izzie to everybody. Surprisingly they are shy, but everybody does their best to make them feel welcome. We have some people in our group and in the other groups that are Spanish speaking so they do not feel quite so alone, of course they know Mary Elaina and her family well, so they feel better by the end of the day. Besides Teddy, Tommy, and Timmy volunteer to take them hunting. Don't worry; Nickie and Bobbi are going with them.

All the other groups start getting here early in the afternoon to help get ready for the big cookout. We have some really nice wood stoves that are made for cooking, like they used before gas and electric stoves were invented. We use these quite a bit when we are going to cook a lot of food on a stove. We have some great grills that we made out of cutting fifty gallon drums in half and welding a frame around them. Some of our people love sweet corn when it is cooked on a grill and some of our people like it better boiled. Personally I will eat it either way, as long as I have plenty of butter to eat on it. We started growing these great red potatoes about six or seven years ago and now they are pretty much everybody's favorite. We still grow several varieties, but the small red ones taste so good. We are cooking about two bushels of them for the dinner this evening.

Several of our people also like potatoes baked in the coals of the grills, so we also make a bunch of those. We have several very large pots that we found in restaurants and restaurant supply houses that we are boiling the water to cook the lobsters, the crabs, and the shrimp in. Of course some of them will be cooked on the grill as well. Personally I went down to the freezer where the beef is curing beautifully and cut several large steaks off the tenderloin of the ribs. Dayna will eat a little of the seafood, but she will eat one of the steaks as will Teddy and Nickie. Thomas and Timmy are not sure if they like seafood or not, but there are plenty of steaks if they decide they don't.

The dinner is a total success. Even Sara, Jenna, Morgan, and Lindsay were satisfied. That is if eating about a bushel of seafood, potatoes, and corn, then leaning back in their chairs and belching loudly, constitutes being satisfied. I know Dayna and I are totally satisfied with our steaks, baked potatoes, and corn on the cob. This was the first time that Lillie and Izzie have eaten steaks like these, but believe me when I tell you it definitely won't be the last. Several people found out that they do like seafood and some learned that they don't really care if they eat it or not. The general consensus is however that we visit the coast at least once a quarter to get more of what we had this evening. It's always great to have all of our extended family come over for a get together.

I told you a while back that we built a covered area, like a pavilion, where we have a cement slab and picnic tables set up with enough room for everyone to sit under the roof. It is open on the sides and ends, but we can drop screen walls that go to the ground if the insects get to be a pain. When we first built it we thought it would be big enough to last forever, but we have had to add onto it a couple of times now and looking at the crowd here this evening, we may want to start planning another addition. LT and Kathy sat with our family, which is pretty good sized when you consider Melissa, Robin, and Becky and their husbands and all the children.

The great thing about having everybody getting together this way is that it takes no time at all to clean up, even after a huge meal like this one. It always makes me feel good when I look around after something like this and everybody I see is helping with the cleanup. Even Kathy and LT notice how everyone helps out. They are carrying dishes over to the large outdoor sink that we have for occasions like this. There are actually several sinks where the dishes are washed then rinsed and handed off to someone to dry and put them away. Kathy mentions that when she used to go to pot luck dinners in their church when she was younger, it always seemed like the same couple of people got stuck with cleaning up and doing the dishes while everyone packed up and left. They really fit in here perfectly. They both remind me that I promised to show them the system of tunnels that supposedly run under most of our settlement. When LT says supposedly, I know that he thinks I was exaggerating, so I play along a little.

I tell them that it isn't really a system of tunnels and kind of let my voice trail off. He picks up on it instantly and tells me he knew I was exaggerating. Nobody goes to those lengths for security, when they have as many men and weapons as we have. Teddy is going by when he hears LT talking. He stops and starts to tell him just how many tunnels we have and how far they run, but I signal him not to say anything, yet. I tell LT that I will show them the tunnels, such as they are in the morning. Sara is going by with some of the leftovers to give them to Doc McEvoy and his wife, but stops long enough to ask LT if he is ready for a rematch yet on the obstacle course. He starts to answer when she starts laughing and says I didn't think so, as she walks away.

LT is looking after her as she walks away. He is still watching her go when he tells me that she can be a real pain in the neck sometimes. I tell him she is only like that until you get to know her well. He looks at me like he doesn't believe me until I tell him, that's because when you get to know her real well you learn how to avoid her. He and Kathy laugh and I get smacked by Dayna, Becky, Melissa, and Robin. They tell me that's no way to talk about my sister. Actually Sara is like a sister to me so when she comes back I tell her I'm sorry for saying what I did. She stops and acts like she is checking to see if I have a fever. Then Lindsay, Jenna, and Morgan come over and say that if what I said has anything to do with getting my butt kicked on the obstacle course, then it's absolutely true.

Then they all walk away laughing, accompanied by my good friends Ryan and Carol. I act like I'm going to cry when my grandson, Little Jon, comes up and tells me he loves me even if Aunt Sara beats me on the obstacle course. I can't help but laugh along with them. Like I have told Dayna since the first day I met her, my life didn't start until the day Tim and I wound up here. We have often talked about why we were sent here, if we were, but to us it doesn't really matter. We think of this as the only real home and family we have ever had. LT told Tim and me that he visited Tim's family in New York after our funeral. He found out that they used the life insurance that we left them to start a restaurant and pizzeria and it was doing very well.

I don't think I told you before that I named Tim's sister as my beneficiary because I didn't have anybody else to leave it to. It made us both happy to hear that his family is doing so well. He sometimes wishes they were here, but then he remembers how much they all fought and argued when he lived with them and says it's probably better this way. We believe in a hereafter, so we will get to see them when we leave this earth or whatever it is. Speaking of the hereafter I have a dream where Gunny and my dad come to visit me and just talk for a while. It's a great dream. We are talking about the trips we just took and about the great friends that Dayna and I met there. Just about the time they are saying they have to leave, Gunny tells me to be careful.

I ask him what he means by that and he tells me that I have to be on the lookout because there are some people out there that would like to see me dead. I ask them who and they tell me that they have already said more than they should, but they wanted to warn me. Ma Horton and my mom joined us just before I wake up and it's so nice to get hugs from them both. When I wake up Dayna is in the bed staring at me. She tells me that maybe someone else should go to the other settlements and we can stay here where we are relatively safe. I ask her if she had a dream where Gunny and my dad came to see me. She tells me yes they did and she is going to make sure we grow old together. I tell her that I want nothing more out of life than to spend it with her and our family for another fifty or sixty years. We start to cuddle a little and we get a knock on our bedroom door. It's the twins Tammy and Tina. They are yelling at us, through the door of course, that there is no reason for people as old as we are, to be in bed this late in the morning.

I look at the clock and it says it's not even seven-thirty yet. I ask them if they would like us to explain in detail, what old people like us might do at this time of the morning. They tell us to please spare them the details, their imaginations have already taken them much farther than they really wanted to go. They tell us that Doc Betty and Josh called and said to tell me that they think there may be a thief running around again. My mind goes back about six or maybe seven years ago when we had several items disappear from pretty much all of the settlements in our group. It was nothing major or nothing that couldn't be replaced from the warehouses, but we never did find out who was taking the items.

Dayna and I figure we better get up because we won't get left alone until we do. I call Doc Betty back on the CB radio and she laughs and tells me that she told Tammy to wait until Dayna and I had gotten up. It's not that big a deal, Josh is laughing on the other end, saying that Sherlock Gorman could have waited at least another hour before taking on this case. Doc Betty tells us that she will have breakfast ready if we want to come over to see what's missing. By this time Lillie and Izzie are up and ask if they can go along because they haven't seen that settlement yet. We can't see why they shouldn't, so we decide it's a nice day for a walk and decide to head over through the woods.

The girls love what they are seeing about our woods. One of the puppies decides to come with us. I'm not sure which one this is. I know her name is either Cricket or Biscuit. She seems to love the girls and the feeling seems to be mutual with them. It's fun just watching her run after the birds and rabbits that get scared up as we walk. I call her a puppy, but she is right around six months old. She and her sister are pretty good sized, but then they are Malamutes that get good sized anyway. It takes a little longer to get to Doc Betty's than they thought it would, so we get told if our breakfast is cold it's our fault. Breakfast is fine; it's hard to ruin oatmeal. We usually eat it with honey and a little milk and most of us would rather have that than bacon and eggs.

This is the first time that the girls have had oatmeal and they seem to enjoy it as much as we do. After breakfast Josh and Doc Betty show us where it appears that someone went into a couple of homes and took a couple of guns, hunting knives, and some dried beef that was there. The people that live in the houses where things were taken said that they would have given those items to someone if they would have asked. There are plenty of guns and knives in the warehouses and dried beef is pretty plentiful around here with the hunters we have. We figure it was probably just someone or a couple of someone's that happened by last night when we were all together and decided to help themselves. The things that are gone are pretty much things someone would need to survive.

We check around for footprints, but there are so many that it would be impossible to pick out any particular ones. We thank our good friends for breakfast and head back to our place. The girls had forgotten that Teddy and the others are planning to take them hunting today. They are worried all the way back that they are going to leave without them. Dayna and I assure them that they will wait for them, but they are not as confident about that as we are. Timmy and Tommy are acting like they are very upset because the girls went with us and now they have to leave a little later than they wanted to. Bobbi and Misty tell them that if they don't want to go hunting with their new sisters then they can stay home and they will go without them. Nickie comes out and says that Teddy has to go as well because she doesn't mind shooting a deer, but she is not going to field dress it, as long as she has a husband to do that sort of thing.

They invite me to go along, but I remember that I promised LT to show him and Kathy our tunnel system. The young people are taking the truck with the hoist and a pickup truck. They are heading to the same area that they went to last time. They saw plenty of game there and we can always use the meat. I tell them about the thefts from Doc Betty's and suggest that they keep their eyes open for anything that looks out of the ordinary. As they are pulling away, LT and Kathy are coming toward Dayna and me. He comes up and says he wants to see this so called tunnel system we put in. Dayna and I smile and tell them we can start at the house they are living in if they would like. He laughs and tells us that now he knows we are pulling his leg because he has gone over every inch of that house looking for anything that resembled the entrance to a tunnel and there is nothing there.

We go into the house and naturally Dayna tells Kathy that she loves what she has done with it. LT is looking around then tells us to show him. The house has a pantry that is just about as large as a small bedroom. The floor in there is tile with a throw rug over the center of the room. LT says he opened ever cupboard in here and didn't find an entrance, so he challenges me to show them. I walk to the throw rug and lift one corner of it. That's actually the only corner that lifts up without moving the trap door under it. I lift the handle and the rug comes up with the doorway down to the tunnel. This house does not have a basement. It was moved here after we got settled in.

LT says something that I won't repeat because Dayna will make me wash my mouth out with soap and I tell them to follow Dayna and me. Down in the tunnel he has to stoop a little, but then so do I. We show them the passages that lead to many of the other houses and to the barns. The last one we show them is the one that goes out to the shed in the woods. They are impressed to say the least. He tells me that this rivals any underground security system he has ever seen, except for some of the military installations where they had pretty much unlimited funding. We tell them about the few times we have actually had to use the tunnels because we were surrounded. On the way back we decide to walk in the woods and we get to show them the peach, pear, apple, and cherry orchards that we have.

The fruit is growing great this year and it looks like we will have a great crop of strawberries and both red and black raspberries. Kathy says that now she knows where the delicious preserves she found in the cupboard came from. Dayna tells them that Doc McEvoy and his wife have about a half acre of currant bushes that make great jelly and preserves as well. Kathy asks if they might be willing to trade for some of them. Dayna tells her absolutely not, then laughs and explains that here we all help each other; even though they found the bushes and transplanted them here, the fruits are for everybody. When the fruit gets ripe we will pick it and we will get together and can and preserve it so everybody can share in the bounty.

Dayna tells them we will have to show them around so they can see the other orchards that the groups take care of and the other fields of fruit, not to mention the bee hives that each group has. I tell them I can't wait until we get a good frost so that we can tap the maple trees to gather the sap to boil down to make maple syrup with. They both say that they are still not sure if they died or not because living here is like being in heaven to them. Dayna and I laugh and assure them this isn't exactly heaven, but it is a great place to live.

18

We get back to our house a little after noon. Dayna and I get to play with some of the younger children and our grandchildren. We have our chores to do like everyone else, so we spend part of the afternoon greasing some of the windmills that need it and do some minor repairs to the homes of some of the people who are not as experienced in home repair as some of us. They are happy to learn, so we always take the time to show them exactly what we are doing and let them do as much as possible. One job that not everybody wants to learn is climbing up on some of the higher roofs to replace shingles that may have been blown off in the wind. Today there are several shingles missing on one of the barn roofs and it just happens to be the highest barn that we have.

It is built into the side of a hill, so on the one side it is only about thirty-five feet up to the first level of the roof, but on the downhill side it is all of fifty feet to the first level and on the very top it is just about seventy feet up. Heights don't bother me, but Dayna hates to see me climb up there. It's really not too bad, especially since after the second time I had to climb up there to replace shingles, Tim and I put a trap door in the roof that allows us to climb out onto the roof from inside. It makes a great lookout post because we can see at least a mile in every direction. There is a huge beam on the inside where we put the trap door that we always hook a safety rope to when we climb out onto the roof for any reason.

LT and I do that today and I use the safety rope to hold me while I climb down onto the steepest part of the roof to change the shingles that have blown off. For doing this Tim and I took the harness off a couple of parachutes that we found at one of the military bases we visited. That gives us much better support than just having a belt harness. LT is handing me the shingles today as I need them. The job takes less than a half hour, so we stand on the roof enjoying the view. We can see the road that the kids will be coming back on. In fact they should be coming pretty soon. LT points to a truck coming on a road that is not the direction I was expecting them to be coming home from. After a few seconds we see the second truck following the first. This is strange and I simply do not like strange, so I go back into the barn and come back with a rifle with a great variable scope on it.

I am not planning on using the rifle, just the scope to see if I can see anything out of the ordinary. Right off the bat I see something that makes me concerned. Teddy and Timmy are sitting in the back of the pickup and they are holding their guns like they are expecting to have to use them. They are at least a couple miles away, but on that road that could take a few minutes to cover. The road is more like a coiled snake, with twists and curves every few yards. That's the main reason we don't use that road unless there is a very good reason. LT and I are back on the ground by the time we can see them coming from this level. They pull into the yard and I breathe a sigh of relief and I don't even know why.

Teddy and Timmy jump out of the back of the truck and come running over to Tim, LT, and me. Tim saw us heading this way quickly, so he joined us in case there is some action. Teddy tells us that they had good luck today hunting and the large buck and the very large steer attest to that. I ask him if they hunted somewhere other than where they said they were going this morning. He tells me that they kind of had to, there were several men on the road that they usually travel when they are hunting and rather than start trouble with the women along they decided to turn off and hunt somewhere else. I ask him if anybody threatened them or got nasty with them. He says that they seemed friendly, but not in a friendly way if I know what he means.

Lillie and Izzie join us and are about as happy as they can be. Apparently they got the large buck with their bow and arrows. Our butchers are guiding the bigger truck down behind the big barn so that they can unload the carcasses and get busy skinning and quartering them to age properly. The girls are following because they want to be involved in whatever they are going to do with that buck. Teddy and Timmy both tell us that Lillie and Izzie are very good hunters and are dead shots when it comes to using those bows they have. After they leave Teddy tells me that he remembers seeing at least one of the men they saw today. He can't remember where or when, but he knows he has seen him somewhere before and he is sure he isn't a friend of ours. Teddy looks like he is trying to decide whether or not to tell me something then says I should know. He tells me that the man told him to say hello to me when they were driving away.

Teddy and Timmy along with Nickie and Bobbi head toward the big barn to make sure they don't need any help, Tim's son Jon catches up to them and tells them that if they need any help they sure won't want to see them. Our kids harass each other as much as we do, if not more. It's great having our children home safe. Dayna asks me why they came home on this road instead of the one we usually use. I don't want to scare her so I tell her they just wanted to check out a different area for a change. She asks if they were able to find any game where they went. I tell her how successful they were and especially what Teddy told me about Lillie and Izzie. She heads over to the barn to check it out and to see the kids. LT and Tim ask me what I think we should do about those men that are setting up camp near here.

I tell them that we should not do anything unless they start something. It's a free country and they have as much right to settle there as we did settling here. Hopefully they do not have anything more than that on their minds, but that warning from dad and Gunny in my dream keeps nagging at the back of my mind. We have a great evening playing with the younger members of the family. Some of them are still young enough that they enjoy wrestling around with dad or Grampa. I just wish Dayna and the other women in this family would learn how to referee. They always cheat so that the little ones wind up winning then the little beggars eat all my ice cream and other treats. I spend quite a bit of my night listening to make sure no one attacks us in the middle of the night.

In the morning Teddy and Nickie come over with Little Jon to join us for breakfast. He tells me he thinks he knows where he saw that man before. He asks me if I remember that night in Rochester when I got wounded. I tell him I don't think I will ever forget that night. He continues saying that when he was going up the stairs in that building to get to me, he saw a man in the building next door looking into the building we were in. He and the man stared at each other for what seemed like a long time before the man smiled and walked away. He tells me that he thinks the man he saw yesterday is the man he saw then. I start to say something and he tells me there is more.

He tells me that this is the second time he has seen that man since that night. He was one of the men who were part of the group that attacked Doc Betty's group several years ago. He knew he had seen him somewhere before, but couldn't remember where until last night. He actually stayed with Doc McEvoy's group for a while before the attack. He tells me that he is so sorry for not remembering before this. I tell him not to worry about it, odds are he has learned his lesson and just wants to settle down and live the easy life. We finish breakfast and one of the first things I want to do is call our friends who moved back up that way to start their own settlement. Tim does the calling on the short wave radio. Luckily someone is on at this hour of the morning to answer the call.

They are happy to hear from us and say they are doing very well. They are having a great summer and their crops are growing like the weeds usually do. I ask them if they have had any trouble with roving bands or two legged predators. Jack, who is one of the leaders at this time, tells us that it is funny that we ask that question. He says that they were attacked about three weeks ago by a band of about six or seven that they were able to fight off. He says that the funny thing is several people are sure that at least one of the attackers used to be in the settlement when they lived here as well. He describes the guy pretty well and I am beginning to remember him, at least I think I do. I ask them if there is anything they can remember about the way they attacked them. He says that he was not there when it started. He came in after it started and luckily they were able to fight them off.

Jack tells us that he remembers that there were some homes that got broken into about a week before the attack. I ask him if the thieves took guns, ammo, knives, and survival food like jerky. He tells me that I must have heard about it on the news or read it in the newspaper because that's exactly what was taken. His wife Elaine comes on the radio and says that she remembers that there were similar thefts in Doc Betty's group just before the attack there. Jack tells us if it is happening again we may want to find those guys before they hurt someone seriously. They had a couple of wounded and those guys didn't care if they shot at a man, woman or child. I ask them if Karl is still in their group. He was from Rochester originally and may know the man we are talking about.

Jack tells us he is, but he is out hunting this morning, however if we listen this evening he will have him call us. Before we hang up Jack asks Tim if the invitation to come back to our group still stands. Tim tells him that Elaine and the kids are always welcome, but he wanted to go up north so he has to stay there. There is silence on the other end, so Tim quickly tells them that he is only kidding. Naturally if they or anyone else wants to come back, they are welcome. Jack says he knew Tim was only harassing him, that's why he didn't answer. He wanted Tim to sweat it a little. We have to be going and so do they, but we promise to take a trip up there before winter to see how much progress they have made.

I decide to go looking for the men that they saw yesterday, but when we get to the place they were supposedly living it is totally empty, although there is sign around that a decent sized group was at least here for a couple of days. There is evidence that they did quite a bit of target practice while they were here. The shell casings are the caliber that was stolen from Doc Betty's group. We are close enough to call on the CB, so we call Josh and ask him to please check their warehouse and see if anything is missing. Josh is in his truck so he heads over to check the warehouse. His son Tyler, who is sixteen, stays in the truck and talks to us on the CB while Josh goes in to see if there is anything missing. The first thing Tyler asks is if Lillie and Izzie are enjoying being here.

I tell him as far as I know they are enjoying themselves. I tell him that they may enjoy it more if one of the groups decided to put on a dance and invited them to come. He asks me if I really think they may come to a dance if they have one at their settlement. Josh must have just come back because we hear him telling Tyler that the only way to know for sure is to ask them. He also says that he doubts if their social calendars are full yet. Then Josh comes on the radio and tells us we were right. Someone made off with a case of military rifles and enough ammunition to fight a small war. He adds that he hopes it's not against us. Tim, LT, and I all second that, but it isn't looking too good at the moment.

We decide to put the groups on a state of alert until we know for sure what we are up against. LT is curious to know what a state of alert is. We explain that when we feel that there is a threat to our groups, we make sure that everyone knows to be on the lookout for anything suspicious or out of the ordinary. Also those that can, carry weapons wherever they go, some of our people do that anyway because you can't be too careful. Tim and I always have a gun with us and LT shows us that he has a gun tucked under his shirt and a small handgun in a holster on his ankle. We already know about the handgun though because we know what to look for. We go back to our group and call a quick meeting of the leadership committee and explain what we fear at this time. Robin's husband is on that committee and as soon as we finish he walks outside and sounds an alarm that we have mounted on the large meeting hall.

It takes about two minutes for every group in our area to respond. We can stand on the porch and see just about everybody in our group headed for their homes to get their weapons. Several of the men stop to ask us if we think there will be an attack. We tell them honestly we hope not, but there are some strange people in the area and we know they are armed. Teddy, Nickie and several others of our children are working at the wheat mill today. That is about a quarter of a mile away over near the river. My son Timmy calls us on the CB and asks if they should cut the day short and come home. I ask him if they all have guns and he tells me that everyone does except Lillie and Izzie, but they do have their bow and arrows with them and they also have the K-bar knives I gave them. He adds that he is betting they know how to use them too.

We discuss how long they should work before coming home. The guys and girls that were working in the fields away from the group pull into the yard and ask if anybody's garden needs weeded. We all use mulch to keep the weeds down, but several people say they could use some help picking and canning tomatoes and the green and yellow snap beans. I know that that is what Dayna was planning to do today, along with the twins, Misty, Paige, and Lisa. Tim and LT are going to their homes to see what they can help with. The girls already have a good handle on the canning. They have it down to a science, where some of them pick the vegetables while others get the canning supplies ready. Then they all prepare the vegetables to put into the jars and pressure cooked or in the case of tomatoes some of our people prefer the open kettle method.

That's the way I learned to can tomatoes from Ma Horton. She always told me that as long as you keep the tomatoes boiling and keep the jars in boiling water while you fill them; there is no danger from botulism. Tomatoes are the only thing that I know of that you can put into jars that way. Beans, squash, corn, and all the fruits we do are either done in a pressure cooker or in big blue enamel covered canning pots. Today Kathy and Charity are at our house helping. The girls have been going to each other's gardens and picking everything that is ripe enough to put into jars. Our house and three others have had extensions put on them to be used for the purpose of canning during the canning season.

We added like a second kitchen onto four of the houses in our group and at least that many in the other groups, to give people somewhere to do the canning without heating up the house too badly. The rooms have windows with screens in them all the way around so they can open them and let the heat out into the air outside. We also added three or four stoves into these rooms so that a lot of jars can be packed and canned in a short time. The ladies are all having a good time visiting and helping each other do the canning. At this time the bulk of the tomatoes are still not ripe, but some of the early blooming ones are, also there is a lot of different kinds of squash and snap beans of both colors that are plentiful. To make sure we have enough beans and squash, we grow about two acres of them along with the individual gardens that just about all of us have.

Tim, LT, and I decide that since the ladies have this part of the plan taken care of, we will go down to the barn where we do the butchering and see if they can use some help. When we go out the back door Kathy is sitting on the porch and she has tears in her eyes. I ask her if she is hurt or if someone said something to offend her without knowing it. I know all of the people in the house very well and they would never offend someone intentionally. She tells us that she is just being silly as usual. The last time she helped do any canning was when she helped her real mother just a couple of weeks before she died. She had no idea how much she missed doing the simple little things that can mean so much to our survival. She tells Tim and me again how grateful she is that they wound up here with us.

On the way to the area of the big barn, where we butcher the meat, we pass the chicken coops where Jennifer and Samantha are busy gathering eggs. There are usually more of them to gather eggs, but today there are a bunch of chicks that are hatching in the incubator so the others are busy with that. We volunteer to help since gathering eggs from as many chickens as we have is a pretty big job. The girls are happy to have the help. Actually we take over the gathering while they candle the eggs that they already gathered to make sure there are no chicks in them. The eggs we are gathering today are for food, so they will be available for everyone that would like some, which is pretty much everybody. The other groups have their own chickens and milking cows.

By the time we get to the butcher area there is nothing left for us to do there so we go looking for someone that can use our help. Frank, who is our most experienced farmer, tells us that one of the tractors is missing on one cylinder. We check it out and sure enough it is. It takes all of about five minutes to fix it. The wire from the coil to the spark plug had cracked and wasn't making a good connection. We decide that it would be a good time to check out some of the other equipment and make sure everything is in good order for harvest time. We get so busy that we don't pay any attention to the time and before we know it our wives have sent the children to look for us.

After dinner we hold a meeting to make everyone aware of the reason for the alert status. A couple of people say that they think they saw two men watching the settlement from the woods using binoculars. They say they think they saw them because when they tried to get a better angle to see them,, they weren't there anymore. Frank says that he was in the farthest field from the homes and could swear that he heard motorcycles or a truck with loud exhaust. He says he didn't think much of it because the young people and some of the not so young people, use the motorcycles that we have when they want to go scouting around. We know that we are not going to settle anything with our meeting, but we like to make everyone aware of what is going on.

The other groups are doing the same thing and in a little while we will meet with the other groups to discuss what we found out, if anything. We also use this opportunity to make sure everyone knows where they are supposed to go if we get attacked. Each individual has a specific place that they are responsible for. The women and girls all carry guns and knives, but if we are attacked, we expect them to take cover in the barns or homes and do any shooting from a relatively safe location. We know from experience that many of our women are as good with a gun as any of the men. It's just that if someone happens to break through the defense, we don't want the women fighting hand to hand with men, even though some of them are just as capable as most of the men. That's saying something because most of our men are very good fighters.

Karl calls just as we get to the radio room. We exchange pleasantries then he tells us that he wishes he had better news for us. He says he knows exactly who is hanging around our settlement and he knows why he is here. He asks me if I remember that guy that Teddy killed to keep him from killing me. I tell him I remember that night well. He tells us that the guy hanging around here is that guy's son. That's a surprise, at least to me. Karl says that he lived in Doc Betty's group for about a month a few years back. From what Karl has heard, he did that to find out all he could about the man who he thinks killed his father. Teddy is listening when Karl says that, he tells Karl, and anybody else listening that he killed that guy's father and if he comes around looking for trouble, he will kill him and any of his buddies as well. He adds that is if his dad doesn't take care of it first.

Karl laughs and says there was a time when he underestimated my ability to fight. He learned his lesson and was smart enough to let it go and he has never regretted it. He tells me that his money is on us. I tell him that I hope we can settle this without anyone having to die. He says he hopes so too, because William and the guys with him are really not bad people. William is eaten up with vengeance and those with him are his friends and will follow him to hell if they have to. Karl wishes us luck and asks if we could please let them know how this ends. We assure him we will and have to be going to discuss the group meetings with the other groups.

19

The meetings with the other groups went pretty much like ours did. When I tell them who we are probably up against, everyone that remembers him has nothing but good things to say about him. I just can't put a face to the name, but I am sure I will know him when I see him. I really hope there is some way to end this without having to kill him, or have him kill any of us. I don't sleep well thinking about how senseless it will be if any of us die because of a killer with no conscience, even if he was Williams's father. I have gone over every possible scenario and it will still come down to how badly he wants to see me dead. I'm not the one who killed his father, but I am not going to let them kill Teddy either.

Dayna asks me if I have a plan yet. I tell her that I am going to try to reason with him. It's not like the other people who have attacked us trying to take our way of life away or trying to steal women to use, and then kill them. We decide that since this guy will probably not shoot me from hiding, we may as well go on with our everyday lives, as if there is nothing wrong. I do notice that wherever I go there seems to be one of my family members or good friends that just happen to be doing the chores that I am today. Actually it is pretty difficult to concentrate today because Rod, Ken, and Gary got together and decided to smoke about half of that hog that the kids shot earlier this week. We make our own recipe sausage and smoke a bunch of that as well and today the odors that are filling the air are pure heavenly.

The problem is that we slow smoke our meat, so although some of it will be done today, most of it will not be done until tomorrow morning. The day goes by with no interruptions other than sneaking over to the smoke house to steal a piece of the smoked sausage. Unfortunately I got caught so I had to go back to work hungry. At least the kids got a laugh out of watching me get my behind smacked by Dayna for it. After dinner, where I do get to enjoy more than one piece of the smoked sausage, Teddy, Tim, and LT come over and ask me if I think it would be a good idea to go looking for these guys, rather than wait for them to make the first move. I tell them how much I appreciate their willingness to help and if something doesn't happen soon then we may have to go looking for them.

I am still trying to think what I might say to William to make him realize that his father was killed in self defensc. I don't think I will sleep very much, but surprisingly I fall asleep fairly quickly and sleep pretty soundly. I have another dream where Gunny and my dad come to me to tell me that William is planning to visit tomorrow. Gunny asks me if I am planning to kill him and his followers. I tell him that I hope that doesn't have to happen. We need all the good people that we can get in this world. Gunny tells me that he hopes we can settle this without anyone dying. He and dad say they will see me tomorrow night, one way or the other then laugh. Ma Horton and my mom smack them both for what they call their sick sense of humor. I thought it was kind of funny myself.

In the morning I tell Dayna about it and she doesn't think it is very funny either. We sit down to eat breakfast when the alarm goes off. I grab a gun along with the sidearm I am carrying and head out the door. I don't have to go far because from our front porch I can see William riding into the settlement with six of his friends on motorcycles. They are all armed, but then so are all of us and we outnumber them at least ten to one. I recognize him and his friends as soon as I see them. They ride right up to the porch, actually William rides up to the porch, the others spread out behind him. When he turns off his motorcycle I call him Billy and offer him and his friend's breakfast.

He smiles and tells me that he remembers sharing some great breakfasts when we worked on some of those projects together, but today he came here to kill me. I smile back and tell him that I remember those projects as well and that I really enjoyed working with him and the guys with him. I take a moment to call each of them by name and say hello. Billy asks me if I heard what he said. I tell him that I did and ask if he would mind telling me why. He tells me that he wants to get even with the man who murdered his father. I ask him if he is referring to the man that was going to kill me back in Rochester. He tells me that his father was a soldier before the war and the only way anybody would be able to kill him, is if they shot him in the back.

I start to answer when Teddy steps out on the porch and tells Billy that he is the one who killed his father and he was looking right at him when he did it. Billy says he remembers seeing a kid going up the stairs where they found his father's body. Teddy tells him that was him. He goes on to tell him that he didn't want to kill anybody, but his father was going to shoot me in my other leg and leave me to die in the cold. Billy is looking at me. I tell him that I was on the roof trying to stop the rest of their group from killing us all when his father shot the roof out from under me, hitting me in one leg and in the ribs. I tell him how I fell through the roof breaking some ribs and my leg and how his father told me he was going to kill me because he wanted the young girls in the group we were there to bring back with us.

I can see that Billy does not want to believe me, but something must be telling him that we are telling the truth. One of the women in the group that came here from Rochester, tells him that we are telling him the truth. She says that Doc Betty wasn't sure I would live for at least a week after they brought me back unconscious. She tells him that his father was a brutal man, with no conscience when it came to hurting people. She tells him he was too young to know what his father was doing and she can't blame him for loving his dad no matter what. I am being quiet because I don't want to say anything that may make this situation go the wrong way. One of his friends tells him that he knows his dad was mean and had a bad temper. Billy yells at him to mind his own business.

The other guys tell him as carefully as they can that if shooting starts, they are going to be just as dead as he is, that makes it their business. He mentions that they have an insurance policy and my son Timmy tells him they don't have an insurance policy anymore. He points to a pickup truck coming toward us, when it gets close we can see four young men tied up in the back. He tells me that they were out in the brush like snipers, but they saw them from the barn roof. The lady that knew him in Rochester has a daughter close to Billy's age. She tells him that she is sorry that his father was killed, but he would have killed all of them if he hadn't been. She tells him that there is no reason for more bloodshed. There is plenty of room for all of us and she is sure if they asked us nicely, we would let them join our groups.

I can see he is thinking about it. He looks at me and Teddy and asks if it really happened the way we said. I tell him that I would not lie about something like that. In the short time I got to talk to his father, I could tell he was a soldier and probably a very good one, except that something made him mean and vicious. I can see that Billy is still torn between wanting to believe us and getting vengeance for his father. Finally one of his friends, a young man named Sam, tells him that he will die for him anytime, as long as the cause is righteous, but he is not willing to die for his father. He says he saw him do some things that he would have killed him for himself, if he would have been big enough.

The rest of his friends tell him basically the same thing. I am afraid that he is going to go for his gun when he tosses it on the ground and asks if the invitation for breakfast still stands. His friends walk up close to him and he tells us that he is sick of eating Sam's cooking. They wrestle a little in the yard then all come into the house for breakfast, including their four friends who were out in the brush. I jokingly tell them that after eating Dayna's cooking, he might think we are trying to hurt them. I get smacked good for that comment, but it does get a lot of laughs. During breakfast I ask them what their plans are for the future. They say they haven't really given it much thought because they have been busy planning how they could kill me and still get away.

I tell them they are more than welcome to stay in our groups if they would like. They all say that they would like that; they really enjoyed living in the group before. We get talking with some of our other group members and the suggestion is made that they might like to go to some of the military bases we know of and bring back some of the buildings they have there. Naturally we would work it like we always have. A group goes out and dismantles a couple of Quonset huts or other steel buildings then they bring them home and get plenty of help putting them back together. Then another group goes out and does the same thing.

They say they think they would enjoy doing that at least once. We make sure they know there is plenty of time for that after they get settled in. The way some of the young single women in the family are talking to them, they may not be in any hurry to leave just yet. With this major problem being downgraded to no longer a danger, we start thinking about the other settlements that we know. We call a group council meeting to discuss the best way to handle this. Several of our friends tell Dayna and me that we have spent too much time away from the settlement this year as it is. They think that some other people should be going to visit the other groups.

James and Jenna, along with Mike and Morgan, say that they received word from David and Kimberly, who are two engineers that came to this world and now live with the Missouri settlement that they have found an oil refinery down near the gulf coast. They want to know if our engineers and scientists would like to come over and see if they can get it working again. They are excited about that because even though we have a large supply of gas, propane, and diesel fuel, it will not last forever. Our scientific people believe that there is nothing they can't do, if they have the process documentation that those who were here before the war used. We tell them that they can go, but not to get any ideas about staying there for good. They all think that this will be a great learning experience for Jennifer and Mike Jr.

They are so much like their parents that it is scary sometimes. Mike Jr. tells us that he will not let his mom and dad stay down on the coast. They want to make a trip north to where the auto makers had their headquarters because they have read that they squelched a lot of technology just so that people would have to buy their cars. They want to see what they can find. They are hoping to find the plans for an electric car so that we don't pollute the world like the people before the war did. They also say that from some of the books they have read on the subject, we are barely scratching the surface of solar energy. Luckily there are a lot of books on the subject that give pretty good instructions on how to make many of the materials needed.

Actually Colonel Bob, Blake, and Trevor, along with their wives, are going with our scientific people to Missouri. We tell them to be sure to be home in time for the fall harvest, which is about six weeks away. Naturally they say they will see us in seven to eight weeks and laugh. We still have to decide who is going to visit the other groups and make sure they are okay. I have been giving this a lot of thought and I think I have come up with an answer. We have several couples in our groups that have always worked very hard to make all of our lives better and easier and they never seem to go anywhere. I nominate Billy and Ramona, Ryan and Carol, and Doc Betty and Josh.

You have never seen people that are more surprised than they are. LT and Kathy get asked to go along primarily because of their knowledge of motor vehicles. Sara tells LT to be on the lookout for a small twin engine plane that will seat six to eight people comfortably. Billy, who is just about seven feet tall laughs and tells her there is no such thing as a comfortable plane. She laughs and tells him that if they find the right one, it will even be comfortable for human mountains. Billy laughs, but only because it is Sara calling him that. He is truly a gentle giant, but don't start thinking that he is afraid of someone because he avoids trouble. He is worth any two other men that I have met in my life and I have met some pretty tough men and women.

They are going to leave in two days to give themselves time to pack and to get ready for the extended vacation. Dayna is just happy that it is not us going this time. Sometimes I wish that our friends and family were not as good at keeping the homes, crops, and grounds so well taken care of. I really have to look for work to do sometimes. Today Dayna and I help out at the wheat mill. This week is our family's turn, so there is a bunch of us there to do the job. Lillie and Izzie are really enjoying being part of our family. Lillie told me this morning on the way to the mill that she would really like to go hunting with me. She was quick to say that others can come along as well, but she just likes spending time with me and Dayna.

Izzie likes to fish more than hunt, so we get her a good solid fishing pole and some bait and let her fish in the river that turns the wheel for grinding the wheat. My sons and some of their friends would rather fish than eat sometimes and this gives them an opportunity they simply can't pass up. They know the best places on the river to catch certain kinds of fish. They are always catching big catfish, bass, and pan fish. Today is just like every time they go, they have quite a stringer full just a little after lunch time and Izzie is as excited as we have ever seen her. She caught a catfish that must weigh all of twenty-five pounds. That's not the biggest we have seen, but it's still a nice fish. The boys start bragging on the CB about all the fish they and their sisters are catching, so it is not long before we have representatives from all the groups that make up our extended family.

They spread out quite a distance from the mill in both directions, so that they don't deplete the fish close to home. We have caught a lot of fish out of this river over the years and there always seems to be plenty every time we go fishing. We do throw them back quite often as well and that probably helps some. We also drive about ten miles to the west or fifteen miles to the southeast and there are a couple of lakes and rivers over that way that we have had great success at as well. Today those of us working at the mill decide to quit a little early and test our luck with a fishing pole as well. By the time we are through fishing, we have enough fish for a giant fish fry with all of our friends.

Lillie, who said she didn't like to fish very much, caught a catfish just about the same size as Izzie and now says that she likes fishing this way. Everyone pitches in to clean and filet the fish, so Dayna and I go ahead to get the large deep fryers we have warmed up. The ones we have now came out of a mess hall on one of the military bases we visited. We used to use mainly lard to deep fry in, but we found a recipe for extracting and purifying vegetable oil. We also have some very nice large ovens in case some of the people don't care for oily food, or we can wrap it in aluminum foil with some spices and bake it that way. We have come a long way since that first fish fry we had here. Doc McEvoy likes fish, but he likes hot dogs better, so we make sure to have some of those cooked over the coals for him and anyone else that might want them.

When the meal is served Lillie comes over to Dayna and me and tells us she doesn't see William and the others here. We know which house they are using because it is one of the few that will accommodate that many people. Sure enough when we get there, they are standing around or sitting on the porch. I ask them why they are not enjoying the meal this evening. They look a little sheepish and say that they didn't help catch the fish or anything else for that matter, so they don't think they should enjoy it. Dayna asks them if they worked today. They say they did and really enjoyed it. She tells them that they are part of this family now and she will not have her sons missing meals.

They all smile and say that they will just have to join us and force themselves to try some of that great smelling fish and French fries. Sam asks me if we still make hot dogs for Doc McEvoy, even if everybody else is having something else. I tell him we have plenty just in case someone doesn't want fish. They all say they are willing to try the fish, but they have never had it cooked this way before. When we get back to the shindig everyone welcomes them back. Very few of the people in our groups know about the misunderstanding this morning and we intend to keep it that way. Lillie and Izzie report back to Dayna and I about how much food our new friends consume. We kind of surmised that they may not have been eating regularly. That makes us that much happier that we were able to work it out.

You would think the cleanup after having a large gathering like this one would take a long time, but when everybody pitches in, it makes light work for everyone else. Sam and the others notice that there are still several hot dogs and sausages left. He hints around that they have a good sized refrigerator in their house and it has nothing in it, if we need a place to put some of the leftover food. The girls putting the leftovers away tell him that is a perfect solution for taking care of them. I apologize for not thinking of it today, but I promise that tomorrow we will make sure they have food in their house. They ask about the garden behind the house and the people who moved out of that house about a month ago, to move into one of the Quonset huts tells them that they are welcome to any of it they can use.

Our new friends are some of the last to leave after the cleanup. They tell us that they really want to thank us for not just killing them and for letting them stay here. William, who wants to be called Billy, tells me it's been a terrible internal struggle inside him thinking that he had to avenge his father's death and liking us all like family. They say that they want to spend the rest of their lives here and be part of our family. The fact that they are looking at some of our daughters doesn't get past me or Dayna. We tell them that we are just as happy as they are that everything has worked out the way it has and that they are welcome to stay as long as they would like. We add that we hope it is for the rest of our lives as well.

20

We help the team that is going to visit some of the other settlements get ready to go. They have been getting on the radio and calling all the settlements we know, plus Charity told Dayna about a settlement that we didn't even know about down in Georgia. They say they came down from Canada at the end of the winter primarily because it was so difficult during the long cold winters. Apparently they have talked to us before, but it has been a couple of years since the last time they heard from us. They are definitely interested in having our team stop by to give them some advice and maybe even help them get their electricity hooked up. They said that they have a bus and a truck that they used to get down here with, but those quit running and they don't have anyone that knows about mechanical things.

Tim asked them how they got the vehicles running in the first place and they told him that a couple of guys stopped by about a year ago and got the truck and the bus running for them. They showed them how to use a siphon to get gas from other vehicles and that's how they made it down. Charity told Dayna that it sounds to her like they were looking for our settlement, but couldn't find it so they pretty much settled where their vehicles quit. Our family knows enough to invite anyone that would like to join us to do just that. We have been expanding since we came here and there is still plenty of room to expand a lot more.

We start looking where we can put a fairly large group of people if they decide to come back with our team and the kids tell us there is still plenty of room over near where the church building is that we use as a gathering place. That is not far from Ryan and Carol's group on the southwest. Our groups almost always meet over this way, which is not a bad thing either. We have built along the road and left the acreage for growing our crops pretty much alone. In most of the homes the crops grow right up to their backyards. It is still common to see deer and other animals come into the backyards from the fields. We decide that today would be a good time to go over to the area that we are thinking of and check it out, to make sure it is big enough and to see how much work it will be to put the number of houses we will need in there.

This is the kind of project that gets our people excited and there is no shortage of volunteers to get started, even though we don't even know yet what exactly we will need, if anything. We have a small crew come with us, at least for the initial walk around. We are met at the site we are talking about by Donny and Kim who are part of the leadership team in Ryan and Carol's group. They are excited about the possibility of having some new people join us. I haven't been over this way in about a year and there have been some changes since then. The biggest change is that the heavy woods that used to run between this section and the road aren't so heavy anymore. The teams that cut firewood for the groups have cleared a bunch of the deadfall out and thinned out the woods so that you can see right through them to the open area.

When we get into the area we are thinking about building in we see that the woods between this area and sixty or seventy acres of farmland have been opened up very nicely. Not only have the woods been thinned out nicely, but there are at least twenty or thirty face cords of wood all nicely cut and stacked for the people that will need it this winter. We decide that a nice mixture of pre-fabricated homes and Quonset huts should work nicely. There is plenty of ground water in this area, so we will wait until we get a couple of houses set up then start sinking some wells and putting in the septic system. With the decision made to at least start bringing in some houses we head for home to lay out the homes in the area and decide where to get the houses and huts from. We know we will also need to have a couple of big barns as well.

There is no shortage of metal buildings that we can disassemble and put back up where we need them, but we have gotten spoiled on the military buildings. We have also gotten some nice buildings at airports, but those tend to be very large, so we don't usually go after those. We are discussing this very point today when Kathy asks if we have tried some of the private airports, or even just some of the smaller ones, where only small planes flew out of. We have been to a few of those, but we didn't really find anything we thought would be useful, however that was several years ago. Now we want to look for a small plane, but something big enough to hold six to ten people at a time. We are trying to figure out the easiest way to find some small airports that we haven't already seen, when Dayna, Charity, and Kathy come out of the back room that Dayna uses for things she likes to collect, with several phone books that Dayna and the other ladies collected from places we have been or been at least through.

I get smacked for my attempt at humor when I tell them I was just going to mention that we could look in the phone book and call ahead. It doesn't take long to see that there are several small airports within a couple hours drive of here. We can identify the ones that we already visited, but we don't want to miss them because we may find something that we simply didn't need when we were there the first time. The group that is going to visit the other settlements is going to look for airports as well. The day flies by and before we know it, we are having dinner with a bunch of our family. This evening Teddy, Timmy, and Tommy want to talk to me about raising our own beef cattle.

They have been reading up on it and with all the open land around us, they feel that we could easily raise a hundred head and by breeding them, we would keep a good number of milk cows for every group. The bulls could be fixed, so that we don't get too much inbreeding and we can find some younger bulls from some distance away so that we are sure they are from a different herd. They must think that my silence means that I don't like the idea, but I am just thinking about it while they talk. Teddy tells me that this way we wouldn't have to go hunting so far away all the time and we could always hunt for venison and pork if we would like to. Finally he tells me that if I don't like the idea just say so and maybe we can discuss it, but please say something.

I smile and tell them I'm sorry I am just thinking about everything they said. Actually I think it's a good idea and we have been doing something close to that whenever one of the cows gives birth to a male. We have raised them to be adult cattle then slaughtered them, but it was not real popular with some of the people in the group who just about made pets out of them. Raising our own cattle will give us a better chance to control the breed of cattle we are raising. I tell them that I have no problems with the plan, but now they have to persuade the committee. Teddy says that's the easy part, when they talked to the committee, they told him to ask me and if I agree they have no objections.

I laugh and tell them to let me know what I can help them with. I also warn them that as soon as people find out we are going to be raising cattle, someone will bring up the subject of raising our own pigs. We have tried that at least five times and every time we try, we wind up butchering them all because of the trouble that they are. The woods are full of wild pigs and we have already proven that there is so little difference in the taste of the meat that it isn't worth the hassle. Teddy laughs and tells his brothers about at least three of the trials when they were too young to remember them. He says when you get the baby pigs they are so cute, but after they start getting bigger and they try to bite and knock you over every time you get near them, you would pay for the pleasure of putting them in the freezer or smoke house.

Lillie and Izzie say that they can't imagine anyone wanting to live anywhere near a bunch of pigs because they smell so bad and are so dirty. Then they ask when they can go hunting again, they want to get another big one like that last one. Teddy and the boys are planning to go hunting again day after tomorrow. The other groups told them that they could use some fresh meat, so some of their hunters will be going along as well. Teddy tells me he would like to hunt an area a little further way than usual because the new guys told him that they saw a lot of very large cattle over that way and several large pigs. He likes to tease his new sisters, he tells them they might even find some rabbits or squirrels for them to hunt. Lillie starts telling him in no uncertain terms what she thinks about hunting rabbits, when there is big game around. Teddy laughs and says she must be related to Gramma Horton. His other sister Amy, who is about the same age as Lillie and Izzie smacks him and makes the announcement that she is going hunting with them the next time they go and she and her sisters are not going for rabbits.

The boys look at me like they are asking me to rescue them from the girls. Nickie smacks Teddy and tells him that it won't hurt him to take his sisters hunting with them. She tells him it won't be too many years before he is taking Little Jon with him. That's stretching just a little, but he is growing up quickly. The boys tell us that they will have a written plan tomorrow for us to look at as far as the cattle endeavor is concerned. I assure them they don't have to be perfectly organized to get started, but the better plan you have the easier it is to make things happen the way you want them to. We have had several people come up with good ideas, but they didn't investigate them far enough before starting, then we found out it wasn't such a good idea after all. It's not a big deal either way, at least we tried something whether it worked as well as we thought it would or not is irrelevant, we learned from it and probably had a good time trying.

In the morning our two teams are getting ready to leave. Our scientific people are about as excited as we have ever seen them. The prospect of getting a refinery going, even if it will be only partially to capacity, will be a huge step for our people. We are still very much interested in alternate fuels and ways to accomplish what we want to do without messing up the environment. We feel that if we do things right now, the future generations will follow in our footsteps and hopefully make good choices where some of the generations in the world we came from didn't.

We have had a number of discussions on this topic and we don't think it's fair to necessarily blame the common people for much of the way the earth was abused. We know that our leaders allowed the big money people to dictate what the average citizen would be allowed to even hear about when it came to scientific and technological advances. Things like more efficient cars and alternate fuel cars were kept out of the reach of the average person until there was almost no choice not to. Even then we could never be sure that we were being shown the best possible choices or if they were just what we were allowed to see. Those of us who are in leadership positions in this world want to make sure that everyone is equal and has the same opportunities as everyone else.

That's why we make sure that every young person and not so young people know how to read and are given every opportunity to attend classes. They are taught about government, math, science, reading, and writing, history, and pretty much anything that we are capable of teaching them. They are also given the opportunity to learn any or every trade that we use to survive. Everyone that lives in our groups is given the chance to try any job they think they might like. For some of us, we have tried every job in the settlement and work wherever we are needed the most on any given day. We also have some people that are what you might call specialists and enjoy doing only a couple of different jobs. Some of our farmers are like this, but they are so valuable to our group that we are happy that they enjoy it so much.

William and his friends are trying a bunch of different jobs before they decide what they might like to do most of the time. Zach and Sam really want to learn more about mechanical things so they are going with the team visiting the other settlements because we know they will be getting a lot of experience that way. After our teams leave, Teddy, Timmy, and Tim's son Jon want to show me the area that they want to start raising some cattle. They picked an area that is close to the wheat mill, but far enough away that the smell will not be bad for the people working there. They are planning to go downstream from the mill as well. It's an area that is walled off on two sides by forest, one side is the river and on the other side, there are is a row of trees that form a natural fence except for about a hundred feet. That they are planning to fence off using barbed wire or a split log fence.

That's where they will put the gate. They are even talking about eventually putting a good sized barn in this area where the cattle could be slaughtered and butchered, then transferred up to the large refrigerators where the meat is currently stored. I am impressed with the work they have done just to present the plan to us. When they mentioned raising our own beef this is the area that I thought of right off the bat. One of the reasons is that it is several acres in size and there is always deep grass in this area. We have cut it a few times over the years to use as straw and hay for our dairy cows. Actually there is no shortage of grass that can be cut for hay and feed around us. We use an area approximately five miles square, give or take a little, so considering how big the state is, we still have several hundred thousand acres of land that could be used.

The boys even have a plan of how they will grow the herd at least to get started. First off we already have about ten head of cattle that are still too small to butcher that came from our dairy cows. The bull that has been breeding the cows we have now is getting old, plus we would like to have some new blood introduced into our herd, I guess we can call it. What they are proposing is to look for younger cattle in the areas that we hunt away from the settlement. They figure if they gather four or five younger cows from each area, we will have a good sized herd in no time. I start to ask them how they are planning to get the cattle home, but Teddy interrupts and tells me that we have had that livestock trailer out beside the big barn since we moved here.

They are going to fix it up and take that whenever they go hunting. When I smile they laugh and ask if they have a good enough plan yet. I tell them honestly that I could not have done any better. I ask them how many people they have that want to help in this project. They name off most of the family then they say that William, Chuck, Noe, and Brandon, who are some of the newest members of our family are excited about helping. I look disappointed and tell them I was hoping there would be room for me to help sometimes, but it looks like they have it covered. They all tell me that they wouldn't think about starting a project like this one without at least one of us oldens involved.

They are running when they finish talking and they are all laughing as well. I run after them, but they are all faster than this olden, as they call us. I can't catch them, but I know where they live, so I will get them later. They are in a hurry to get started running the fence that they need so we head into town to get the materials needed for the fence, along with some other things that they think may help the cattle feel at home there. We have a pretty good sized load by the time we head back to the settlement, but we take the materials over to the area they will be needed and drop them off.

There is still several hours of daylight left so the boys and some of the girls decide to get started putting up the fence.

While we talked about it in town they decided that it might be better if they run the wire fence through the woods as well to make sure the cattle don't roam too far. It will be more work, but since the wire and posts are available, why not use them. Actually they are marking off where they want the fence to go through the woods. Then they will clear a path through them to have a nice flat area to work and to run the fence on. Today all they accomplish is to mark off where they want to go and then they moved the backhoe and bull dozer over to that area to start work tomorrow. Tomorrow some of them will work on the pasture while others go hunting. We are planning to scout around for young steers wherever we go.

The girls are excited about going hunting tomorrow morning. Lillie and Izzie have not used guns much at all, so they want to spend some time practicing after supper. Target practice is always a good thing to do before a hunting trip so that you can make sure your rifle is shooting where you are aiming. To me there is not much worse than wounding an animal and having it run away to eventually die. If you are going to kill an animal for food, make sure that it goes down quickly with a good shot that doesn't make the poor thing suffer. The girls are better shots than I thought they would be, but they have been shooting a bow and arrows almost since they could walk, so they have excellent hand, eye coordination.

We let them pick out whatever gun they think they would like to use. They both picked a really nice .308 with a variable two to nine power scope. Anywhere from a hundred yards out to about two-hundred and fifty yards they are deadly. At three hundred yards they are a little off, but they would most likely hit what they are shooting at. Our daughters have been shooting pretty much since they could hold a gun steady, so they are ready for tomorrow. We are looking to bring back enough meat for all the groups. They will be represented by their hunters as well, so this should be a good trip. The fellowship will be fun, but it is never fun to take the life of an animal or a man, unfortunately, sometimes it is necessary to survive.

We get up early in the morning so that we can get an early start. We are taking two of our trucks with the hoists on them and a couple of pickup trucks in case we get as much meat as we are expecting to. We are going to an area that we haven't hunted in about ten years. We like to mix up our hunting areas so that the game has a chance to replenish itself. On the way there we see several small herds of cattle and even some bunches of pigs in the fields. Most of them have probably never seen a man before, so they don't act at all scared when we go by. We make a mental note that there were several cattle in those herds that are just about the size we are looking for. When the fence is up we will come back this way and see if we can catch some of them.

We get to the area we want to hunt and before we can assign everybody hunting areas, we see one of the biggest, meanest looking bulls I have ever seen. He must be all of fifteen or sixteen hundred pounds and he is one impressive sight standing in the field just looking at us. Teddy asks me if we should take him and I honestly don't want to kill that magnificent beast, but if he gets much older he will be too tough to eat. While I am debating the issue in my head, the bull makes up our minds for us and charges the group. He is about a hundred yards away, but he is covering that distance very quickly.

Teddy starts to move to the right and I am moving to the left to get a side shot at the bulls head because experience has shown us that the bullets will just bounce off the thick skull in the front. Lillie is moving with me and Izzie is right beside Teddy. The bull has covered about half the distance and seems to be picking up speed as I am sighting just below the ear on the side of his head. I am ready to fire when I hear the report of a gun next to me and another shot almost right over the first one and the big steer drops right where he is, which is now about twenty yards away from us. Lillie and Izzie are walking toward the downed bull carefully. It twitches a couple of times then lays still. Teddy walks over to me and says that he didn't have time to get a good shot before Izzie fired and I have to admit that Lillie beat me as well.

Timmy tells them that they killed it they have to field dress it, but they already have their knives out walking toward it. I am impressed that they stop and say a prayer thanking the steer for giving himself to them, so that they will have food for the coming winter. The boys tell them to wait a minute and they will hoist it up so that they can get at it better. We have some large containers that we catch pretty much everything in so that nothing really goes to waste when we kill an animal, even if some of it only goes for fertilizer. Teddy and Jon stay to help the girls get the steer ready to transport home and the rest of us break up into pairs and continue hunting.

21

I go with my daughter Amy and Sara's daughter Misty. They have never been big on hunting, but since Lillie and Izzie came to live with us I think they feel the need to show that they can do it as well as anyone. We go to an area that is between a mile and a mile and a half west of the people dressing the steer. It is pretty warm today so we don't want to stay very long before getting the meat back to the settlement. We brought several coolers full of ice to pack inside the animal where the insides used to be. When we get to the spot where we are going to hunt, the girls tell me that if we see anything to shoot that I can do it, but they want me to tell the boys that they did. I smile because I kind of figured that they were going to do something like that.

We are walking toward the woods with our rifles at the ready because you can never tell when you will run into something that flat out doesn't like you. We go about fifty yards into the woods and come to a good sized clearing. We stop quickly because on the other side of the clearing are about twenty large hogs feeding on some green apples that have fallen off a couple of trees over there. These hogs are not as large as some of them we have shot, but I am guessing some of them are over five hundred pounds. The pigs are about fifty yards away and I am hoping that they ignore us and continue eating. I motion for us to back out of here, when one of the biggest boars in the group starts walking toward us with his head lowered.

He looked up when we first came into the clearing and I was hoping he would ignore us, but no such luck. He is staring straight at us while he walks steadily toward us. He has tusks that are about six inches long, but from here they look to be all of a foot long. I raise my gun and the girls spread out to either side of him. The boar gets about halfway across then lets out a very loud grunt and breaks into a run right at me. I fire and the bullet enters right beside one of his ears, but he doesn't even slow down. I jack another shell into the chamber and hear the roar of two guns that sound like a single shot and the boar takes two more steps then falls forward onto his stomach. He rolls on his side and his feet kick a couple of times then he is still.

The girls are so excited that they start to walk right up to it, but I warn them that he may not be dead yet, so it is better to wait. The other pigs look toward us, but they do not seem to notice that one of their fellow pigs is no longer with them. I check the one we shot and determine that he is totally dead, so we start field dressing this one when Amy, who is standing guard, tells me conversationally that I may want to get my gun because three more of the large pigs are coming this way and they do not look like they are too happy. We stand up and just have time to raise our guns and each choosing one of the pigs we fire. One of the pigs goes down and stays, but the other two stumble and keep on coming. All three of us fire again and this time they go down, but not more than ten feet from us.

We look back at the group eating and they move to a tree farther away from us and continue eating. We hear something coming through the woods from the direction of the road and turn quickly to make sure we are not being attacked again. This time it is Teddy, Jon, Lillie, and Izzie. They come up and looking at the four dead pigs ask us if we left any for next time. Amy and Misty are so excited they start talking so fast that I can't understand them. Teddy says that he will go back and get the pickup back in here to drag them out before we field dress them. It only takes a few minutes to get the first one out, so some of us stay with that one while the others go back for another one. By the time we get them dressed and loaded onto the truck, there is very little room left.

We are getting ready to go back and meet up with the rest of our hunting party when Lillie asks me if we would like some venison. Teddy tells us that Doc Betty specifically asked for some venison this time. There are several large white tail deer feeding in a field just past the first part of the woods. There are several bucks in the group which strikes me as odd, but Teddy tells me he has seen the deer like this before. There is a really nice one that is at least a ten or twelve point and will weigh at least three hundred pounds. Jon has already grabbed his rifle and is working his way a little closer. He gets to about a hundred yards from the herd, takes aim and shoots the biggest one in the herd. The herd is startled by the gun shot, but they only run off about thirty or forty yards and go back to grazing.

He looks back at us as if to ask if he should take another one. I look at the truck full of meat and I have to think the others had pretty much the same luck we did and tell him to save some for another day. It's going to take the rest of the day to just get what we have skinned and quartered. He and Teddy run to get the one he shot and drag it out to the truck where they field dress it and fill the cavity with ice. We meet up with the others and they have a truckload just like we do, only they have another steer, three deer and two pigs. Our butchers are going to be very busy for the next couple of days. The boys are excited because they saw several head of cattle that are just about the right size to start our herd. Now they want to get the fence up so that they can start capturing some cattle.

All the groups are excited with the amount of meat we were able to get today. It's getting on toward the time of year when we cook and can a bunch of the meat so everybody has some for the winter. Our winters here are not so bad that we can't hunt, but it's nice to have enough to survive without having to hunt all winter. It also comes in handy to barter with some of the other groups for things that we don't get all the time. A good portion of the beef and the venison will be dried and made into jerky as well as some of the best pepperoni I have ever eaten. We will make some great Italian sausage with the pork as well. I hate to brag, but we really do make some of the best pizza that any of us from the other world has ever eaten.

We get a call from both teams that went out telling us they reached their destination. Of course the one team will help the settlement if they need it or want it and the other group will try to get an oil refinery running again. I am amazed at the things our people can do sometimes. James and Jenna, and Mike and Morgan can go into a factory or practically any kind of business and make it work by using the process instructions that are in the place. Some of the places we have been, they don't even have instructions and they figure it out. As our world grows and progresses, those of us from the other world expect that we will probably get more people with that knowledge coming to this world.

Dayna and I were discussing that topic just the other night and we agree with the others to a degree, but we feel that the people of this world are getting better and better educated so we won't be surprised to see many of the technological advances that were here before the world changed, being opened again by the people that are here and even making those advances better. The one thing that we all agree on is that we don't want to make the same mistakes that our world made. That's one reason Dayna and I think that the major advances will come from within because some of the people that have come from our world think like we do, but there are still some who look at being here as a way to do whatever they want to, no matter who it hurts.

Jenna must have talked to Sara after we left because she comes over to tell me that she knows where we can find a couple of planes that seem to be exactly what we are looking for. The airport or airports are over in Tennessee. Sara has very detailed directions to where they are and she wants to know if we can go get them tomorrow. I start to tell her that we have other projects that have to be done first, but my sons tell me that they can finish the projects that we are working on and if there is any work left when I get back, they will do me the honor of letting me finish it. Actually I would like nothing better than to drive that bulldozer of ours along the lines that we chose as the boundaries for the pasture. I'm betting that the only thing left to do when we get back is string barbed wire, but that can be fun too.

Because of the possibility of the planes and the hangars we are going to leave tomorrow. According to Sara it should take us a little over a day to get there, so we are planning to be gone for three or four days at least this first time. We are taking two of the new guys, Jared and Tyler, along because they want to learn as much as they can about mechanics and pretty much everything that we do. In the morning Sara and Gary are ready to go when the sun comes up. Dayna and I have traveled with them enough to be ready when they come knocking on the door. Misty is staying with Teddy and Nickie, but Sara has to embarrass her daughter by telling Nickie to make sure that Misty and Thomas are not alone long enough for any hanky-panky.

Misty tells her that she has convinced Thomas to do a little hanky, but so far he isn't interested in any panky, which makes Thomas turn about as red as I used to when people talked about that stuff. Sara looks like she is not so sure about leaving Misty home now. Misty laughs at her mom and tells her that she has nothing to worry about. She will wait until she is the same age as her mom was when she started having sex. Misty asks her mom when that was. Sara tells her she was thirty-five before she started having sex, but since she is only thirty-six now and Misty is thirteen, something doesn't quite add up. Sara is trying to convince Misty that she is adopted, so Dayna takes Sara by the arm and leads her out the door telling her to quit while she is behind.

We are almost to the car when Lillie and Izzie come running out to ask if it's okay for them to learn to drive the backhoe and the bull dozer. Teddy is standing on the porch. He yells over that he will be happy to teach them as long as I don't mind. I tell him to go ahead. All the other women in the family know how to drive them. I do tell them that whenever they are doing something in the woods to make sure they have a loaded gun with them because you can never tell what you may run into. Teddy tells me and them that he will take them to the armory this morning and get them fitted with a good handgun. That reminds me of something and I turn to ask Tyler and Jared if they have their handguns with them. They both proudly show me that they have brand new .44 magnums and enough ammunition to fight a small war.

We are taking a military vehicle that will seat six comfortably and will go through just about any terrain we come to. When you go anywhere with Sara, she always wants to drive, which is okay with me because I would rather sit in the back and neck with Dayna, but since that's not going to happen at least I can sit with her. For the first part of the trip the roads are not bad. We have driven on them before so the cars are pushed out of the way and the larger buckles in the pavement have been smoothed out some. It doesn't take long to get into Tennessee, but we have to go almost to the far side of the state to find what we are looking for. As soon as we turn off the roads we know, we find out in a hurry that we are going to have to push some cars off the road and fix a few very rough spots in the pavement.

Our other group came this way, but in the interest of time they worked their way around a lot of the stuff that we will take out of the way, in case we have to come this way again on the way back or for future trips over this way. The going is much slower through here, but not as bad as we first thought it would be. We are about two hours into the new road when Sara tells us that must be the surprise that Jenna told her about. I was looking out the side window when she says it so I turn to the front and almost directly in front of us is a huge store that specialized in outdoor equipment. The road curves around in front of it so we decide to pull into the driveway and check it out. The store is like finding a buried treasure. There is pretty much everything you could need to survive in the outdoors along with enough guns and ammunition and fishing equipment to supply at least five or six settlements like ours.

Tyler and Jared ask me what we will do with the stuff we get here. We tell them that it will probably go into the warehouses until someone needs something or we find another group that needs some of it. They think it's a great idea. Then they ask if it would be okay if they find a good winter coat because they don't have one yet. We all tell them that they can pick two coats if they want to, but it might be better to wait until the trip home. Then we will get a truck running and load it to take back. One thing we do take with us though, is some canned chocolates that the seal has not been broken on. Sara and Dayna both tell me that one of the next projects we have to do is find a factory that used to make chocolate and learn how to make our own.

I make a note to see if the cocoa beans grow in Cuba or any of the islands in that area. Gary, Jared, and Tyler are talking about the bass boats that they have on trailers around the store. They are thinking that we could probably catch a lot more fish if we had some of those boats to take to the lakes around us and fish them more. I can't argue with that logic, I wouldn't mind trying out one of those boats myself. The rest of the day we are moving cars out of the way and filling in huge pot holes and flattening areas where the pavement has buckled over the years. We find four gasoline tankers that the gages read almost full on and three propane trucks that are close to full as well. When it is time to quit for the day, we figure we are only a couple hours from the first airport. According to Sara the second one is about an hour from that one.

We camp in a couple of travel trailers that were probably used before the war, but they are still comfortable and reasonably clean. We have discussed getting some of these for when we travel, but they use so much gas that we always decide against it. We are waiting for our scientists to find a way to run them on solar power. James and Mike both say that when they were in the other world, they read articles about solar powered vehicles. That's why they want to go up to what was Detroit in our world, where the major auto makers had their headquarters. We leave early in the morning and get to the first airport about three hours later. If we didn't have good directions we would never have found it. It's just a small airport where mostly small private planes came and went from it.

The planes that we can see are in pretty rough shape from the weather, but when we go into the largest of four hangars we feel like we have hit the jackpot and the lottery in the same day. There are four planes in this hangar and they all look to be in good shape. We can see where our team had to force the door open, so it was locked up tight since the war. The largest plane is a sixteen seater with four engines. That's probably a little bigger than we need at least for now. The next one is exactly what Sara has been talking about. It will seat ten and still have a little cargo space, it also has four engines. Sara and Gary start looking for fuel, but I tell them we have three more hangars to check out.

The other hangars do not have the jackpot that the first one does, but there are some nice small planes in them and another helicopter that looks like it might have been used for flying in supplies. Most of the planes we find are twin engine planes that will hold from four to six people at a time and there are two single engine planes that look good. It takes us about an hour to get the tow vehicle running so that we can move the planes around enough to work on them. We have to get good tires on the ones we want to try to get started, so Jared, Tyler, Dayna, and I start doing that while Sara and Gary work on the engines. Sara keeps commenting on how clean the engines are and how she thinks they will run with very little work.

They find a fuel truck with some in it, but they go to the area where the pumps are and fill the truck to the top. Naturally we try some of the fuel to make sure it will burn before we put it into the planes. By the time we get the tires either inflated or changed on three of the planes, Sara and Gary have the plane with ten seats running. It's a little rough, but it doesn't sound too badly at all. We check the running plane over for leaks of any kind and find a small hydraulic fitting that is leaking, but a quick tightening of the valve stops that one. Sara taxi's the plane out of the hangar onto the runway, but doesn't want to test fly it yet. We really haven't had time to check it out enough to trust it in the air yet. Sara really wants to work on the largest plane, so rather than waste time talking about it, we decide that she and Gary will work on that one and I will work on one of the smaller planes.

We get them running at almost the same time. Our new friends Jared and Tyler are impressed with our skill as mechanics. While we have been working on the planes they have been checking out the hangars and think that we could easily get two of them, but two of them don't look like they will come apart very easily at all. They also found something that skipped the rest of our attention. Down the road, only about a quarter of a mile away, are several military Quonset huts in a row. We go down the road to check them out and find out that there are actually six of them and it looks like they got setup here and never used. They should come apart fairly easily. Now all we have to do is find a truck large enough to take the buildings back on. Naturally they will be taken apart, but they still take up quite a bit of space.

We find a nice flatbed truck that breaks apart for loading heavy equipment and get to work seeing if it will run. While we have been looking at the other buildings and finding the truck, Sara and Gary have been checking out the planes that are running. The runway is not in very good shape for taking off on, but while I am trying to figure out how we can smooth it out, Sara taxi's the largest plane out to the road and uses it for a runway. It's not as smooth as it could be, but it's a lot better than the runway. The plane sounds powerful as she starts the takeoff and lifts as gracefully into the air as a large bird. We are all listening for any missing in the engine, but it sounds great. She makes a large circle around the area then lands on the road where she took off. We have not seen Sara this excited since she got the helicopter flying.

She tries each of the planes that we have running successfully then says she will take all of them right now. We are discussing how we are going to get them home, when James and Mike call us on the short wave radio. They laugh when Sara tells them she has three beautiful planes ready to be flown home. They along with Jenna and Morgan want to guess which ones she has ready to go. They get all three of them and only miss on one of their guesses. They tell us to start moving the hangars and they should be heading home about the time we get at least one of them home and setup. If we need their assistance flying any of the planes home, they will be happy to stop by here on the way home. Sara wants to fly one of the planes home tomorrow and return with more help in one of our small trucks.

We agree to that, but we all know that if we are going to have airplanes and helicopters we are going to need a larger supply of aviation fuel to run them. Regular gas for cars and trucks is not pure enough for airplanes. We spend the last couple of hours in the day to work on more planes and to start taking apart the largest hangar. It was funny because when Jared and Tyler heard us say we were going to start taking the hangar apart, they started looking through the tool box for wrenches. Dayna went over to the tool box that we keep the pneumatic impact wrenches we use for this purpose. We carry a small generator and a compressor to run the impact tools. We find the lift that pretty much all places like this one has and make sure it is safe before taking it up to the roof of the hangar.

This hangar is not very high compared to some of the buildings we have moved. I go on the outside while Tyler and Jared work on the inside, taking the panels apart. When one of them is loose, I use ropes with special connectors on them to lower the panels down the side of the building. They are trying to save the nuts that they remove from the panels, but I tell them not to worry about that. We have thousands and thousands of the common sizes that are used in buildings like this. If they can catch them without losing any time that's great, but if they fall don't worry about them. That speeds things up somewhat and we get quite a bit more done than I thought we would. We can all sleep after the day we had, but we all know we will start over again tomorrow. Tyler and Jared thank us again for letting them be part of our family. We thank them for letting us be part of their family.

22

We find some cots that must have been here for when pilots got grounded for some reason, but they are nowhere near as comfortable as the travel trailers that we slept in last night. Dayna and I agree that if we are going to be here for a few more days, or possibly even a week, or more at different times, we need to find better sleeping arrangements. We are getting ready to go looking for some travel trailers that we can tow here, if nothing else, when Sara tells us she will take the plane up and circle the area quickly to see what might be available. Gary goes with her because she is just going to check the area, then head for home. Sounds like a plan to us and it works better than we expected it would. She no sooner gets in the air when she radio's that she can see a large selection of them about a mile east of where we are.

She circles the airport, waggles her wings and takes off for home. In the airplane the trip should be less than an hour or at least no more than that. Having a good airplane will open up a lot of doors that have been closed to this point. We can get pretty much anywhere we need to go in a fraction of the time it would take us to drive. We take the military vehicle with us so that we can tow the trailers back to the airport. We don't really want to spend half the day getting them running, so our plan is to fill the tires and tow them back. It doesn't work quite that easily, but it only takes a little over an hour to get three of the trailers back to the airport. We only need two for now, but there will be others coming and they will need somewhere to sleep as well. We will wait to hear from the group coming back how many more we will need.

We get a call on the radio telling us that Sara and Gary got back safely and everyone is totally impressed with the airplane. Naturally we are all happy to hear that. Between removing panels from the hangar and getting the flatbed truck running, and getting good tires under it, the next two days go by very quickly. We are very happy that we took the time to bring the trailers over here. We are going to get two more tomorrow for the group coming back with Sara and Gary. We load the panels that we already have off the hangar onto the flatbed. We mark them very carefully to make sure we can put them back together in the order they go. When we get the panels loaded, we work on finishing the dismantling of the building. Tyler and Jared keep telling us how much they are enjoying this kind of work.

I know how they feel. I have always enjoyed working with my hands and moving heavy loads. We work until just about dark then sit back and relax until bed time. While we are sitting here, just looking around, we see several large herds of deer and cattle standing out in the fields around us, grazing on the grass there. They don't seem to even notice that there are some crazy humans not far away. I mention to the others that if we are going to be here much longer we may need to shoot one of those deer to have food to eat. We brought canned meat and vegetables to last about a week and we are getting close to that now. When we work as hard as we have been there is no trouble at all getting to sleep at night. Every night we make a list of what we need to accomplish the next day, to remind ourselves to stay focused.

In the morning we get up, eat a quick breakfast and check our list to see what we need to do today. The list shows us that we have to finish taking down the hangar and stack it neatly on the truck. Then we have to tie the load down so it doesn't move on the way home, then we have to get a couple more travel trailers brought over for the people that are coming. Dayna asks if we can get the trailers first because she has a feeling we will need them today. I have learned to trust Dayna's feelings, so we take our tow vehicle over and start bringing back trailers. By lunch time we have three of them and Dayna has this feeling that we are going to need at least one more, so we go get it. While we are hooking up to tow the last one, we hear the sound of vehicles coming our way.

Some of them sound like motorcycles and I am starting to worry a little because we didn't bring any rifles with us today. All we have are our side arms, which are good, but mainly if you are fighting in close quarters. I personally don't want to get into any fire fight in close enough proximity to fight it with hand guns. We hear the vehicles getting closer now and by the time we walk to the front of our vehicle, four motorcycles with riders pull up and stop right in front of us. There is a small bus and a couple of vans that stopped back about a hundred yards. The riders before us look tough to me. They are wearing sun glasses and helmets, which is a little odd here. They take off their glasses and then their helmets. The one on the right in the middle seems to be in charge; at least he is starting to talk.

He smiles and introduces himself as Wyatt Tremont. He introduces the men with him Max, Trey, and Junior. They all smile and offer their hands to shake. We introduce ourselves and shake their hands. Wyatt asks if we have a settlement near here. He says they heard about some settlements, but never could get a location on them, so they have been driving around hoping to find one sooner or later. I tell them that our settlement is over in Virginia, about a day and a half away. They say they have talked with someone named Tim, from a settlement over east of here. They ask if that may be the same place we are from. I am being a little careful until we find out what exactly their intentions are. They ask if it would be okay if the rest of their group gets out of the vehicles. They assure us that they mean us no harm and hope we don't mean them any.

Naturally Dayna goes to meet the new people as they get out of the vehicles. There are several women and children in the group and many of them speak Spanish and they all speak some English. The men ask if we can use a hand getting the trailer moved to wherever we are planning to take it. Dayna is showing the others where we are staying, so we finish hooking up the trailer and tow it back to the airport. When we get it there we decide to fix some lunch, which is a very popular decision with our guests. They say they ran out of food yesterday, which is why they would really like to meet up with a settlement. Feeding them all puts a serious dent in our food supplies, but we are not going to see people go hungry, as long as we have food.

Jared asks if he and Tyler should go see if they can shoot a nice buck for meat and see if they can find any vegetables growing wild in the fields near here. Max says if he can borrow a rifle he would love to go along. We have an extra gun, so he goes with them to hunt the woods not far off. The other men stay and help me finish taking down the hangar and load it on the truck. While we work I tell them about our settlement and they say it sounds like heaven to them. Wyatt asks if it might be possible to go back with us and if we don't have room in our groups, at least they could possibly settle near us. I assure them that we have plenty of room. I also mention that we have a very solid security system in place in case of attack.

Wyatt and Junior laugh and say they will take my word for it. They have no intentions of testing it. While we are talking and working, Wyatt mentions that he has heard of some people in the settlements that came from a different world. I joke about it and ask him if they are little green men or some other kind of alien. He laughs and says that from what he heard on the radio, they look just like him and me, only they have skills that are needed in this world to help the people that survived the war rebuild this one. I tell him that's an interesting theory, I wonder if I have ever run into any of these people and just didn't know it. Wyatt smiles and says he wouldn't be a bit surprised. He no sooner says that when a young woman, that must be his wife, comes running over and tells him that I came from the same world that he did.

We both laugh and I ask him what he was doing when he wound up here. He says he was working on an oil platform in the Gulf of Mexico when a huge storm came up and they had to ride it out on the ocean. When the storm was over, he, Max, Junior, and Trey were the only ones left on the platform. They were able to get a small boat running well enough to get back to shore in Mexico only to find that they were no longer in the world they had been in. They found a small group of people who were living together and were asked to join because there is safety in numbers. They met their wives in that group and the rest is history as they say. They say they have been in this world for about five years now.

They were barely surviving down in Mexico and when they heard about a group with over five hundred people in it, they decided to see if they could find it, hoping they could join us. I tell him Tim and my story and about the rest of the people we know of from the other world. While we are talking we hear gun shots coming from the direction that our hunters went. I tell him that if the deer here are as big as the ones back home we better drive over to help them. At first they think I am kidding, but when we get close and they see two very large deer being field dressed, they see what I mean. Our hunters have also found a good sized field of carrots, potatoes, and green beans growing wild. There are even some tomatoes mixed in the field. We go to the next field over and find a nice long row of wild blackberry bushes that are heavy with fruit.

The women and children, from our new friends group, pick more than enough for a great dessert and Dayna, along with Wyatt's wife Tori, mix up a great big pot of venison stew. They even found some onions growing behind the airport. With the four new trailers we moved over here we have just enough room for everyone to sleep. Before they turn in for the night, Tori tells us that she knew if they put their lives in the hands of the Lord he would lead them to the best place for them to be. Wyatt told us this evening that they found us by listening to the noise we made taking down the hangar. They heard it yesterday and followed it hoping to hear it again today. They were disappointed when they didn't, but they did hear our engine when we started towing the trailers and they followed that to us. We are very happy that they did.

In the morning we are making fried potatoes for breakfast when Sara and Gary, along with four other members of our group, pull into the airport. We are watching them pull up and get out of the vehicles when Wyatt asks if these are strange people or do we know them. I can't help myself, I tell him we know them well, but they are still strange people. Sara comes over, punches me in the chest, takes my plate of potatoes, and starts eating them. His wife is laughing when she says if she had to guess, Sara is my sister. Sara says she is close and starts introducing all the new comers to our new friends. When she sees the children, she tells them to get one of the boxes out of the back of the truck she was driving.

They run to get it. When they bring it back their moms can read that the box is full of cans of chocolate candy. They ask Sara if she is sure that she wants to give a treasure like this away. Sara tells them to enjoy it. She made arrangements to start making our own chocolate in a very short time. The children have never had chocolate, but when they smell it, they are more than willing to try it. Sara wants to fly the largest plane home this time. We get it ready to take off, and then she asks if any of our new friends would like to go for a plane ride. They decide to send the women and children along with two older men that are with them, the rest of the men will stay with us and help get the hangar home. We are also going to drive one of the tankers full of aviation fuel back with us as well. Since we cleared the road on the way up, we may even make it back today. If not it will be early tomorrow. Tyler and Jared decide to stay and help take another of the hangars apart with the new crew that came back with Gary and Sara.

We watch the plane until it is out of sight then head for home ourselves. We were going to stop at the outdoor store on the way back, but we decide to get the trucks home and come back for the store later. We do get home, but it is getting dark when we pull into the driveway. We see the plane parked next to the other one and we no sooner stop the trucks when the people that came back with Sara come running out to greet their loved ones. They are so excited about everything we have here that they can scarcely believe it's true. Wyatt and his wife come up beside Dayna and me and tell us that this looks like heaven to them.

We have to agree when we stop to look at all the homes that are lit up and the fields full of crops right beyond the houses. Junior and his wife come up and he tells us that he used to have a calendar that he liked that had a picture almost exactly like what we are looking at. He says the caption on that picture said, Coming Home, now he knows what it meant. The new families have been assigned at least temporary homes to stay in until they decide where they would like to live. As they are heading for the house they are going to stay in for now, their little girl who is about three, asks Wyatt if they are going to stay here. He tells her that he sure hopes so and she tells him she does too. We have lots of kids to play with and plenty of food to eat.

Dayna tells me that Wyatt's wife Tori told her that she never dreamed that people were living like we do here. She also tells me that all the families that just came to live with us are Mormons. I joke and tell her that I will try not to hold that against them. She smacks me and tells me I'm terrible. When I finally get home we have some very excited kids that have been working to fence in the pasture for the past several days. They can't wait to tell us all about it. They are so excited that they want to show us what they have accomplished right now. I finally convince them to let it wait until morning to go see the progress. As soon as they finish telling us about the pasture project, they all ask if they can learn to fly one of the planes that we are bringing back. I can't see any reason why they shouldn't be able to, as long as we can find aviation fuel.

The travel trailers were nice for sleeping in, but our own bed is like heaven. In the morning we get up and fix a nice breakfast and invite Wyatt and his family over to share it with us. All the new people got invited to someone's home for breakfast, so Wyatt's family is the only ones left. When they sit down to eat, I remember that some religions don't eat pork so I quickly ask them if they are one of those. Wyatt tells us that he sure hopes not because he hasn't had pork sausage since he came to this world and the sausage on the table smells better than any he can remember before that. Their little girl, whose name is Ariel, already has a big piece on her fork and is chewing on it. She asks between bites if she can have some milk and Wyatt tells her it's not polite to ask for things when you are guests.

She tells him that she had two glasses of milk with dinner last night and Aunt Dayna told her she could have all she wants. Dayna tells her that she can have all she wants, as long as her mommy and daddy don't mind. They have a son as well, that looks to be about two, and he is putting away the sausage and scrambled eggs as fast as he can. Dayna fills a Sippy cup full of milk for him and he almost drains it before putting it down. His mom apologizes and says that the children have only had cow's milk a couple of times before this and apparently they really like it. Dayna tells her that most of the people in our groups never had cow's milk until we moved here. Now we don't know what we would do without it. She adds that we all love the butter and the ice cream we make from the milk as well. Little Ephraim, that's the two year olds name, smiles and looks at Dayna and asks if he can have some more, "I keem" today. His mom tells him that we will have to see. Wyatt says that apparently he missed a lot that happened before we got home last night.

He says he's not complaining because the ham sandwich and fresh garden salad were perfect. He asks Ephraim what kind of Ikeem he had last night. Ephraim stops eating long enough to look at his mom and say, "black rapserry". His mom tells him close, but it was black raspberry and I wanted to save you some, but I was afraid to ask for more as nice as everyone was to us. Dayna apologizes for not thinking to send some home with them, but says she will make up for that when they leave after breakfast. While we eat, we talk about what they would like to do. They both say that if it's okay with us they would love to stay here as part of the settlement. We tell them about the other groups and tell them they are welcome to stay in which ever group they would like.

Wyatt says they talked about it with the other people that they came with and they would all like to stay right where they are, unless we need the homes for someone else. They both say they are furnished so comfortably they are afraid that they may mess up someone else's furniture. We explain how we do things here and that they can go to the warehouses and pick out new furniture if they would prefer. We will help them move the furniture in the house now and move in the new stuff. Dayna tells Tori that she will show her what we have to choose from and also where she can find all the clothing that they may need for the entire family. She makes sure they know that goes for the others as well. She tells Ephraim and Ariel that we may even be able to find them some toys to play with as well.

My children have been waiting patiently to show me what they have accomplished this week, so while the wives go shopping, we men go with the young people to inspect the pasture. Wyatt is even more impressed in the daylight. He is excited when he sees that we use windmills and solar panels to generate electricity for our homes. We have to go by the wheat mill and he is even more impressed that we use the river to drive the wheel and the quantity of wheat that can be ground at a time. He tells us that his wife is going to go crazy when she sees all this. We are joined by Max, Junior, and

Trey along with Rob, Tim, and Frank. They are comparing what they had for breakfast and it looks like no one was disappointed. We follow the kids to the pasture and it is obvious that they have done a tremendous job in the time that they have had.

They have three strands of barbed wire surrounding approximately forty acres with a beautiful gate that is as solid as any I have seen. Max, Junior, and Trey are really impressed. Apparently they were raised on a cattle ranch in Idaho. The kids even brought the steers over here from the barnyard and also went out and caught several head of young stuff to add to the herd. Max and Trey say that they went down to the barn where our milk cows are kept and are very much impressed with what they see. They also say they saw the largest hide they have ever seen hanging in the barn and they want to know how big that steer was. I start to tell them about that steer, but Teddy asks if he can tell them.

He tells them about that day when that steer chased our hunters and almost got one of them. They are listening intently and saying that they have run into some ornery steers like that. Tim asks them if any of the steers they worked with weighed over a ton. They are not sure that they believe that, but they will take our word for it. Teddy tells them he will take them hunting in a couple of days. He says he will try to find them one like it. They all say it's a date. They can't wait to see some of the large animals we have here. They remember that those white tail deer we shot are the largest they have ever seen.

23

We spend the rest of the day introducing our new friends to the rest of the group and the other groups. I warned Wyatt and the others about what was going to happen when their wives see the selection of home furnishing that we have. The furniture that was perfect a couple of hours ago, is now being replaced by some that they found in the warehouse. After the introductions, we spend the remainder of the day helping them get the new furniture to their houses and taking the furniture that was in the houses to the warehouse. The new children found no shortage of children to play with, not to mention the puppies and the kittens we have around the settlement. Today is Saturday so we have a movie in the big meeting room.

Not everybody comes to watch the movies anymore because we have so many other things to do as well. Some like to bowl or play miniature golf and some just enjoy sitting home with their families sometimes. Our new friends all come to the movie night and really enjoy themselves. I'm not sure if it's the movie, the friendship, or the hot buttered popcorn that they enjoy the most. We invited them all to our church service tomorrow morning. In fact when Dayna and I invited them all, I told them since they are Mormons perhaps they wouldn't mind speaking to the rest of us about their religion. We didn't tell them that we meet in what used to be a Mormon chapel. Many of us have read a book that we are sure is part of their scriptures called The Book of Mormon, but we don't really know what they believe.

Dayna is so excited about our new friends that she can hardly sleep tonight. She tells me that Tori's parents were serving a mission for their church, by being what they call a Mission President, when the war interrupted everything. She was born after the war even though her parents were older in years than most people have children. The other wives of the guys joined them where they were living. They just walked in one day saying that their parents died and they had nowhere else to go. Dayna tells me that the girls were all thirteen or fourteen at that time. Tori's parents raised them until they married Wyatt, Max, Trey, and Junior. Her parents passed away about two years ago and that's when they decided to go looking for other survivors.

It took them a while to put together enough food and supplies for the trip because they had no idea how long it would take. She says that their supplies ran out almost two days before they met us, even with the adults not eating so the children could have the food. Dayna tells me that you will never convince our new friends that Heavenly Father didn't lead them to us. I tell her that I agree totally with them, they are going to help our groups out in so many ways. It's a good thing we don't have to get up early on Sunday mornings. We meet our new families waiting outside on their porches on our way to church. They ask if we hold our Sunday meetings in the big meeting room that we used for movie night and we tell them that we have, but we prefer to use an actual church building for that.

We explain on the way to church that we don't usually have a sermon or anything like that. We usually just discuss what we think religion is and wind up reading some passages out of the bible or some other book that we feel is worth hearing. Today as usual we have a good sized group walking to the church building. If someone was to come by they might think we were some kind of a parade or march for some cause. When we get to the small lane where the church building is, we let our new friends go first to see their reaction. When Tori sees it she says "Oh my goodness" and turns to tell us that this building is like the one they had down in Mexico where she grew up. We use the building for more than church services, but we left the chapel area untouched other than to clean it properly and keep it that way.

Today we get our first lesson in what they call the Plan of Salvation. It makes good sense to all of us; at least no one disagrees with what they are teaching us. It feels good to spend the rest of the day relaxing and visiting our friends and family. Of course we don't get to relax much when we play with the grandchildren, but for us that's the best kind of relaxation. We hear from both groups that are out right now. Our scientific people are having a good time and are actually being able to get the equipment running that is needed for the processing of oil to gasoline and other flammable products.

Wyatt and his family are with us when we talk to them. When they mention going up to Michigan to look for information on electric cars, he tells me that he and the other guys can help us a lot with that technology. Mike and James get to talk to him for about forty-five minutes, but most of their conversation is above my education level.

Josh calls us after the conversation with Mike and James. He tells us that the settlements they are visiting are doing very well. They have been able to help them get more activities for recreation like bowling, miniature golf, and the obstacle courses, but they all seem to be doing well. Today they are at the one we recently helped get started in Florida and they are doing very well. They have talked with the ones in Cuba on the radio and they are doing better than ever. He says to tell Sara that they have found a lot more cocoa trees both on Cuba and on the islands around it so she can have all the pods she wants. They did say that when she figures out how to make eating chocolate out of those nasty beans in the pods, they would like some.

That's what she means when she says she made arrangements to make our own chocolate. Even with the beans, we will still have to have special equipment to process them and recipes to tell us how to get the different kinds of chocolate. I'm sure we can do it. We just have to find somewhere that did that before the war and use their equipment and processes. Wyatt tells us that Junior may be of some help with that because he once worked for a very large candy manufacturer in Orem, Utah when he was in his teens. I know that I have seen the name of a large candy manufacturer somewhere in our travels right here in Virginia. Misty tells us she can't remember the name of the company, but she remembers that it had the same name as one of the planets that they studied in their science books.

Now I remember the name of the company and where it is. It is just about an hour away by car. I'm sure we will not have any trouble getting people to volunteer to work on that project. We are all happy to hear that the other settlements are doing well and that the ones in Florida and Cuba are doing better now. Our new friends are surprised to hear that there are as many settlements as there are and that they are as advanced as this one is. Sara comes over and tells us that she hears we found out about her plan to make our own chocolate. She and several other members of our group have already been over to the company here in Virginia and have been reading about it for a couple of months now. They have just been waiting to see if they can get the raw cocoa beans.

As soon as it becomes common knowledge, she has half of the settlement volunteering to help. Later in the day Wyatt comes over with his family and tells us that he recalls some car manufacturers in Kentucky and Tennessee in the other world. He is just not sure if this world had the same technology before the war. He is not totally sure where they would be exactly, but is pretty sure one of them would be fairly close to where we were at that airport. Sara wants to go back and get at least two more planes to bring back. She thinks that if we can get two pilots flying those planes home, we can look for the auto plants from the air much more efficiently than from the ground.

We have already organized a crew to start putting the hangar back together, so we have to go back anyway because we couldn't get the whole thing on the flatbed truck, but we messed up by getting quite a bit of the roof on first. But when we discovered we couldn't get it all on, we had to leave some of the middle sections behind. At least the crew can get a reasonable amount of work done before they need the other sections and we still have a crew taking the next one apart as well. This time we decide to take two trucks back hoping to get the rest of the one and the entire smaller hangar on the other truck. We decide that Wyatt and the others will stay here and help with reassembling the hangar and we will go get the rest of the one and hopefully the other one. Dayna reminds me that we should get at least one truckload of supplies from the outdoor store we found over there.

We decide to get a truck running from there, rather than burn a bunch of gas or diesel fuel getting a truck over there. In the morning Wyatt catches us before we leave and asks if we would mind taking Heber and Joseph with us to help look for the manufacturing plants over that way. At first I don't know who he is talking about, then Dayna reminds me that they are the two older men that came with Wyatt and the others. I haven't really gotten to know them very well because they have been going to some of the older members of our group's homes to visit. I am guessing that they are in their seventies, but they get around as well as some people half their age. They were both engineers before the war and will recognize the plants when they see them.

We climb up into the cab of one of the big trucks we are taking and Heber asks me if he can drive part of the way today. I ask him if he has a license to drive trucks this size because I would hate to get a ticket out of state. He just laughs and says his brother in law is a judge over that way so he can get the ticket fixed if we get one. I bet everyone watching us pull out of the yard laughing is wondering what is so funny. We have some very interesting conversations on our way to Tennessee. He really can drive that big truck and in case you're interested we didn't even see any police officers along the way. Actually we don't see anyone that isn't part of our team. We stop at the outdoor store on the way over and find a very nice truck that has been indoors since the war that we get running pretty quickly.

We leave the truck at the store and complete our trip to the airport. Our crew that was left there has both hangars completely down and laid out on the ground so that we can load them on the trucks in the reverse order that they will come off. Sara and Gary are more interested in getting the planes that we want to take back checked out to make sure they will fly the distance they are supposed to. Joseph and Heber help them get them smoothed out. At first Sara didn't know how much they know, but apparently they convinced her that they do know what they are talking about. They even ask if we would like them to fly one of the planes home. They both flew private planes when they were young and even flew crop dusters up in Utah and Idaho.

They say they can cover more ground with two teams flying rather than one. They get both planes flying smoothly and decide to take a quick trip around the area just to see if there are any large manufacturing facilities. Loading the trucks takes a while because of the size of the panels. If we get careless someone could get hurt badly and we definitely don't want that. The planes take off and start their surveying of the area around us for between fifty and a hundred miles. At least that was the plan when they took off. We spend the rest of the day loading the flatbeds and securing the loads. There are some items in town that our team would like to pick up before we leave.

When we go into town there is a really nice truck, with what appears to be a twenty-five or twenty-six foot box on it, parked in front of a sporting goods store. We stop next to the truck and the guys show us that they have pretty much emptied the store of all the guns and ammunition, as well as archery supplies and coats and other clothing for active people. That's what the sign in the store says. I ask them if they checked for special guns and ammunition and they have no idea what I am talking about. I tell them what to look for and with all of us looking we find what I am looking for in just a couple of minutes. There is a trap door in the floor that has a set of stairs leading down to what appears to be about a half basement under the store.

It only covers about half the size that the store is and is finished very nicely. This is where the best guns, as well as some that were probably illegal to own by the average citizen. There are also some dehydrated and freeze dried rations that are still in the foil pouches in containers that they came in. We will have to test them to make sure they are okay, but we are going to take them with us now. The guns we are finding are very nice, but hardly worth going to this much trouble to conceal. I am looking around the walls when I see what appears to be a door built of cinder blocks in the wall.

I push inward on it and nothing happens, but when I use a pry bar that is just lying down here, I am able to move the door outward enough to get a hand hold on it. When I pull the door it opens to show us a very nice variety of military weapons from several countries along with enough ammunition to fight a decent sized war. There are also several cases of the K-Bar knives that we all like so much. Since most of the guys here are new to our group, I tell them they can take one of the knives for their own use and they can pick out a couple of guns for their own when we get back. They can take a handgun now if they would like. It's just that the rifles can be as much of a bother as they are good when you have several people in each vehicle.

There is just about enough room in the truck for our treasures, so we load them all and bid farewell to the five skeletons that were in the closed room. Unfortunately we still find the remains of those that didn't make it through the war, or if they did, they died shortly afterward. We get back to the airport just in time to see the two planes landing. They report that they did see a couple of manufacturing plants, but none of them were automotive plants. We are pretty sure that we will have to go to Detroit, or possibly to Washington D.C., to the patent office to find plans for electric cars.

We still have a couple of hours until dark, so our pilots are going to head for the settlement tonight and we will try to get to the outdoor store tonight and leave from there after we load the truck in the morning. We get to the store and decide to sleep inside of it. There are plenty of sleeping bags and even cots that we can use. We heard on the short wave radio that everyone got back to the settlement safely so we are happy about that. We do spend some time looking around for what we want to take with us in the morning. This store has some very nice cold weather gear as well as heavy duty clothing, like outdoorsman would wear to do farming, construction work, and just being out in the cold for long periods of time.

We have quite a bit of this kind of clothing in the warehouses back home, but with all the new people we can always use more. Plus we share with the other groups that may not be as lucky as we are at finding this kind of stuff. I am sleeping soundly when all of a sudden I hear something outside that sounds like a door closing on one of the trucks. I am up instantly and heading for the door so that I can look out. Sure enough the cab light is on in the truck we brought from the town and someone is looking around in it. I push the door open as quietly as I can and creep around to the front of the truck. I hear someone say that there is no food in there, but there are some guns and knives.

I am right behind the people standing outside the truck talking to the one in the cab. There are three of them on the ground and they all appear to be smaller in stature and they sound like women, but they are whispering, so they could be young men. One of the people on the ground tells the one in the truck to get a couple of the guns and a couple of the knives so that they can defend themselves and maybe even be able to hunt. I figure now is as good a time as any to introduce myself so I tell them that if they are hungry we have food inside that they are welcome to share with us. That startles them and now I am trying to keep from getting beat to death, while they are trying just to get past me. We must have woken up everybody because there are suddenly several flashlights shining on us and I hear Jared's voice telling us all to stand where we are or he will shoot.

Now I can see that we have four very frightened young ladies trying to find some food. I tell them that we mean them no harm and that we really do have food inside the store that they are welcome to share. One of the young ladies asks if we will bring it outside for them. She says no offense, but once they are inside they will be almost helpless. I tell them that I understand their fears and we will be happy to bring enough food outside for them. We also bring some chairs and a table for them and us to sit at while we get to know each other. They tell us they were living with their parents until about six weeks ago when they passed away. They are not sure where they were living and where we are now for that matter.

While their parents were still alive they heard on the short wave radio about settlements in the south, but they were too weak to make the trek to find them. When they passed away the girls decided to go looking for those settlements that they heard of. They have been looking with no success until this evening, when they saw our trucks drive past them on the way here. They heard us coming and hid as we drove by. They followed the road hoping to find the trucks to see if they could get some food. I tell them about our settlement and invite them to join us. I tell them we will be going there as soon as we load the truck in the morning and they are welcome to ride along. I assure them that in the morning we can contact our settlement so that they can talk to some of the women there.

If they get to the settlement and don't like it we will arrange transportation to another one for them. They say they will sleep in the trucks if we don't mind and they would like to talk to the ladies at our settlement in the morning. It's getting on toward fall so it is a little chilly out. Jared and Tyler go back into the store and come out with some really nice down filled jackets and sleeping bags for all the young ladies. The flatbed trucks that we have also have sleeper compartments and we tell the ladies they are welcome to use them and we will see them in the morning. It makes me wonder how many other people are living out there alone, when they could be sharing our bounty.

I think maybe Colonel Bob and some others should be out looking for these people again. Maybe Dayna and I should go on the trip up to Michigan and look for people along the way. The thought of those young ladies spending six weeks alone, wandering the countryside, keeps me from sleeping. They are not much older than Lillie, Izzie, and my daughter Amy. I must fall asleep for a little while anyway because the next thing I know is the sun is starting to shine through the windows of the store. We are all awake so we decide to load the truck before we wake up the girls. We have it loaded along with a couple of trailers with very nice boats on them hitched to the smaller trucks to tow back with us.

The young ladies seem to be a little friendlier this morning. That could be because they are warm and had a decent night's sleep for the first time in who knows how long. I was going to call home on the short wave, but Dayna beats me to it. She calls us because she says she had a dream last night that we met some very scared, very lonely, young ladies and she called to encourage them to trust us and join our family. Since most of us men will be driving, I guess they feel safer so they agree to go with us. Since we have been this way several times now, the road is cleared pretty much, so we make good time getting home.

The welcome the young ladies receive makes them feel like they have finally found a home. Our house is big enough for them to stay with us, at least for tonight. We even got home in time to unload the two smaller trucks with all of our treasures. There are a lot of people that will benefit from the items we were able to find and bring home to make our lives a little more comfortable. The young ladies asked if they had to return the coats and other items that we gave them last night. Dayna told them they are theirs to keep, unless they see something they like better.

24

In the morning Jared and Tyler stop by to see if the young ladies would like a guide to show them around. The young ladies that reside in our home tell them that they can do what men do best and wrestle with those big metal slabs that are used in building the hangars. Amy pretends to be a man giving someone a guided tour of the settlement and even though she does take it a bit far, it is still funny. She pushes one of the young ladies ahead of her, then points at something across the yard and grunts the word barn. She then points at one of the cows in the pasture and says cow. Jared and Tyler are laughing as much as the girls are. They tell the girls it wouldn't be that bad, at least they would say red barn and white cow. They ask the two oldest girls that since their morning is already booked perhaps they would like to play some miniature golf after work.

The girls all look at each other and ask what miniature golf is. Bobbi tells them that she and Timmy will be happy to go along with them and show them how to play the game correctly. The girls tell Jared and Tyler that since they have no other plans, they will be happy to go, as long as Bobbi and Timmy come along. As soon as the boys leave and the door is closed the girls are all shrieking that they have only been here lest than twelve hours and they have a date already. Now they all have to go to the warehouse and pick out some new clothes, especially since all they own they are currently wearing. I give Dayna a kiss goodbye for the day and tell her that if she had played hard to get, we may never have gotten married.

She smiles back and tells me and the girls that she knew the moment she saw me that I was the only man for her, so there was no reason to play games. My daughters all say that you have to keep the guys guessing at least for a little while. Otherwise they take you for granted. I have to agree with them on that. Not all men, but some will even in our group. I start to leave when Nickie, who was in the kitchen, tells the girls that if that sort of thing happens around here, Daddy Jon will have a man to man talk with that young man and they always see the error of their ways. We men take our leave to help with the hangars, but first my boys want to show me how the cattle business is going.

We get to the gate to the pasture and find Wyatt, Junior, Max, and Trey here. They smile and greet us as if we have been friends forever. Teddy asks them if we had any other new guests for our steer resort this morning. Wyatt laughs and says as a matter of fact we had a sight more young steers waiting patiently at the fence to get into our resort. All the boys seem to be carrying note books that they write down the new numbers in. Teddy is laughing when he tells me that we now have fifty-seven head in the pasture and after the first day all they have had to do is open the gate in the morning and let the new steers in. Junior tells us that at least five of the cattle that have come up to the fence are carrying calves, so we will have to watch them closer than we normally would.

I ask them if they got to go hunting while I was gone and they just look at me and smile. Max tells me that he owes me an apology for doubting me when I told him how big that steer was that we got that hide from. I tell him that no apology is necessary, I'm sure he will get his chance to see one at least close to that size. He smiles and says that they all got a firsthand look at a steer that looked like a mini-van. Max and Trey both say that when they were younger they rode some of the meanest, biggest bulls in the country and they never saw anything like the one that came up to the fence and acted like he was challenging the bulls in the pasture to a fight. Then he must have seen us coming toward the pasture from the mill road and decided that he would warm up by stomping a couple of us. He bellowed louder than any bull they ever heard and just charged them from about fifty yards.

They barely had time to get their rifles up and fire before he was almost on them. They say two of them hit him square on between the horns and that didn't even slow him down. Timmy and Teddy stepped off to the side and shot him just below the ear and he dropped about ten feet from them. They still had to jump because his hooves were flailing the air and could easily break a man's leg or possibly even his back if they hit him. Teddy tells me that they broke the chain on the backhoe trying to raise it up and finally had to get the truck with the hoist to get it off the ground. Our scale tops out at twenty-five hundred pounds and that steer pegged the needle. They say it is quartered and hanging in the meat freezer in the barn.

We are all looking forward to seeing the number of great steaks and roasts we will get off that bull. We join the group putting the hangars up. With the amount of equipment we have and the number of people we have working on them, we are doing both of them at once now. The cement slab has been poured for the second one and is dry, so we get started on that one. We have done this a number of times now so we know pretty much what we are doing. Our new friends are not quite as experienced in this kind of work as we are, but they know how to use a wrench and they are strong and willing to work. The rest is a simple matter of doing the job a few times to get the experience. By lunch time we have a pretty good amount of construction done. When it is going this well sometimes I hate to quit even for lunch because sometimes that can change the rest of the day.

We have enough workers that don't mind working through lunch to keep moving. Dayna and some of the other wives bring us cold water and sandwiches that we can eat in a few minutes then get back to work. When the others come back we continue with the same vigor we had before lunch. We have what I consider the best day we have ever had putting these building together and we still have at least a week's work to get them completed. None of us mind though because we know that when these are done, we will simply find another project to work on. This is one of the more physical projects we get into, but that's what keeps us young. When we get home we hardly recognize the young ladies that joined us last evening.

They have all new clothes on and they have had their hair done differently. They are all very attractive young ladies. Jared and Tyler come over to pick them up and there are a couple of their buddies with them, in case the young ladies would like an escort. Sara follows them up to our porch and asks me if I am in the mood to get my butt kicked at miniature golf this evening. I tell her that she couldn't beat me if I only had one arm and that one was broken.

She laughs and tells me that I'm going to have to put up something as a bet after that big talk. I already know what she wants so I tell her if she wins Dayna and I will go with her to get a load of the cocoa beans. She tells me that she was thinking more along the lines of sex, but since Gary and Dayna have this thing about monogamy, she will settle for the trip.

I think the new members of the family are a bit confused, so Sara tells them that she wouldn't really bet sex with me, but she likes to get me excited. We head for one of the miniature golf courses that we have here. The young people are trying to explain to the new people what miniature golf is, but they have nothing to compare it to that they will understand. Dayna finally just tells them they will probably enjoy it because we haven't met very many people who don't. They don't have to wonder for long because we are only a couple minutes away from one of the courses. We older people start out ahead of the young ones so that they can see how easy it is. After the first couple of holes they are all having a great time. Sara, Dayna, and I are tied going to the last hole, but I miss a three foot putt and wind up losing by one.

When everyone is through the course we go home and have a nice bowl of ice cream. For now we have to make fruit flavored ice cream, but hopefully soon we will be able to make chocolate ice cream. Our new members don't seem to mind a bit. We get to find out that my little buddy Ephraim and his sister Ariel, like strawberry ice cream as much as he does black raspberry. My daughter Amy asks the new girls if they have experienced enough in the last twenty-four hours to convince them to stay with us, or would they like to look somewhere else to live. They all say that they would really like to stay here with us, if it is okay. I tell them they can either stay with us or we can fix them up a house of their own. They say for now they would just as soon stay with us, if we don't mind.

I tell Dayna that it's probably a good time to consider adding that third bathroom to our house, with the number of people we have in it. Dayna laughs and tells me that we added the third bathroom five years ago and the fourth about two years ago. She says we could probably use a fifth, but we will have to add onto the house to make room for it. Our new friends tell us that they wish their parents were still alive. They would have loved getting to know all of us. Tori tells us all that they still can, only it probably won't be in this world. That gets everybody's attention then she says that will be part of our lesson on Sunday. I have already told Dayna and the people in our house about the conversations I had with Heber and that was one of them.

In the morning we find out that we have a bunch of vegetables that are ready to be picked and canned. Just about everybody has been picking them in their individual gardens so it makes sense that the larger crops will be ripe soon as well. We have been doing this for quite a while now so our ladies and most of the men have it down to a science. As I mentioned before we have four houses that we put additions on in each group specifically for the purpose of canning and sometimes cooking if we are having a group meal. The men and women that prefer to pick the vegetables and fruits, go to the fields to pick the ripe vegetables, then send them to the places where the team that will wash, peel, or prepare and put the treasures into jars.

In the kitchen at our house today they are making spaghetti sauce to be canned. Before the season is over they will can enough sauce for everybody that wants some. Like everything else some people prefer to make their own sauce, so they don't request any of the premade. We also can jars of meatballs and Italian sausage to go with the sauce. Today two of our newest friends decided to try their hand at canning and the other two decided that they would like to help with the chickens and egg gathering, and with the milking of the cows. We have too many to do by hand anymore, so they get to use milking machines that make life much easier for them. I don't know if I mentioned it or not, but we now have too many chickens to keep them in the barn, so about six years ago we built a much longer building for them to roost and live in. Three years ago we had to build a second building, even larger than that one.

We have some chickens that we grow primarily for egg production and some that are raised more for their meat than their eggs. Each group has their own facilities like ours for their food. It's a lot of work to live the way we do, but we can't think of any other way that we would want to live. We get the tomatoes that are ripe picked pretty quickly. I was under the impression that we planted two acres each of the green and yellow beans, and tomatoes, but I was shown today that we have four acres of tomatoes total. Our farmers tried planting them farther apart to make it easier to cultivate and weed them throughout the season. They thought we might need the extra acreage because of the fewer plants, but it looks like we will get more from the plants this year than we did in previous years, so two acres may have been enough. The groups have grown by about thirty people this year so I'm sure the extra will get used. If not we will have some for next year.

From the looks of the fields we will have to pick tomatoes again in two or three days. We like to pick them when they are ripe and get them in jars because they taste so much better that way. When we get done in the field, at least for today, I stop back at the house to see how things are going. The sauce they are making smells great, I ask Dayna to keep enough un-canned for dinner tonight. She laughs and says that she is keeping the last bushel or so of tomatoes to make sauce for those that have requested it for tonight. She tells me that I might want to make a big batch of Italian sausage to go with the sauce. She tells me that Nickie is baking bread today and she promised to make a bunch of French bread to go with the spaghetti sauce.

I'm not sure if I told you or not, but we found the equipment needed to make white flour out of wheat. It separates the kernels somehow so that all you have left is the middle of the kernel, which according to our nutritionists, is not as good for us as whole wheat bread, but several of us like the white bread better, especially when it is made into rolls or Italian or French bread. I also like the spaghetti we make better with the white flour as well. My mouth is watering just thinking about it as I head over to the largest barn to make some fresh Italian sausage, and while I am at it, I think I will make some of the great breakfast sausage we make. When I get there Rod, one of our regular meat cutters, is showing Wyatt, Max, Heber, and Joseph how we cut up the meat when we butcher a steer for example, and seal the best cuts of the meat in plastic to do what is called wet aging.

Heber and Joseph both mention that dry aged beef is the best. We agree with them, but it takes quite a bit longer and you lose probably twenty percent of the meat that way. I tell them that we used to just butcher the beef and eat it. We still do that with the hamburger, the ribs, and some of the, what might be considered lower quality steaks and cuts. Actually we make a lot of beef jerky out of the leaner cuts. Rod tells me he heard through the grapevine that we need to make a big batch of Italian sausage for dinner this evening. He goes into the large refrigerator and drags out a stainless steel table on rollers with at least seventy-five pounds of ground beef on it and asks me if I can get the other table with the ground pork on it.

The other guys are very interested now. We dump the meat together in a large mixing vat. It must be a vat because it's too big to be a bowl. There is a paddle that mixes the meat and then we dump in pre-measured spices for this much meat to make Italian sausage. Both Joseph and Heber want to smell the seasoning before we dump it in. They both say that the biggest problem they found with people making Italian sausage was that they didn't use enough fennel. They also say that our mixture smells heavenly to them. They start to say something else and I tell them that we will separate out a little less than half and add more red pepper to make it bite back when you eat it. They both smile and say I read their minds.

While we are waiting for it to mix well we talk about the breakfast sausage that I want to make. The biggest thing about making food like this, is making sure that you make enough for everyone that might want some. We discuss the fact that we now have more than twenty new people to think about. We decide that we probably better add about ten pounds more of both the pork and the beef. We have packets of spices made up for varying sizes of batches, so we add the correct amount of spice as well. Some of our people like their sausage in the casings and some like it in the bulk. We fill the casings first, and then measure out the number of packages of mild sausage we need, then add the extra red pepper and mix it thoroughly. We then put some in the casings and the rest in bulk.

We have a list of which of the families in the group even want certain items and we make sure that the others have a chance to either take some or not. We get the breakfast sausage mixing while we deliver the sausage to the group. Everyone must be in the mood for sausage today because we deliver all we have, but everyone that wants it got their share, even the new people, which made them very happy. We go through the same procedure with the breakfast sausage except we leave it all in bulk. Pretty much everyone wants some of that as well, but as with the other we have plenty to go around. While we have been delivering the food, we have been smelling the fresh bread baking in the ovens. I show the new people where the bakery is and make sure they know that they are welcome to come here every day and pickup fresh bread.

I also explain that they will be asked to help out in the bakery just like everyone else in the settlement from time to time. We have some people that love working in the bakery and that's their everyday job, but they need help so we take turns helping. Joseph and Heber say if they get to sample what they bake, they will be regular volunteers. Nickie hands me a bag from under the counter with some of my favorite sub rolls in it. She tells us that they are still warm from the oven and gives each of us a small sample to taste. Heber and Joseph are savoring their piece of roll. They ask if they could have another sample for their wives. They haven't tasted anything even close to that good in over thirty years. Heber says it wasn't very often even back then that you could get bread this good.

Nickie takes out bags of the rolls for anybody that wants them. She has to tell some of the people that they will have to wait a half hour, if they want rolls as well as bread. They all say they will either be back or send one of their children to get them before the bakery closes. On the way back to the houses the new people are telling us that they can't believe that we live as well as we do. I tell them that we are able to live like this because of the great people we call our family. Heber and Wyatt say that they have talked to a lot of people and they all say they owe their way of life to me. I tell them that Tim and I showed them a better way to live than scavenging for food and living afraid to even talk to other people. But it has been the willingness of everybody in all the groups to keep it going and making it better all the time.

They all say they will thank the Lord this evening for all of us and for the opportunity to share this bounty with us. As we get closer to our homes, we can smell the spaghetti sauce and the sausage cooking. The new guys all yell to their wives and families that they have got to taste the rolls and bread they just got at the bakery. Their wives say that they got to taste some earlier and they kept some for them to taste as well. I smile and tell them that this is what I believe heaven is. Being with people that love you so much they want to share everything that is good with you and be there when things aren't quite so good. All of our new friends say Amen to that.

Ariel asks her mom if they are being missionaries like her Gramma and Grampa. Her mom tells her that she thinks it's them that are being taught how to live the plan of salvation. Dayna invites the new people over for dinner, but they decline saying that they want to have a special meal together to celebrate becoming part of this great family. Our daughters tell them that they should wait a while before they call this a great family. Dayna asks them what they have to complain about. Amy tells us that for one thing there is never enough hot water and it is impossible to get any privacy around here. Dayna and Becky both yell Lindsay at the same time. She comes up smiling saying that she simply mentioned that it would be nice if the women in the family that would like to could have a place to go, to relax and talk without male interruptions.

I tell them I totally agree with that. In fact I think it would be nice if both sexes had a place they could go that is off limits to the opposite sex. I tell them that personally, I do not need nor want, any place that I cannot be with Dayna and my children, but I have heard some people talking about that very topic, so we should do something about it. I challenge the girls or women to come up with a solution and we will help them build it and the men should do the same thing and I ask for a volunteer or volunteers. Chuck and Noe say they will come up with some suggestions, but that's only because they do not have any members of the opposite sex in their lives at this time. That settled, we all head to our homes for a great supper.

25

It is truly a great meal. Our newest daughters are all very much impressed with the food we serve and all agree that they better find husbands soon, before they start putting on weight. Naturally the other young girls start teasing them about their dates last night. Sara and Gary come over to discuss the possibility of going to either Washington, which is not that far away, or Michigan, which is a pretty good distance away. Sara says being practical, we should probably try Washington first. That way if we don't find anything, we can always run down to the settlements in Florida and pick up some of the cocoa beans that are being sent over in boats for her. I ask her why she didn't ask our other group that has been visiting the other settlements, to pick them up for her.

She tells me that they are bringing back a small truckload of the beans, but our friends in Cuba and the other islands there, are continuing to send the beans over whenever they have a boat coming to the mainland. We decide to leave in the morning to go to Washington, but I insist that we drive, primarily because we have a limited amount of aviation fuel, so we need to save it for what might be considered almost emergency situations. I know what she really wants to do, so I ask her why she doesn't take a small crew over to the chocolate factory, for want of a better description, and get it ready for when she gets her first crop of beans. Sara and Gary say that's a great idea, they will put a team together and leave tomorrow morning.

Our daughter Amy tells me that we all know that is what Aunt Sara wanted to do in the first place. She is driving poor Misty crazy talking about it all the time. I tell her that I know all that, but if I would have said it to Sara like that, she would have been embarrassed and she wouldn't have gone because she would feel guilty. This way everybody is happy and I get to drive up to Washington to see if we can find anything in the patent office. We all decide to head off to bed a little early tonight because tomorrow will be a pretty busy day unless I miss my guess. The girls are all planning to go help Sara get the facility cleaned up for when the beans get here, which should be in just a few days.

In the morning Wyatt and Junior are ready to go with me to check out the patent office. Of course we are assuming that it is basically in the same place as it was in our world. Pretty much everything else has been, at least close to the same geographic location, so we figure we have a good chance of finding it. We take one of our pickup trucks in case we find something we want to bring back with us. We have been over this way before, so the roads are at least partially cleared and we can make good time. We pass many large herds of deer, cattle, and even pigs in the fields. Many of them have probably never seen a human being or a truck, so they are not the least bit afraid of us.

It only takes a couple of hours to get to Washington, but then we have to find the patent office. Surprisingly we have a map that we found at what was once a tourist information center and it tells us right where it is. We have to move some cars and trucks that are blocking the road, but we manage to get to the office and try to find what we are looking for. Luckily Wyatt and Junior have had occasion to look for different subjects in the patent office in the other world, so they have a pretty good idea how to find what we are looking for. We start scanning some documents that seem to tell us where we can find what we need, like in the old libraries before everything got put on computers. We find a whole section on electric cars and solar powered cars, and a section on multi-fuel engines. I mention that we have some really cool dune buggies and motorcycles that are multi fuelers. They both want to see those when we get back to the settlement.

Rather than dig through the filing cabinets that contain the information we are looking for, we decide to take the cabinets and everything in them with us. There are four cabinets full of information. On the way out of the city we see a library that is at least twice the size of any I have seen so far in this world. I ask the others if they would mind checking it out and possibly getting some books to take back with us. We find plenty of empty boxes inside and the shelves are loaded with books of every kind. I know the young people like to read the books that are generally written in a series, so I look for some that I know we don't have all of them and take every one I can find for that series.

We load the remainder of the truck with boxes of books and make ourselves a promise to come back and get as many more as we can. We go past an Air Force base on the way back and we all think at once that it might just be a good place to find some aviation fuel that we could use. We turn in just to make sure there is some before we tell the others we found some. Actually we may have just found all the aviation fuel we will need at least for the next several years. There are several trucks full of fuel and there are at least three large tanks that are very close to full. We don't spend too much time looking because we want to get home early today. We keep a lookout for anyone that may be living alone or in a small group, but we don't see any signs of it.

We get back to the settlement and everyone is excited about the good luck we had at the patent office and at the library. We already have many of the books we brought back, but having another set allows more than one person to read them at a time. We have people that already want to take the new books out, but we have to get them cataloged into our library first. Sara and the team she took with her today, get back in plenty of time for supper. They did not complete the work that needs done, but according to them they put a good sized dent in it. I am totally surprised when Sara tells us that she would like a few more men to come along next time because there is some heavy equipment moving that she is sure will need done.

My daughters tell me that they are sure that they can move anything that needs moved, but there is an air about the place that's kind of creepy. I ask them to elaborate and they say that it feels like you are being watched sometimes and they heard some strange noises at different times during the day. I tell our sons that they should probably go next time because I am afraid of ghosts. All our children tell me that I am not afraid of anything, much less ghosts. I tell them that actually I am afraid of many things, but the main one is that something might happen to the people I love and I might not be in a position to help them. We wind up having a pretty serious discussion about being careful not to let ourselves get into situations we can't get out of. Basically we need to think before we act sometimes.

In the morning Teddy and I go with the girls, along with Sara and Gary. The candy factory is a pretty impressive place to be. I only wish that I could have visited one of these places when they were making chocolate. We are barely in the door when we hear a noise that sounds to me like someone leaving quickly. We brought one of our dogs, named Biscuit, along this morning as well, but she is so friendly I'm not sure how much protection she will be. When we hear the noises I look at her to see what she is thinking. She is looking in the direction that the noises came from, but she didn't bark or anything, just stared in that direction. We tell the ladies to go ahead and clean and we will look around to see what we might be able to find. Teddy and I go through the stock room which is where the sound was coming from and we don't see anything right away.

There are several hundred bags of cocoa beans in the stockroom that are obviously no longer any good, but we do find a large supply of canned chocolate candy that still appears to be sealed. We go through the stock room and out the back docks to find a large warehouse behind the building. We also find some sign that makes us pretty sure we know what the girl's ghost is. The warehouse has several fork trucks that will come in handy when we start making the candy and will also come in handy getting the spoiled beans out of the stockroom. Teddy, Gary, and I go to work cleaning up the stock room, while the girls clean the equipment that we will use. We use one of the fork trucks to move the pallets of bad stuff outside and find enough evidence to verify what we are thinking.

The day goes by quickly. The stockroom is cleaned out and swept. Several of the cans of candy have been loaded safely into the truck we brought with us today. Teddy and I ask the girls if they felt like they were being watched today and they say they didn't, but then we were close by all day and that always makes them feel safer. That definitely makes us feel better, but since they are trying to get me to let them sample the candy in the cans again it loses a bit of its sincerity. Just before we are getting ready to leave, Biscuit is looking at the stockroom and scratching at the door leading to there. We open the door and she runs in causing a bunch of noise like someone or something trying to get away quickly.

Biscuit is barking, but quietly and looking up into the rafters of the stockroom. We all look up and see what she is seeing. There are three very large raccoons up in the rafters looking into the main manufacturing area. Teddy tells the girls that there are their ghosts. The girls get defensive saying they never said there was a ghost, they said that they felt like they were being watched and they probably were. We shoo the unwelcome guests out the back, then cover up the holes in the wall that they are getting through. We don't need any critters bringing in who knows what to get mixed with our candy. Sara figures one more day will get the place cleaned up enough to get started. Naturally once we actually start making candy, everything that comes in contact with that will be sterilized.

Speaking of sterilized the guys at home today spent a large part of it neutering as many of the young bulls that they can to prevent them from becoming more aggressive as they get bigger. Our herd continues to grow by new ones coming up to the fence or the gate and watching the cattle in the pasture. Usually all they have to do is open the gate and the new members of the herd walk right in to join the others. Our friends that went to the other settlements must have made great time because they get home just before supper. Naturally we harass them about that, but we are very happy to see that they are home safely and that they had a successful trip. They brought two more couples that came to the mainland from either Cuba or one of the other islands. They are going to live in the group that Ryan and Carol are in.

We spend several hours talking about the settlements that they visited and whether or not they need our assistance to get where they want to be. They say that the biggest thing they noticed is that some of the groups haven't done much for entertainment, so they showed them how to have more fun. We can attest that entertainment is very important when you work as hard as our groups do and we know the other settlements have the same issues we do. Our team thinks that we should go back in the fall and make sure they are learning to enjoy life a little more. We all turn in feeling relieved that the other settlements are doing well and that our family members are back safely. Tomorrows another day and from the look of the fields, we will be picking and canning again tomorrow. Sara is taking another group to the chocolate factory to finish the cleaning and to get the cocoa beans that were brought back ready to be used.

We know it is not a quick process, but we have good documentation on the processes so we feel confident that we can make our own chocolate. LT and Kathy are through with traveling for a while. They are excited about helping with the canning tomorrow along with Ramona and Billy. Doc Betty and Josh say that they already received word that they are canning tomorrow as well in their group. When the crops start to ripen, they are usually pretty close to each other no matter what group you are in. Sometimes one or two of the groups will get done sooner than the others, but we always help each other if we have the time and the resources.

Actually if someone needs help, we will make the time and the resources to help them. That's what our way of life is all about. If another group had their crops destroyed, we would share ours with them. That's why all of our groups have always planted more than we need. There is always a surplus that can be shared with anyone in need. The day goes pretty much like it did the other day. The guys who worked the cattle yesterday have some very interesting stories as well as some minor injuries to tell us about today. We are all surprised to find out that LT and Wyatt knew each other in the other world. Wyatt did some contracting in the Middle East and LT was his contact with the military there. They had only met a couple of times, but it shows us what a small world we used to live in.

Since Junior, Max, and Trey have all worked at a candy factory, they are going with Sara and her team to get the process started. The bean pods have to be broken and the cocoa beans inside have to be prepared. That's as much as I know about the process. Well that and the fact that if I open one of the cans that we found at the candy factory, I will probably get some pretty darn good chocolate. It doesn't take long in the field to pick all the ripe tomatoes and the beans. We will have to pick again, probably twice, before we get them all in. Even the canning goes quickly today. Everything we picked along with a bunch of stuff from the individual gardens is in cans at about lunch time.

Some of the ladies in the group mention that they were walking in the forest earlier in the week and it looked to them like the peaches are getting ripe. We had a bumper crop of cherries this year and it looks like the peaches will be at least as plentiful. The apple crop is looking very good as well. We keep as many apples as we can in the root cellars to keep them fresh for as long as possible. The ones that get bruised are made into apple slices that we can some as well as make apple sauce and dehydrate a bunch more. In past years and I know we will do it again this year, we have gotten bunches of bananas and dehydrated them as well.

This year some of our people, primarily Sara, Dayna, and Kathy, are talking about getting some mangoes as well as some of the other tropical fruit and dehydrating it for the winter. That will require a couple more trips there before winter gets here. I almost forgot to mention our pear orchards. Last year our crop wasn't very good, so Frank and Tom trimmed all the trees and this year we have almost twice as many as we did last year. The same thing happened with the apricots, but last year's crop wasn't that bad. It's just that this year's crop was fantastic. We canned a bunch of them and made preserves out of a bunch of them. We are planning to do the same thing with the peaches in the next couple of weeks.

Actually when we check the peach orchard, we can see that we will be canning at least some of them within the next week. We make our own pectin to thicken the preserves when we make them. Apples are full of natural pectin. We found a recipe for making our own, since we can't go to the store and buy it. There is still a lot of the boxed pectin in some of the stores, but we prefer to do ours naturally. The preserves don't get as firm or thick, but most of our people have never had any other kind and they are not complaining. We get a call on the radio from James and Mike. They have had very good success in being able to process the crude oil in the plant they are working in. Their goal is not to produce millions of gallons of gasoline to pollute the air again, as it did in the world that we came from. They are hoping to be able to separate the crude and process natural gas, liquid propane, and aviation fuel. They would also like to make some diesel fuel for running the boats for the settlements that count on the seas.

They are excited that we were able to get the files from the patent office, but they say that if it's anything like our world, the government was in cahoots with the big automakers to squelch any invasion into their profits. They are pretty sure that the only place we will find that technology, is at the headquarters of the big automakers. They are excited that Sara was able to get the larger plane in flying shape and are hoping that perhaps she can fly over there and pick them up, and then go up to Michigan. They would also like Wyatt and at least one other member of his group, to come along as well. Sara tells them that the only problem could be getting aviation fuel where they are going. James tells her that there is plenty where they are and he is counting on there being some in Michigan. One of the largest airports in the world is not far from where they want to go.

We are about to hang up when James asks if I would be able to come along. I ask him why they would want me along. I don't know anything about electric cars. He says he is well aware of that, but it is always comforting to have daddy Zeus along in case there is trouble. I agree, but I am sure we have other men in our group that are just as qualified. We start making plans for leaving in the morning, so we can get this part of the project behind us, before we get very busy. Junior and Trey, along with their wives, are going to continue working on the chocolate project in Sara's absence. Everything else is just the natural running of our settlement. In the morning we get ready to leave. LT asks if he can come along in case we need more than one pilot somewhere along the way.

There is plenty of room in the plane we are taking, so no one has any objections to it. When we are in the air, Wyatt and Max tell us that they can fly pretty much anything up to a C-130 military cargo plane. Sara says that she has always wanted one of those since she came to this world. She is dreaming out loud about how much sea food and cocoa beans she could get every time she goes down to the islands. Gary good naturedly tells them that they should not have mentioned that because now she is not going to be happy until she gets one. When we get to the appointed pickup place, we are all happy to see Trent and Patricia and David and Kimberly. David and

Kimberly are going with us to get any technology that we get, that will help their group.

We have plenty of room, but we are quickly running out of room, so hopefully what we find will not be too big. We were able to fill the plane before we left after picking up the others so we have plenty of fuel to get there and at least part way back, so we have to find some fuel while we are there. That will be our job while the others look for the information they want. We see the first headquarters building from the air, so we look for a place to land not far away. We find just such a place not far from that building and as luck would have it, we are not far from the other two as well. We are also not far from the airport, so we commandeer a couple of vehicles and get to work making them run. We have learned from experience that in the harsher climates it is better to look for vehicles that have been inside since the war. They are much easier to get running.

We work on the vehicles while our scientists head for the big corporations to start looking. I ask Sara if she made reservations in a hotel for tonight because she knows how difficult it can be to get rooms without one. The vehicles we are working on are brand new and we have everything we could need because we are in a dealership here. Actually we already have the generator running here and they have a very nice showroom and lounge area, so we think that if the others don't have any objections, we could camp here tonight. When we get the vehicles running, Sara and Gary go to meet the others at the corporate offices. LT and I go looking for an airport where we can find fuel to get us back home. While we are looking we both comment that we wouldn't mind driving this SUV back home.

We find the main airport not far from where we landed. I forgot to tell you that Sara landed the plane in a mall parking lot that is as big as a runway. Finding fuel is no problem with all the trucks still parked at the terminals. We find one that is still just about full and work on getting it running. It tries, but we simply cannot get the engine to turn over. The winters up here can be very harsh so it isn't surprising. We find a vehicle that is used to tow the airplanes into line at the terminals and this we can get running. We decide since we can't drive the truck to the plane we will tow it. We are towing the truck when we notice a sign that catches our attention. It says Michigan Air National Guard on one of the biggest hangars we have seen in this world. Naturally two former military men have to check this out.

We pull both vehicles over to the hangar and go inside to check it out. As soon as we do, we know we are in trouble, because there are two C-130 cargo planes sitting right in front of us and they are in beautiful shape. The first thing we do is check the runway to see if there is enough room to take off in one of them. We are both very happy to see that with a little work we can probably do it. Next, we have to check them out, to see if we can get them running again. It takes less than an hour to get the engine turbines running and two of the four Allison T56-A-15 turboprops running. Each engine has

4,300 horsepower. LT knows a lot about these planes and he is sharing that knowledge with me as we work. We also find several cots that must have been where the people in this unit slept, when they stayed here.

Luckily we also find enough new mattresses, still in plastic bags, to go with the cots. We get back to the plane with enough light to fill the fuel tanks. It didn't take as much fuel as we thought it would to get here. The others join us shortly after we finish fueling the plane. They are excited because they were able to find some of the information they are looking for, but more than that, they found some communications, that must have taken place shortly before the war, that says this car maker actually made some electric and solar vehicles to test. The communication tells which facility they are supposed to be at, so they are going looking for them in the morning. They are talking about how much they hope to be able to actually find a working model that we don't get to mention our find until we are getting ready for bed.

The others don't mind staying at the dealership, there are plenty of offices for privacy and the cots are actually quite comfortable. As everyone is getting into bed, I tell them that we almost forgot to mention that we found two C-130 planes in a hangar at the airport. That gets the reaction I was expecting, except I didn't expect Sara to come out of the office where they are sleeping with so little clothing on. Everything is covered, but just barely. When she realizes it, she goes back and puts on some more clothes. We spend another half hour telling her and the others about the planes. Dave and Kimberly both say that they would love to work on those planes and possibly take one back to their settlement.

We now have several volunteers to help with the airplanes and somehow I got picked to help the other group find the place where the electric cars may be. Looking at the city map it appears that the facility that holds those cars is not far from here. I really don't mind going looking for the cars, if we can make that technology work well it could change the whole civilized world such as it is right now. We have tried to make electric cars in the past and were not very successful, maybe this time we can do everything right. In the morning LT takes one group to the airport and I go with the other group to find the electric cars. Actually we go down the road we are on for about a mile, turn right and the facility is about a hundred yards down the road.

I have never seen people get out of a vehicle so fast in my life without someone tossing a hand grenade into it. The door is locked, but Jenna has it opened before I catch up to them and I am only about two steps behind them. We go inside and it looks like we have hit the mother lode. There are six cars that we can see and there is at least one other large room in the rear. James and Jenna walk over to one of the cars and Mike and Morgan go to another one. Dave and Kimberly and Wyatt go to two of the other cars. James is saying that it almost looks like someone knew that the war was coming and put all of the data and information about the cars right with them. The others agree with him, they all say there would not be any reason to do something like this, unless they knew that someone else may be looking into this technology someday.

While they are checking out these cars I decide to go to the next room, just to see what might be in there. There are six more cars back here and they have all the paperwork with them as well. There are also four skeletons in here with the cars and what appears to be a letter addressed to whoever finds this. I call the others because I know they will want to see this. They come back and they are pretty excited, until they see the skeletons sitting around a table where the letter is sitting. They start to be a little boisterous, but when they see that they quiet down and get pretty reverent. James comes over and picks up the letter and begins to read.

To whom it may concern,

> An hour or so ago we heard that much of the population of the world has already been destroyed and that we have only a short time before we will join them. My colleague and our wives decided to make amends for at least a part of the damage we have done to our own countrymen, or at least what we have allowed our employers to have us do. We have squelched the technology that you see before you, to allow the big automakers and the oil concerns to

> dictate what we can drive. We were allowed to build these cars just to see if the technology was as good as it appeared. The test data along with the specifications are with each test vehicle we built, along with a bill of materials for each vehicle. The blueprints and other information are in the file cabinets along the back wall filed under the vehicle number. If anyone survives this terrible war, please do all you can to improve the technology we started. Good Luck.

Most of the people in the room have tears in their eyes. James says that we will definitely take up where they left off and all this will make it that much easier. They are all heading for the file cabinets and I am heading for the generator for the building. It takes a while to get it running, but it does run and we have all the power we need. The first thing they want to do is get at least a couple of the cars charged up, so that they can test them. Wyatt mentions that one of the cars he looked at in the back room said that it has a small gas engine that will get the car moving then it has the ability to generate the electricity that it needs to keep running. Mike and James both say that they have always believed that there is a way to accomplish that, but the so called experts always told him that it couldn't be done.

We make sure that the tires on the cars will hold air then we get the gas engine running and drive the car out the back door of the facility. There is a test track behind the building that Jenna starts driving around. There is more than one of these cars, so Morgan does the same with the second one. The top speed with the small engine appears to be somewhere around thirty miles per hour. It takes a couple of laps before we notice that the gas motor has shut off and the vehicles are running on their own generated electricity. They can accelerate up to about fifty or sixty miles per hour, which is faster than we can usually drive on the roads anyway. By the end of the day we have tested six of the twelve cars that we found. We are discussing how we should take the cars back home with us, when we see a car carrier that will easily hold six of the cars and if there is one, we are sure there is at least one more.

All three of our scientific couples drive one of the electric cars back to the dealership where we are spending the night. The others are shocked at how much success we had today, but they have quite a bit of success to brag about as well. They were able to get the other two engines running and they were even able to taxi the plane out of the hangar and just a little around the grounds. They also got three of the four engines on the second plane running as well. They say they are sure they can have the other plane running by noon tomorrow. That will give us time to get the car carrier running and hopefully find another one as well. There is some conversation about taking the cars home in the C-130, but the logic that if the plane doesn't make it all the way back at least the crew can parachute to safety, we will lose the cars and all that technology if they go down with it.

Actually we have just about enough people along to accomplish what we want to do. Actually I should amend that to say that we have just enough people to do what we need to do, if we want to get one of the C-130 planes home. The second one will have to wait until we can come back. Our scientific people still want to check the other automakers here to see if there is more information that we can take back with us. In the morning we go three different directions. Wyatt, Junior, Gary, and Sara all head to the airport to get that last engine running. The reason it takes so much time is that we have to drain all the hydraulic fluid and put new in as well as check about a million things to make sure everything works correctly. When an airplane engine quits running, it's a little different than when your car engine stalls.

LT and I are trying to get the car carrier trucks running. We did find another one inside a large warehouse. There is another outdoor store not far from where we are, so we decide to go there and see what we can find before we leave. The first truck doesn't take long to get running and even the tires hold air. The second one doesn't take much longer than the first, so when we are done we drive them both over to the facility where the electric cars are. James, Mike, and Dave along with their wives get back just as we are trying to decide if we should put the cars on the carriers or wait for help. Our car carriers will hold up to ten cars, but we are going to split them up so that some of the cars come to our settlement and some go to the Missouri group with David and Kimberly.

We get them divided the way they all agreed on and loaded so we are pretty much ready to leave first thing in the morning, provided the C-130 will fly. We get our answer on that point when we hear the roar of the engines directly overhead, as the big plane is circling the area. We decide to go to the outdoor store after we drop the trucks off at the dealership we are staying in and head for the store. When we get there I can tell that someone has been coming and going fairly regularly and may well still be in the area. I tell everyone to let me and LT go in and see what kind of reception we get. I open the door and ask if anybody is here. We do not get an answer so we continue in to check out the contents of the store. We come to an area that has camping equipment and right away we see that there are cots setup and obviously being used. LT and I decide to split up to look for whoever is here. The smell of cooked food is strong and the stove in the area where the cots are is still hot.

I am thinking about drawing my gun, but something tells me I'm not going to need it. I am walking through an area where there are several large displays of sports clothing close together. I get about halfway through the department when I hear a very small voice ask if I am going to hurt them. I look in the direction the voice came from and I can make out the shapes of people crouching in among the clothes. I tell them in a conversational voice that I am not going to hurt them and ask them to please come out so we can meet them. By now we have everybody in the store, which may make it easier to believe because people tend to believe that if women are along, they are probably safe. Boy could I tell them some stories about some of the women we met when I was with the Seal team.

A man and a woman, who I am guessing is his wife, come out from behind the clothes rack with two very cute children. They look to be about the same age as Wyatt's children. We ask them what they are doing here and they tell us that they were living in Canada with some other people, but his wife got sick and the others left them to look for a settlement they heard about in New York. That was at the beginning of the summer. His wife recovered from her illness and they were heading for that settlement, but somehow got way off track and wound up here. They had a car that ran, but it died not far from here, so they have been staying here for what they believe has been about two weeks.

They found food and shelter and since they aren't hurting anyone, they didn't see anything wrong with it. We tell them they are perfectly welcome to stay here if they would like or they can come back with us to our settlement in Virginia. They say that they have heard about a settlement in Virginia that claims to have over five hundred people in it. We tell them that's the one and they are more than welcome to join us if they would like. That is unless they prefer freezing up here all winter alone. They ask when we are going back because they don't have a car or any way to get there. We tell them that we have two planes and at least two trucks going back tomorrow. We have plenty of room for them and anything they would like to take with them.

The woman has been very quiet up until now. She starts crying saying that her prayers have finally been answered. Her little ones are rubbing her hands telling her that everything will be okay now. We tell them they can either join us tonight at the dealership, or stay here and we will pick them up in the morning. They say that if it is okay with us they will join us where we are staying, as soon as they put together some bags full of clothes and some of the dehydrated food. We help them as well as helping ourselves to boxes of the clothing and dehydrated foods as well. We also take all of the guns and ammunition that we can carry. We will come back in the morning for one more load.

When we get back to the dealership our friends are excited about the way the plane worked and about finding some new friends. We discuss how we are going to get everybody back to the settlement, along with the electric cars. Sara is going to fly the plane we brought here home, while Wyatt and Max will fly the C-130 with the help of Mike, James, and David. Jenna, Morgan, and Kimberly will go back with Sara. LT and I will drive the trucks back and Gary will ride with us in case we need some help. The new family will go back with Sara in the smaller plane. Matt, the new gentleman tells us that he will be happy to ride with us, if we need help. We tell him we think it's more important for him to stay with his family this time. There will be plenty of opportunities for him to come with us later. With everything settled, we eat supper and get ready to turn in when we see headlights coming our way.

It turns out to be Colonel Bob, Blake, and Trevor. They knew we were coming this way and got a message from Karl up in the New York group that they had some new people join them that are worried about a family of four that they had to leave behind. Apparently they are really worried about them because as soon as they got to the settlement there they went back to get them and they weren't there. They were afraid that they might get turned around and cross the border into the US near here, instead of over that way. They look at the new people and say it looks like we found them. Colonel Bob winks at me and asks them if he can see their passports. At first they think he is serious, but when all the women in our group smack him, he laughs and says he is only kidding.

Blake and Trevor say that if they let me in, anybody can get in, so welcome. They say their job is done, so they will be going. They turn and start to go back to their vehicle. Bob turns around and asks us if we are at least going to invite them for supper. We tell them there's a KFC a couple of blocks over. The new family has no idea what we are talking about, but we have talked about the fast food places we had in the other world. This is actually the first time that Bob and the other guys have gotten to meet LT. We toss them some dehydrated meals that all they have to do is add hot water and they are happy. We discuss it and now Bob, Blake, and Trevor will drive back with us. That will give us enough people that we should be able to make it back without stopping for anything except fuel, and with tanks as large as the ones on these trucks we may make it without stopping.

In the morning we take one of the car carriers to the outdoor store and load as much stuff as we can get on it, then take it to the airport where we load it into the C-130. It looked like a lot on the truck, but it barely makes a dent in the plane's cargo area. Bob and the others are excited to see the newest airplane to add to our list.

They are also excited that we will be coming back for the second one in the not too distant future. We decide to have the C-130 take off first. We make sure all the hydraulics are working fine and that the fuel is topped off at around sixty-thousand pounds of fuel. With the load we have in the plane it should go approximately fifty-two hundred miles on that much fuel. Wyatt tells us that he will take good care of our $23 million dollar airplane, give or take a couple hundred thousand.

They taxi it out onto the runway and take off just as smoothly as I remember them doing in the other world. Sara says they better get going or they will beat them home. The military plane will cruise at about 374 mph at about twenty-thousand feet. They will probably fly a little lower than that and probably not quite that fast, but it will still only take a couple of hours to get home at the max. We load the other plane with everybody going. The new family is a little nervous because they have never seen an airplane before and the thought of being at the settlement within a couple of hours is pretty exciting.

Under normal conditions we could easily drive the trucks to the settlement in one day, but the roads are not all that good and we will probably run into a lot of traffic, so it will probably be tomorrow sometime before we get there. I'm just kidding about the traffic, just seeing if you are listening. We make sure that our loads are riding properly; check our tires to make sure they are inflated properly check the oil in the engines and make sure all of our tanks are full. We found several five gallon cans at the dealership so we fill up several of them with the diesel fuel we use and a couple of them with gasoline and we are ready to leave. We are planning to meet Trent and probably one or more of their people to take the one truck, with the electric cars on it, to their settlement. That will be fairly close to the airport we found the first planes at.

27

Hello everyone this is Dayna. Jon is on the road bringing the trucks with the electric cars on them back. There has been so much going on that our heads are spinning. Jon called us last night on the radio and told us that they found another family of four that has had a rough go of it and they will be here in just a couple of hours. The guys just finished putting up three more of the Quonset huts between our group and Doc Betty's, so first thing this morning one of the groups of single men moved out of the house they have been living in to one of those huts. The younger people seem to love living in them, so who are we to tell them they can't. The house they moved out of is only five houses from us and is between the house Wyatt and Tori live in, and the houses where the rest of their friends live.

Junior and his wife are the ones right next to the one that just became open, so we asked them and the others if they would like to move into that house, so that their friends are all together. Jon will love this when I tell him, they all said that the new people will be their friends as soon as they meet them as well, so what difference does it make. Our new friends fit in just like they have been here from the beginning. Anyway we formed a couple of teams and while one team was cleaning the house, the other team was moving furniture out of the house so that they can choose their own. We stocked the shelves and cupboards with canned goods and filled the refrigerator with fresh vegetables and meat. As soon as the bread is baked for today, we will have some of that in the house for them as well.

Jon told me that the mother in the family has been ill and still doesn't look all that well. I spoke with Doc Betty to come over and see them when they get here; just to be sure she is okay. Jon was a paramedic in the other world and said that she looks like she may be somewhat malnourished, which wouldn't be surprising, the way some of the people have to eat. A good steady diet of fresh fruits and vegetables, along with a little protein, will do wonders to help people feel better. Charity and I are going over the rooms to make sure they have been cleaned properly, but now we are hearing a roaring noise coming toward us. We run out to the yard in time to see the biggest airplane any of us have ever seen, fly directly over us then turn and it looks like it is landing in the large field over by the mill.

Everybody is headed that way, but at least we know not to get in the way before it is safely stopped. A second plane is coming in for a landing on the road where they landed the last time they brought the new planes home. Again we wait for it to come to a complete stop before anyone even goes near it. The big plane is very impressive, it is painted in what Jon calls camouflage, so it is probably a military plane. I should smack him when he gets home for not telling us about the new plane. The entire tail section opens on that plane and now we can see Wyatt, Max, James, Mike, and Dave coming down the ramp. There is a bunch of boxes and large totes in the back of the plane as well.

Sara and the other wives are coming from the other plane. That must be the new family getting out of the plane now. Tori is meeting them with Ephraim and Ariel. That will make them feel welcome if anything will. Doc Betty is on her way over with Josh to meet them as well. The mother does look a little peaked and like she could use some good meals and some rest. We will help them get their furniture picked out and their curtains and bedding and then we will help them get it all setup for them. Tori is bringing them this way, I meet them halfway and welcome them to the family. The little boy is just about the same age and size as Ephraim. I ask him if I can carry him to their new house and he tells me that he has to take care of his mommy. Always the thinking one, Teddy pulls up in one of the golf carts we have, and asks if we could use a ride back to the houses. Tommy, Timmy, and Jon are right behind him so we have room for the new family and some of us older people.

When the new people see their new home, they both have tears in their eyes. They see it is unfurnished and say that they can find furniture in town maybe. Tori tells them that all they have to do is come over to the warehouses and pick out what they would like and we will get it here for them. I finally find out that the new families names are Matt and Sandy and the children are Erica and Aaron. Erica checks the refrigerator and comments that it is full of food so they must be in someone else's house. I explain that we filled the cupboards and the refrigerator to give them something to start with. We ask if they would like to pick out their furniture, but they say that if we don't mind they would like a few minutes alone to thank Heavenly Father for guiding us to them.

I don't know about anyone else, but I am a little embarrassed that we didn't think about that as well. They come out of the house and say let's go shopping. They pick out the furniture they want including beds and everything they will need for their house. We even have some really cool kid's beds and dressers that the children really like and they get to pick out the sheets and other things they will need. The boys carry everything over and into the house putting it where they are instructed. It only takes a little over an hour to get the house setup the way they want it then we invite them over for lunch. We are having a special treat today; the boys made a very large batch of hot dogs for Doc McEvoy and actually for everybody, and the girls baked up a large batch of hot dog buns so we are having a special lunch today.

Nickie, our daughter in law, says that we better save some of these for Jon or he will be very disappointed. We already have a couple of pounds of them put away especially for him and the others. Doc Betty corners Sandy and tells her she would like to check to make sure she is okay. She starts to say that she is fine, but her husband tells her it won't hurt to make sure, so she goes upstairs with the doctor. They come down in about twenty minutes and Doc says that all she needs is some good food and some rest and she will be fine in no time. We can help with both those prescriptions and are happy to do it. She eats a hot dog and a pretty good sized fresh garden salad to prove that she is on the mend already.

After lunch we show them around in one of the golf carts and they are very much impressed to say the least. They didn't even know that most of what we have and do here ever existed. Matt says that he has a lot to learn, but he will do all he can to pull their share of the weight around here. Teddy tells him that we all work together, which makes the load much easier to bear and we have no doubts that they will do all they can. Teddy tells Aaron and Erica that we sometimes have too much milk so we have to make ice cream out of it. He asks them if they are willing to do their share and help eat all that ice cream. They are not quite sure what to say because they have never had ice cream.

Teddy says he should have known better because he still remembers the first time that he and the others got to taste ice cream. He pulls up in front of our house and runs in to get four bowls of ice cream, so our new friends can try it. After one taste Erica and Aaron say they will definitely help eat all of this they can. Their mom and dad keep saying that this has to be a dream because it's like finding a whole new world to live in. They ask us how we ever learned to do all of these things. Teddy tells them that we all owe everything we have to his dad. They ask which one of the men they have met is his dad. He tells them that they probably met him yesterday. He is always the first one to go where there may be danger and he is the strongest yet gentlest man he has ever met. They say that they know who he is talking about, but the man they met didn't look old enough to have a son his age.

Teddy tells them that he is not actually his father, but he is the only father he has known. He tells them that he remembers living in broken down buildings and being afraid of the predators until Jon and Tim came to them. They organized them and moved them down here to this farm, where Jon taught us how to live, instead of just existing. Others have helped, but Jon has been the driving force that has kept all of the people here together and inspired other groups to live the same way in other places. He continues saying that Jon will never take credit for any of the things that he has done, but that doesn't change anything. Other people from the group, including Tim and Charity, overheard what Teddy is telling them and they all agree totally.

Sandy and the children are pretty worn down and tired so they ask if they can continue the tour at some other time. Matt asks if there is anything he can help with while his family gets some rest. Teddy tells him that if he really wants to help, they still have to put away the stuff they brought back from the outdoor store. He is more than happy to assist with that chore. The day slips away like they always seem to when Jon isn't around. He does call on the radio to tell us that they got to the airport where we found the other planes we now have and met some of the people from the other settlement in Missouri. They took the truck that was meant for them and left a couple of hours ago.

They brought enough drivers to get back without stopping. Jon says they are only stopping long enough to get another fuel truck running so that we have a good supply of aviation fuel. They should be leaving within the hour, they just have to fuel the truck and make sure the tires will hold air. He tells me that they will be driving all night and should be here about lunch time tomorrow. I remind him that tomorrow is Sunday and he tells me to take notes so we can talk about what we learn in our lessons. Naturally he asks about the new people, he has been concerned about them. It can be a shock to see what they have been missing. Jon asks how the C-130 performed and for that Wyatt has to answer. He says it flew like a dream. David and Kimberly want to go back and get the second one on Monday. They are getting flying lessons on the one we have here until then.

We can't say all the things we would like to say to each other on the radio, but I do tell him that I love him and that he is not going back to get the second plane, unless I go with him. He tells everyone listening that they heard the boss, so don't even think about asking him to go unless there is room for me. We will discuss that when he gets home. He says that they are ready to roll so he has to go, but he will see me as soon as he can get back here. I'm afraid that I can't hold the tears back any longer. My daughters hug me and tell me that dad will be okay, he's the most self-sufficient person they ever met. I know that, but I still miss him terribly when we are not together.

The night passes, but I don't sleep very well. Finally I fall to sleep when it is almost time to get up and I dream about Ma Horton and Jon's mother coming to tell me that he is fine and that they should be home earlier than he expected. I always enjoy dreaming about them. Tonight they tell me that we should listen carefully to what our new friends are teaching us. They can't tell me what to do, but they do say that our decisions could have eternal implications. They won't or can't elaborate and I wake up to the smell of someone cooking bacon for breakfast. Bacon is my favorite, especially the way we slice it nice and thick. When I go downstairs Amy tells Lillie and Izzie that she told them that would get me up. They both say that it would get them up too.

We eat breakfast and then walk to church with just about the entire settlement. We will have to setup a bunch of chairs in the overflow. We have so many people coming today. Our church service is different than it would usually be. Our new friends tell us about their beliefs and then we talk about it. This morning Matt and Sandy along with the children came as well. I was surprised to find out that they are members of the same church as Wyatt and the others. Today they are talking about the importance of baptism as an ordinance that must be performed in this world right now. They are not saying that we have to be baptized right now, what he means is that the Lord does have ordinances that can be done in temples that allow us to be baptized for our ancestors.

A lot of people have questions about the temple. They have some pictures of the temple in Utah and the one that was in Mexico when they were there. There is also one in Washington, but there is no one at the Mexico and Washington temple with the authority to perform those ordinances. The topic of being baptized for ourselves comes up and they tell us that Wyatt, Junior, Max, Trey, Heber, and Joseph have the required priesthood to perform baptisms and the confirmation as a member of the Lords church, which includes the gift of the Holy Ghost. There is a lot of conversation today. It's not that people don't believe them because we do, it's just different. Not that any of us from this world know anything about religion, other than what we have read and talked about.

Wyatt asks if anyone would like to be baptized. Several people say that they can't see how it could hurt anything, but they want to hear what Jon thinks about it first. Everyone seems to agree with that statement. The meeting ends with a hymn and a prayer. On the way home we find out that Matt has the same priesthood as the others. They ask me if I think Jon will agree with getting baptized or not. I tell them honestly that we have discussed this topic a couple of times and he is open minded about it. When we get home, I look to the west, which is the direction they will be coming from and see the car carrier as well as two tanker trucks and a fourth truck that looks like a pretty good sized box truck.

I run in and change into some jeans so I can help unload the trucks and get back out just in time to run over to Jon as he steps down from the cab of the car carrier. The other guy's wives are as happy to see their husbands as I am to see Jon. He picks me up off the ground and hugs me and it feels so good. He does the same for all of our children that came out to meet him as well. He tells me that he found a nice SUV that he really likes, so he knows I will like it. It looks really nice, but I will not be able to tell until he gets it off the truck. The cars are unloaded and driven into one of the hangars that we have all built. That will become more of a lab for the electric cars in the weeks and months to come. I get to drive the new SUV and as usual Jon is right, I love it. Now all we have to do is keep it away from the other members of the family.

The two tankers are full of aviation fuel for the planes and the box truck is full of supplies from the outdoor store in Tennessee. We unload it into the warehouses that are for the goods they brought back. When all the work is done for today, we can finally go home and I can show Jon the special lunch that we made for him and any of the other guys that would like it. We made Italian sausage with peppers and onions and some nice fresh rolls to eat it on. All the guys take the time to at least fix a sandwich before heading for home with their wives. It's a good thing we made a bunch because the wives want a sandwich as well. David and Kimberly were already here, but they want a sandwich and the recipe for the Italian sausage.

After lunch we go over and visit Matt, Sandy, and the children. They are happy to see him again and he is happy to get to play with the children. He asks them if they have any questions that he can answer for them and makes sure they realize that they are part of the family for as long as they want to be. He also makes sure they realize that we hope they will want to part of our family forever. That comment prompts Matt to tell him that the topic of forever came up in church today. We start to discuss baptism when Wyatt and Tori drop by with the children to play with their children. We continue the discussion and even I am surprised at how much Jon knows about this topic. When they ask him if he will give his blessing on the members of the settlement getting baptized, he shows them that he has a bit of a mischievous side as well.

He tells them that he will let them know at the meeting tomorrow evening. He also says that his sons tell him that we have some great steaks that are ready and begging to be cooked on a grill, and this meeting would be a good place to eat one of those steaks. Wyatt and Matt both laugh and say they will come and enjoy a steak, whether Jon wants to get baptized or not. Sandy, Matt's wife, says she will enjoy one as well, even if she isn't quite sure exactly what a steak is. Jon asks everybody if they would like to have a baseball game tomorrow afternoon. It's been a while since Jon and I have been able to participate in either a baseball or softball game. David and Kimberly both say they will even stick around, to either watch or play in the game. Our new friends ask how we pick a team with so many people to choose from.

Jon tells them that everyone that wants to play can play. We have enough fields to satisfy everyone. Wyatt says he is surprised that we play baseball and softball. His experience with sports even in the church was not very good. Competition always seemed to bring out the worst in some people. Jon smiles and tells him it sounds like they have some of the same types of experiences and that's why when we play games like baseball we don't have set teams and we don't keep score. Sara tells him that's because he doesn't like to lose. I remind her that the groups all voted to quit keeping score when two of the group's teams got into a fight over a close call. Jon wasn't even at that game, but when the people involved asked for advice to avoid that sort of thing happening, Jon recommended not having set teams and not keeping score.

That way everyone has fun and nobody has to feel like a loser. It looks like we may have at least five games tomorrow before the get together. It's a typical Sunday afternoon. People are playing horseshoes, miniature golf, playing catch and pretty much all the things that we do to relax and spend time together. Our new friends are mostly sitting on their porches or visiting with new or old friends and as far as Jon and I are concerned it can't get any better than this.

As the evening starts creeping up on us you can hear ice cream makers going at pretty much every house around us. We see Matt and Sandy trying to figure out how to use theirs, so Jon and I go over to show them how. In no time they are old pro's and have that ice cream machine churning away making some of the most delicious treats anywhere.

When we turn in for the night, Jon tells me that I'm one of the few people that we know that hasn't asked him what his opinion about getting baptized is. I tell him that I already know what he is going to say. I tell him he will tell everyone what you are going to do, but that it is up to each individual to do what they feel is best for them. He agrees with me, he just wishes that our friends and family didn't depend on him so much. He says that we have several men in our groups that are just as capable as he is and are probably much smarter than he is. I tell him to give them time, someday they will all see him the way Sara does and they won't listen to him anymore.

He smacks my behind and tells me that they don't have to go that far and we start wrestling around. Apparently we are making some noise because our kids come to our bedroom door and tell us to keep it down. Some people actually sleep when they go to bed. I yell back at them that it sounds like a personal problem to me and I can hear them laughing out in the hall. They tell us that we better start acting our age because we are role models for our impressionable children and grandchildren. They are laughing so hard they can barely get the words out. We tell them we will try harder to be the examples that we should be. As soon as they walk away Jon starts tickling me and I let out some slightly louder than usual laughter and our children tell us we are hopeless. Jon looks at me and says that he doesn't think we are hopeless, we were hoping that they would go back to bed and they did. This is one of those nights when everything is funny to me. I think I am just so relieved to have Jon home with me again. Good night.

28

Good morning everyone, I am sure that Dayna was better company than I usually am, but she is so busy today that she asked if I could talk with you again. It's going to be a pretty busy day for all of us here. One of the jobs that we really should do before winter is to get a big enough hangar to put the C-130 in, to keep it out of the weather during the winter months. That is not going to be our average building project because the plane is 97'9" long, 38'3" high and has a wing span of 132'7". We know we can find some hangars large enough to hold the plane not far from here, but a project of this size takes some planning. To do the project correctly we should find the building we want to use, get the measurements then do the preparatory work like marking the location and getting the ground ready to pour the concrete slab.

The group in Missouri is going to have to do the same thing, so Dave is helping us find the right building and get all the measurements we will need. Sara told us that she passed an airport on the way to the chocolate factory. We decide that's as good a place to start as any, so we head that way. It will be great if we can find what we need a little over an hour away. There are a couple of big hangars there, but they are just not large enough. One of the maps we have shows an airport a little over an hour south of here, so we head down there. This is more like what we need. This used to be a reserve unit before the war. There are no planes to be seen, but there is definitely a very large hangar here. We measure it and sure enough it will hold the C-130 with room to spare.

We find a scissor lift that will get us up close to the ceiling on the inside of the hangar, which looks to be between fifty and sixty feet up. I think it's one of those that they used to use for getting up to the windows on the big passenger jets, but it will be perfect for what we need. I can tell from the looks that I am getting from David that he has never moved a building this size. I don't want to embarrass him, so I ask him if he will come up to the top inside the building then tell him I am going to go over the steps to moving this thing, just to make sure I haven't forgotten how. He says that will be good and will act as a refresher for both of us. I always carry a notebook to write in so I tell him I will write down the steps because who knows how long it may be until we have to move another large building like this.

I mainly just wanted to check the bolts at the top to see if we can get them off easily. Surprisingly they come off easier than I thought they would. Now the biggest question is how do we control the large panels that were put together to make this thing. We go outside and look around, finally we see what we need, but we will still have to get the crane running and get it over here. On the way over to the crane David tells me that the list I made looks complete. He makes the suggestion that perhaps the two settlements could work together to get the hangars back and setup. He continues saying that their settlement is much smaller than ours, although they are growing and they don't have as many people that have the kind of experience that our people have.

I agree that it would have its advantages because our people have worked on about forty projects of varying size, although this will be the largest to date. We check the crane over and after trying to get it to turn over we decide that we can get this thing running again, but we don't need it for at least a couple weeks, so we will take care of it then. When we get home Sara, Wyatt, and Gary have already marked off where they think the runway should be based on the conversations we had yesterday. The construction guys are already laying out where the hangar should be and are just waiting for the okay to start digging the foundation and area where we will pour the concrete floor for the hangar. As big as this is going to be, we will have to pour it in sections. I'm sure there are or were people who would have the knowledge of doing this work easier and probably better, but we have what we have and we make do with it.

I give them the dimensions of the building we found and they get more excited than they were. It is still almost an hour till the baseball and softball games start, so we lay the outline out with string and posts. This is going to be a ways from the houses because of the noise and just because it takes so much space to even move it around. We also decided that all the planes should be in the same area, so that we only have to maintain one runway. We will have probably three hangars on either side of the runway. David and Kimberly are impressed with how we make important decisions here. They told us that sometimes they will get several opinions in the mix and it takes a long time to get things done doing it that way.

We explained to them that when we have an important issue like this one, the leadership council at that time will listen to two or three proposals from the people we consider our experts. We then discuss these proposals as a joint council and the council will make the decision. So far we have a couple of instances where people were not happy with the decision, but unless there is a safety issue or we didn't take everything into consideration, they simply have to live with it. I tell them we only had one mutiny over a decision and we had to give in for the good of the groups. Kimberly asks me what was so important that you actually had a mutiny.

I ask Teddy and Nickie to tell them about it, it's too painful for me even talk about it. Nickie pats my shoulder and says they will make it as painless as possible. She tells them that it all happened when she and Teddy were still single. We had constructed some miniature golf courses for the groups to play and some of the older people wanted to design a course primarily for the younger people, but the younger people wanted to design their own course. For some of the older people it became almost a challenge and they didn't want to give in. Kimberly asks how we resolved the issue. Teddy says that they simply refused to play miniature golf until they were allowed to design their own course. It finally took Jon telling the others that the young people deserve the right to build their own course.

Dave and Kimberly both say that it doesn't sound like all that bad of a problem. I tell them they wouldn't, but before I intervened I had to cook all my own meals because my wives at the time agreed with the kids. I did as well, but I don't like telling the groups what they should do. It is now time for the baseball games to start, so everybody that wants to play meets at the baseball fields and we pick teams. Today it looks like we will have enough people to play three maybe four games. Some of the people want to play hardball and some want to play softball. Jenna, Morgan, and Kimberly all played softball in college in the other world, so they have taught the women in this world all about the game.

Since all of our daughters play softball, Dayna and I, as well as Becky, Robin, and Melissa, and their husbands, watch the softball game. As I said we don't keep score when we play. The players do get three outs, but if they don't get three outs the team up to bat gets to bat around and then the inning is over. The nice thing about not being able to lose, it gives players the chance to try different positions because it doesn't really matter how good they are at it. Actually, when we first started this we had quite a few players that were not very good, but now pretty much everybody plays good baseball or softball.

All the games this afternoon are interesting and there is not one argument in any of the games. We have some players that are competitive and will sometimes question a call, but we always tell them the same thing and they usually wind up laughing and agreeing with us. Oh, you want to know what we tell them. Actually it is more of a question than a statement. We always ask them if it really matters since there is no loser and everybody wins. Our new friends all agree that they like the way we play. All the wives of the new people got to play and this is the first time for all of them. While the games have been going on, some of our friends have been starting the charcoal grills for cooking dinner on.

For some of our new friends this is a new dining experience. We have everything to eat from hot dogs and hamburgers to some of the best steaks you will ever find. We also have Italian sausage for those that prefer it. The corn on the cob is a big hit as usual and so are the caramelized onions that we wrap in foil and cook right over the coals. When the meal is over and everything is picked up and put away, several of our friends ask me what I suggest they do about baptism. A hush comes over the entire group of people here and that's not easy because we now number over six hundred members.

I tell everyone that this is a very personal choice, but if they want to know what I am going to do, I will tell them. I tell them it is no secret that I, as well as many other members of our extended family, have dreams in which they are visited by loved ones who have already left this world for what we refer to as the hereafter. I tell them that I have had some very long conversations with Heber, Joseph, Wyatt, and the other members of the church we are thinking of joining. That coupled with the conversations I have had in my dreams, Dayna and I feel that we should get baptized and do those things that will help us be reunited with our loved ones after this life is over.

Where before you could hear a pin drop, now the noise levels are pretty high, Tim asks me if Gunny or my parents told me what we should do. Several people hear the question and ask for quiet so they can hear my answer. I tell them the truth, no they didn't. In fact they told me that they couldn't tell me which way to go because it could have affected my free agency. I listened to our new friends and most of us have read the books we found in the church, so I decided that if what they say is true then I should get baptized and have my family do the same thing, if that's what they feel is best. On the other hand if what they say isn't true, then what difference does it make? We already live the kind of life that they speak about in their books. It may even help us be better at what we do than we have been.

Many of them say that they have been thinking the same way. I'm sure they have, it's difficult sometimes to be the first to say you will do something. The next question is when do we want to get baptized? Our friends, that are already members of the church, say that it would be best if we learn as much as possible about the church as they can before they get baptized. They say that we should be able to have the lessons within two weeks. I tell them that I appreciate that because it gives me more time to sin before I have to be good. The next hour goes by quickly with our new friends answering questions about the church. The biggest question seems to be what we will have to do differently when we join the church.

Heber tells us that he has been a member of the church all of his life and he has never seen a group as large as ours that is already living the gospel principles. That makes us all feel good to know we are doing something right. We all enjoy our way of life and it's nice to know that we are living in harmony with Heavenly Fathers teachings. It's not all that surprising because we have used the bible as a guide for how we try to treat each other and everyone we meet. That is enough talk for tonight. Some of us are planning to get up early and head back up to Michigan to check out the other automakers and to help David and Kimberly get the other C-130 back to their settlement. I was asked to go so Dayna told everyone she is going as well. We made it clear that if one of us is invited to go somewhere, we are both invited.

We get an early start and the flight up only takes a couple of hours. We land in the same location we did last time and it looks just like it did when we left it. LT and I go to find us a couple of small trucks or SUV's that we can get running. The others are going to fly over the city low and see if they can find the other large automakers from before the war. LT and I find several nice vehicles that will do perfectly at the dealership we stayed at last time. We have two of them running in no time and are working on the third one when the others come back and say they have found the other automakers buildings and they are not far from here. They take the two vehicles we have running and go looking to see what they can find.

Dayna and Kathy are staying here with us this time. Dayna tells us that when they were flying over the area she saw at least two more large stores that look like the outdoor store variety. We get the other vehicle running, which just happens to be a van that will seat between twelve and fifteen and go looking for the stores. She is right when she says they are not far away. They are just about as close as the first one we went to here, but in the other direction. There are no people staying at this one, but they do have a very large selection of items that we can always use. We go looking for the other one and it is just as big a treasure as the first one. Since we are so far north these stores have cold weather gear that is better made for the very cold temperatures that they get up here.

We find a nice size truck in a dealership nearby and proceed to get it running. We go back to the second store and load as much of the cold weather gear and other items that we can and still leave room for about the same amount from the other one. LT is looking out the window of the store we are in when he asks me why we don't get a nice diesel semi running so that we can get two or three times the amount per load. There is a dealership not far from here where we find a really nice new tractor and a whole bunch of trailers out behind the place. We get it running and are driving it to the last store we were at when our friends get back. They say it as they thought with the electric cars. The big car manufacturers were working together on the project we found.

That solves that part of the trip. We don't unload the other truck. We figure we will just take them both back with us. We are loading the big truck when Dayna calls me and says that we have company. I look through the glass doors and see a young man running our way and to be honest he doesn't look like he could run much farther. Several of us meet him and just about have to hold him up or he may fall flat on his face. When he can finally get enough breath to speak, he asks if we are form Virginia. I tell him that yes we are, but how does he know that. He says that he lives with a group way up in Michigan and they heard our radio calling a settlement in New York to tell them that we had found a family here and that you were going to take them home.

I tell him that's all true, but that was last week, why is he here now. He says that they could not answer us on the radio because the one they have only receives messages. He says that the people in his group cannot walk to this place to be found so he came down to see if he could catch us. They heard that we would be coming back to get some more things. We ask him several questions about his group or family and he answers them all. He says that they are three days walk north of here and the weather is already getting cold again. He says he does not think they can survive another winter.

There is still a couple hours of daylight and if the roads are not too bad we can drive as long as we have to. I am thinking that three days of walking couldn't be more than seventy or eighty miles. We take the large van and a good sized SUV as well as some food and we head out. There is Dayna, Kathy, LT, and me along with the young man. He is very much relieved that he doesn't have to walk and run back to his people. It takes us about four hours to find the settlement the people have been living in. It is actually a store much like the one the other people we met south of here were living in.

What surprises us all is that there doesn't appear to be anyone over eighteen or nineteen years old and there are several children between the ages of three and six. When we meet the oldest young lady in the group she tells us that she has never been so relieved to see anybody in her entire life. She tells us that there were six adults with them when summer began, including her and her brothers parents. There was a terrible sickness that took all the adults. They buried the last one just two weeks ago. They had no idea what to do when they heard our broadcast and knew that if they could get down to where we were, we would take them to Virginia as well.

Dayna and Kathy are feeding the children. They appear to be so hungry and thirsty. The young lady that is talking to us tells us they ran out of food yesterday and she was afraid to go looking for more until her brother got back. We ask them if they have anything they would like to take with them and they do have a few small things, but they are just happy to be getting out of here. We get back to our group before sunup and introduce everybody to each other. Today a crew is going to take the C-130 to the Missouri group, Sara is going to fly down there and pick up our people to take them home and Dayna, Kathy, LT, and I are going to drive the trucks home. Our new friends are more than a little afraid to get into one of those airplanes. I tell Sara that they must have heard about her all the way up there.

Dayna and Kathy are going to take turns driving them in the van while we drive the trucks. The others get off the ground and are on their way to Dave and Kimberly's group. We finish loading the trucks and then start out driving home again. The new people want to hear all about their new home so Dayna and Kathy take turns telling them about it. It takes us a little over two days to get back home and there is a welcoming committee for our new family members. When they see that we were not exaggerating they are really excited. Kathy has fallen in love with all of the children including the oldest ones and wants to know if they would like to live with her and LT. They are more than happy to become part of their family.

The others all got back safely and the work on the base for the new hangar is going along smoothly. Sara got to go over to the candy factory and reported that the beans are fermenting perfectly and that they should be ready for the next stage within a couple of days. I have no idea what that is, but if it gets us closer to making our own chocolate I am all for it. Our scientists are getting ready to start working on those electric cars to see if there is any way we can mass produce them. The less we depend on gas and other oil products, the better off we will be. We get both trucks unloaded and stored in the warehouses for when the goods are needed.

Dayna and I take a walk with LT and their new family to show them around. From the looks of the crops in the fields, we will be canning, freezing, and drying for the next couple weeks. We continue our walk through the woods to show them the orchards. The little ones see ripe peaches on the ground and hanging low on the trees and ask if they can try one. The older ones are worried that they will get into trouble, but we tell them to all help themselves, there is plenty for everybody. Actually it's the first time any of them have tasted fresh peaches. There were apples and pears growing where they were, but no peaches.

We tell them that they will probably learn many new things and experience many new adventures living here, but we want them to know that they are part of our family now and we will take care of them. Kathy and LT tell them that they have not been here very long either and this is the first real family they have ever known. Wyatt comes up with Tori and their little ones. They are excited to meet the really new ones that just joined us. Wyatt asks us when we want to get baptized and become part of Gods family. I have my arm around Dayna while we are looking around us. I tell him that I believe we found heaven right here on this farm about fourteen years ago. Getting baptized won't change that, but it will help get us on the right track to enjoy this life we live even after our time here is through.

Sorry everyone, but Sara just came up and told me that I need a shower badly, so Dayna and I are going to take her advice and go take one. We are going to be pretty busy with one project or another for quite a while. We will get back to you as soon as we can. May the good Lord bless you all as much as he has us.

Other Books by Ed & Eunice Vought

2nd Earth: Shortfall

When you fall asleep on the subway you can wake up to some out of this world experiences.

When we get to the surface it is not dark so now we are totally confused. We couldn't have slept all night and most of the day on that train. The crowds during the morning rush would definitely have woken us up. While we are looking around for Tim to recognize where we may be we hear what sounds like someone screaming for help. It sounds like it is coming from a couple of blocks over so we head in that direction. By the way there are cars all over the place but no people on the street. This is starting to get kind of spooky. When we turn the corner we see three young men running. They are being followed by a young lady who is apparently the one yelling for help because following her are four other young men who look like fugitives from a punk rock concert. I don't stop to analyze the situation because the punks are gaining steadily on the young lady who is yelling at the guys running in front of her.

When Jon and Tim boarded the subway to visit Tim's family they had no idea what kind of life changing adventure they were going on. They will need all the training that they have had as Navy SEALs to survive in a world that is familiar yet totally different.

2nd Earth: Emplacement

Jon and the other members of their settlement family are awakened by calls for help from the other groups. What they find is more than they were expecting.

We have a radio downstairs, as well as the one upstairs and we are starting to get calls from some of the men in our group, telling us they are okay, but that was a close one. We are also getting calls from the other groups telling us that they ran into the same thing we did when they started to go to the Docs aid. While we are talking, trying to figure out what is happening; a voice comes over the radio that I have never heard before. He is telling us that we are surrounded and have no recourse, but to surrender. He tells us if we do that, he will allow us to take our personal belongings and leave. That is everyone except the women they decide to keep. The voice tells us that they intentionally fired not to hit the men the first time, but from now on they will shoot to kill if they see anyone or if we try to resist.

Join Jon, Dayna, and the others as they continue to meet the challenges of living in a world where the only law is what they can enforce.

Best Friends: The Beginning (Published 2009)

Sometimes being in the wrong place at the right time can be a good thing.

Oh well, I will go in. I close my eyes as I get into the girls locker room though, I can live with bruises, I'm not sure I could explain a black eye to my mom's satisfaction. I am ready to call out when from inside I hear a voice that is plainly angry and plainly Mindy. I know that voice well, but now I hear boys' voices laughing. I shouldn't be hearing that in here. I follow the sound and wind up just outside the girls shower room. This is not good, what in the heck is going on? I hear Kathy's contemptuous voice.

"You will never get away with it and when Ed catches you, you'll be very sorry."

I hear a boy's voice answer.

"Well, he will never find out will he? Because if you tell anyone the next one we get will be your aunt or maybe your mom." Then he laughs a very evil laugh. I know that voice, I pinned him tonight. Now I am mad but I want to make sure I get as much information as I can before I go in to break this up.

Join Eddie, Mindy, Kathy, Ramona and Amy as they forge a friendship and share life's adventures together. This first book in the Best Friends series introduces you to Eddie Marlow and his ever increasing group of friends as they experience growing up in a world where true friendship is a very scarce commodity.

Best Friends 2: First Summer (Published 2010)

Sometimes when you love someone you may be asked to do things that make you uncomfortable.

I don't like the way Mindy is looking at me. She leans close and whispers in my ear.

"Do you want to sing a song with me? *Pleeeeeease?*"

"I don't know how to sing."

"What about that song you like that your dad plays sometimes, you know that Marie Osmond and Dan Seals song?"

"I don't know. How does that thing work anyway?"

"They show you the words to the song on a screen and you sing to the music."

Before I know what is happening she is out of her chair dragging me up to the stage. It's a good thing she knows how this thing works, wait a minute scratch that, no it's not. Anyway the music starts playing and I see the words coming up on the screen but I can't make any sound come out of my mouth.

Join Eddie, Mindy, Kathy and the gang as they encounter uncharted area's in their relationship and in life.

Best Friends 3: Sophomore Year (Fall 2010) &

Best Friends 4: Sophomore Year (Fall 2010)

Sometimes being in love is a good way to expand our horizons and do things that we wouldn't normally do.

"Eddie, you love me don't you?"

"You know I do. What do you want me to do this time?" Now I know I am in trouble.

"It's nothing really, did you hear about the play the sophomore class is putting on in the spring?"

"Yes, each class is putting one on." I am sensing impending doom.

"This year the class sponsors got together and decided to do something different. Instead of doing traditional, well known plays they decided to allow each class to choose a theme and let them write their own play and put it on."

We are going in a circle so that everyone gets an opportunity to participate. It seems every time I think of something someone else has the same idea. Finally I have an idea that I think might be worth something and nobody else said it first.

"Maybe we could do something with a patriotic theme, everyone here is talented, except perhaps me, with either musical instruments, singing or dancing. I know a lot of you have been hoping our play would be a musical so you can show those talents off. What if we did something like a USO show, we could pretend we are holding auditions for acts to visit our troops and the people auditioning would do it for our audience. The grand finale could maybe be a song everyone knows and could include the audience." Everyone is looking at me like I just grew a second head. "Or not, sorry it was just a thought."

Eddie, Mindy and the rest of their ever expanding group of friends are now sophomores. Their experiences and challenges grow right along with them. Join them as they continue to learn about themselves and the world we live in.

Best Friends 5: A Time of Maturing (Coming soon)

When Mindy's mom asked Eddie to spend the night there was no way any of them could imagine how much and how quickly their lives could change.

Somewhere around midnight I must have dozed off but now I am completely awake. Did I hear something or is my imagination playing tricks on me? I have stayed here enough to know the night sounds the house makes, every house is different. There it is again, it sounds like someone at the back door. Not knocking, working the doorknob or something like that.

I get up and grab an aluminum baseball bat that is in the family room for some reason, I'm glad it is. I walk as quietly as I can into the kitchen staying close to the wall so I won't be highlighted by the light in the family room. Every sense in my body is alive and I have a very sick feeling in the pit of my stomach. What if someone breaks in and gets past me? I'm still just a teenager, and these may be men, mean vicious men. The mind has a tendency to over react at times like this.

I am almost right by the door now, there is definitely someone or more than one someone's outside that door, I can hear voices. I definitely hear one tell the other.

"The women are home, I saw them this morning, the old man isn't, his old lady says he's in Arizona." These guys are some nasty customers, they are not just interested in stealing, they want Mindy and her mom. If I have anything to say about it they will have to take them over my dead body. That sounds a bit dramatic but that's the way I feel.

In the next few seconds all heck breaks loose, I am getting better I don't even swear in times of stress now. They must have used a pry bar because the door breaks inward and the first guy is through into the kitchen in a step or two. He is followed by another one but I am not sure if there are more or not, can't worry about that now.

Join Eddie, Mindy and the rest of their ever expanding group of friends in their most challenging experiences and adventures yet.

They Call Me Nuisance (Published 2010)

With a name like Nuisance life can be challenging to say the least.

Dakota horse stops dead in front of the general store, there's a wagon out front and he stops right next to it. I am sitting here looking stupid, well stupider than usual. A few minutes after we stop here a very pretty young lady comes out of the store yelling at someone inside. She is dressed in a man's clothing which is strange for the west these days. She is talking like a man too, this lady can cuss with the best of them. She looks around and sees me staring at her. I've never seen a woman as pretty as her.

"What are you looking at? Maybe the question should be what are you?"

Now I'm embarrassed, I'm trying to get that horse to move but he ain't going nowhere.

When Nuisance, Dakota horse and the dog ambled into town they had no idea what they were getting into. Not that it would have changed anything, they are simply not the type to allow anyone to ride roughshod over a lady. Join them as they help Miss Emily and prove to the bad guys that he is only a nuisance to them.

Made in the USA
Monee, IL
08 April 2021

65125462R10148